Scribe Publications
HOUSE OF STICKS

Peggy Frew is an award-winning writer and musician. *House of Sticks* won the 2010 Victorian Premier's Literary Award for an unpublished manuscript, and her story 'Home Visit' won *The Age* short story competition in 2009. She has been published in *New Australian Stories 2*, *Kill Your Darlings* and *Meanjin*.

HOUSE
OF STICKS

PEGGY FREW

SCRIBE
Melbourne

Scribe Publications Pty Ltd
18–20 Edward St, Brunswick, Victoria, Australia 3056
Email: info@scribepub.com.au

First published by Scribe 2011

Typeset in 12/16.5 pt Dante MT by the publishers.
Printed and bound in Australia by Griffin Press. Only wood grown
from sustainable regrowth forests is used in the manufacture of
paper found in this book.

National Library of Australia
Cataloguing-in-Publication data

Frew, Peggy.

House of Sticks.

9781921844270 (pbk.)

A823.4

www.scribepublications.com.au

For Mick

SHE STOPPED THE CAR. 'SHIT.'

'What, Mum?' Edie's eyes were round in the rear-view mirror.

'Oh, it's ... nothing. Don't worry.' Bonnie noticed her window was down a bit and she pressed the button to close it properly. 'Looks like Doug's there.'

'Douggie! Douggie! Douggie!' went Edie, bouncing in her seat.

'Douggie! Douggie! Douggie!' went Louie, bouncing too. The baby started crying.

'Shh, shh — you guys,' she said. 'Shh, Jess. It's okay.' She twisted and reached into the capsule to stroke the baby's head. Jess cried harder, throwing out her red fists. Bonnie could feel tears spurting under her fingers, the furious heat in the tiny face, the mouth, warm and soft and open, the vibration of the wails. She reached further and tucked the blanket back in where Jess had kicked it off. 'Hey,' she said to the twins. 'Should we go to the park for a bit?'

'Yes! Yes! Yes!'

Bonnie took her foot off the brake, and the car started rolling forward. She pressed the accelerator, and they moved past the house and past Doug's old yellow panel van parked out the front of it.

'Can we go back and get the bikes?' said Edie.

'No.'

'Why not?'

In the mirror Bonnie watched the back of Doug's van receding, shuttered and blank.

'Why not? Why not? Mum?'

Jess cried on.

Bonnie kept driving. It wasn't far off dark. Another hour maybe. She turned into the street where the park was. Her scarf was too high up the back of her neck and cold air was getting in underneath it. She tugged at it, and checked the heater knob. It wasn't working properly. She switched it off and on again, held her hand in front of the vent. The air coming out was hardly even warm.

She pulled over by the park. Looked out at the bare winter branches of the huge oaks, the swings hanging empty, the cold gleam of the slide. Everybody else, every sensible, normal person, would be home making dinner.

'Why can't we get the bikes, Mum? Why can't we get the bikes?' went Edie.

'I'm hungry,' went Louie.

Jess cried.

An old woman came along the street, pushing a shopping trolley. Bonnie watched her. Then she undid her seatbelt, opened the door and got out. Shut the door. Not slamming — a neat, controlled push.

Silence. Amazing.

She leaned for a moment against the side of the car. Smiled across its roof to the passing woman. 'Cold, isn't it?'

The woman nodded and bent her head to her trolley.

Bonnie closed her eyes and counted slowly to ten. She did three deep breaths in and out. Then she went round and opened the back door on the footpath side.

'Let's go,' she said.

When they got back the panel van was gone.

Pete was in the kitchen, still in his work clothes. There was a food smell, warm, rich and salty. Three empty beer bottles stood on the table.

'Daddy!' The twins ran to climb on him.

'Hi, guys!' Pete opened his arms. 'How was kinder?'

'We went to the park.'

'Did you?' Pete glanced up at Bonnie. 'I wondered what happened. I tried to call you.'

'Sorry. I must've left my phone in the car.' She stooped and slid Jess into her bouncer chair. 'These guys are starving.' She went to the fridge, opened the door. There was nothing — cheese, an almost-empty tub of yoghurt, a couple of carrots. The useless background forest of old jars and bottles, sauces and jam. 'Oh god, sorry,' she said. 'I didn't get around to doing the shopping again.'

'That's okay,' he said. 'I've made soup.'

'Oh.' She shut the fridge door and looked with surprise at the back of his head. He had sawdust in his hair. She stepped over and flicked it off. 'That's great. Thank you.'

'No probs.' Pete stood and lowered the twins into a chair each. 'It should be ready. Pea and ham. Never tried it before.' He came over and put an arm around her. 'Douggie brought us a bacon bone. From some friend of his at the market.' He gave her a don't-be-angry squeeze.

She tried to relax her shoulders. 'Thanks for cooking,' she said. 'Sorry about the shopping. I just — the day got away from me.'

'That's okay.' He let go of her. 'I'll just go and get properly cleaned up. There's fresh bread too.'

'Okay.' Bonnie took the lid off the pot on the stove. Her mouth was watering. 'This smells amazing, Pete.' But when she looked up he'd left the room.

'Are you pissed off with me?'

'No.' Bonnie lowered her book. 'Why?'

'Just wondering.' Pete came closer, sat on the edge of the bed. 'Thought you might've been pissed off that Douggie was round.'

She sighed. Folded the corner of the page and closed the book. 'So was it just a visit? Or is he after some work?'

Pete stared at the floor. 'Work. But, you know, he brought that stuff from the market. That was nice.'

'So why didn't he hang around for dinner?' The words came out with an edge she hadn't intended. 'I mean' — she tried unsuccessfully for a joking tone — 'he does like to hang around.'

'I don't know.' Pete was muttering now, head low. 'He had something on I think.'

'A better offer?' *Shut up*, she told herself. *Stop being such a bitch.*

He didn't answer.

'So are you giving him some work?'

Pete licked his lips. 'Yeah.'

'Pete.' Bonnie ran her thumb over the cover of the book. She was struggling to keep her voice even. 'It's just — you know what'll happen. You know what he's like. He's not … You can't … The thing is, he doesn't operate like normal people, and, like Mel said, you've got to be clear with these people about where the boundaries lie. She said —'

'Bonnie, would you listen to yourself?' He stood up. 'Listen to what you're saying. *These people*? I don't know about Mel. Sometimes I wonder — that job of hers. It's like she thinks everyone's crazy.'

'That's not true. I just asked her for some advice about Doug, that's all, and she said — I've told you what she said.'

'Yeah, yeah, I know.' Pete ran a hand through his hair. 'But. Look. He's a friend. He's an old friend, and he … he needs a bit of help, you know? He's broke and ...' He turned to face her. 'Bon. He's cheap. I need some help in the workshop, and he's here, he needs the work, and he's cheap.'

She breathed slowly, tried to speak calmly. 'I know that. We've had this conversation before. What I'm saying is, either hire him or be his friend, but mixing the two things up is ... well, it's messy and ... dangerous.' She lay back on the pillows. She felt exhausted all of a sudden. 'God. It's not like he's even a good worker. I mean, look what happened last time.'

'Yeah, well, I'm giving him another chance.'

She closed her eyes. 'I know I sound mean. It's just —'

'I don't think I can keep talking about this now.'

'Pete!' She sat up straight again. 'You always do this!'

But he'd gone.

She tossed her book onto the floor. 'We need to talk about this,' she said to the empty doorway. 'We need to work something out.'

Jess woke for a feed at five, and after that Bonnie couldn't get back to sleep. She huddled round the house in her ugg boots and the horrible blue wool dressing-gown that had been her mother's and that she only wore because it was warm. She stood in front of the bathroom mirror and looked at the glimmer of her own pale face in the light from the hallway, her still-heavy body a solid mass below.

She opened the back door. Complete darkness. No birds singing yet. She went back to the living room and grabbed the crochet rug from the couch, wrapped herself in it, and stepped out onto the back porch, easing the door shut, hardly even stirring the rope of bells.

Inside the workshop she switched on the lights, and they flooded everything with such sudden harshness that her eyes smarted. She was tired. Maybe she should go back and try to sleep again, get another hour in before everyone else woke up. The thing was, it almost wasn't worth the effort. It took her so long to get to sleep, and then chances were something would happen: Louie crawling in beside her, or Jess waking again. She was probably better off just staying up now. At least she was getting a bit of time to herself.

She stood looking at Pete's latest table, its unfinished surface only faintly reflective, his big stained gloves sprawled empty-fingered at one end. She touched one of the fingers, watched it give and then pop back out again. God, she loved him. She really did love him so much. A ripple went through her, between her legs, where there was still a trace of that swollen, ragged feeling even nearly five months after Jess's birth. Maybe she should go back to bed, slide in beside him, kiss him all down his sleeping chest, bring him gently awake and hard, take him in her mouth. The feeling had needled through her breasts too. She clamped her hands over them to stop the milk leaking. Held them until the needles stopped. Pulled the rug tighter and went around the table to the storage shelves.

There was a veil of fine wood dust over her guitar case. She found a cloth, checked it was clean, and rubbed it over the scratched black surface with its layers of stickers. The flight tags from the last tour were still attached to the handle. Tears pricked behind her eyes. What was this? Regret? No. You couldn't regret kids. Her breasts ached again at the thought of Jess in her cot, the twins in their beds — the sweet abandon of children sleeping, the absolute perfect beauty of them.

She wiped the cloth around all the metal clasps and under the handle. The tears were drying without having fallen. She sniffed and shook her hair back. God, her hormones were all over the place. She had no regrets. It was just a bummer not to be able to fit everything in, that was all. But there was plenty of time, like she and Pete always told each other. The kids wouldn't be little forever.

She opened the case and took out the guitar. Pulled the sheet off her little practice amp. Sat down on the battered old chair. Plugged in and turned the volume right down so that when she started to play it was almost like the music was coming from some other place — from the house next door, from a car radio, or from a party somewhere, far away, an all-night party that was still going, still sending out its sounds into the sleeping dawn.

She played until it got light and her neck was stiff. The dog next door started barking, and she could hear someone thumping around inside the house. She rolled her shoulders and stretched out her neck. Her fingers hurt — her calluses were long gone. She switched off the amp. Unplugged the guitar and lay it down in its case, its coiled lead beside it. Draped the sheet back over the amp. Then she turned off the lights and went out.

Doug was in the kitchen. 'Mornin', Missus Bonnie,' he said, tapping his fingers to his forehead in a mock salute.

'Oh. Hi, Doug. You surprised me.' She drew the crochet rug closer around herself. 'Sorry, wasn't expecting you here so early. Still in my pyjamas.' She was acutely aware of how ridiculous she looked, with her layers of gown and rug and ugly clumping ugg boots. She motioned to the shed. 'I was just doing a bit of guitar practice, while I had the chance.'

Doug smiled, folded his arms, and leaned against the bench, head tilted back.

Shut up, you idiot, she thought. *What do you need to explain yourself to him for?* 'Well, I'll just go and —'

'Mummy!' Louie burst in and threw himself at her legs.

'Louie! Good morning.' Bonnie hefted him up on one hip and kissed him. 'Where's Edie? And Dad?'

'The boss's just in the shower,' said Doug. 'And I think the little princess must still be sleeping. Louie's been keeping me company, haven't you, little man?'

Louie giggled into her neck.

'Oh.' She clenched her teeth. God, she hated it when people said *little man*. Or *boys will be boys*. All that bullshit gender stuff she and Pete were trying to keep their kids away from.

'Yes. He's been helping me sort out me tools. While we were waiting for you to finish out there.'

'Oh — sorry.' *Stop apologising. It's not his bloody workshop.* All she wanted to do was get out of the room, go and have a shower, and get some decent clothes on. 'Well,' she said, and pulled back her lips in a smile, 'it's all yours now.'

'Mummy?' Louie sagged outwards in her arms, and she put him down.

'Yes?'

'Can I go with Doug to the workshop?'

'No.'

'Why not?'

'You know why not, Lou-Lou. It's not for kids out there. There's dangerous tools and things only for grown-ups. Would you like to come and listen to a talking book until brekkie's ready?'

'Yes!' said Louie, but Doug spoke at the same time.

'Oh, don't worry about all that namby-pamby nonsense,' he said, pushing himself off the bench. 'I was driving the car up and down the back lane when I was six. Come on, kiddo, come out to the workshop with Douggie and we'll see if we can find some bits of wood to nail together.' Doug picked up the toolkit that was lying on the table. He held out his hand, and Louie took it. Doug winked at Bonnie. 'Don't worry, Missus Bonnie,' he said. 'I'll look after him.'

She stepped back as they passed her, Doug striding, ragged pants flapping, Louie trotting along beside, not even glancing round. She caught a whiff of Doug's smell: cigarette smoke fresh and stale, and unwashed hair. For a moment she stood, frozen with shock and fury, and then she followed. She could hear herself beginning to gabble, but she didn't know what else to do. She couldn't just let him get away with this.

'Actually, Doug,' she said. 'Pete and I've made a rule. Since we moved. I mean, with the workshop right here, in the backyard, well, we thought —' She went tripping down the porch steps, rug flapping, heart thumping. *Come back here, Louie, you little bastard.* 'I mean, we decided we had to make some kind of distinction between what's home and what's work, and … I think we'd better just … stick to the rules,' she finished weakly, coming to a halt on the path.

Doug, at the workshop door, turned and lifted his free hand in a gesture of surrender. Louie clung to the other hand.

She fixed her gaze on her stupid ugg boots. 'We just — we decided to have a blanket rule. No kids in the workshop.' She couldn't meet Doug's eye. She looked at the child instead. 'Sorry, Louie. Doug didn't know.'

Doug glanced down at Louie. 'Sorry, kiddo,' he said, hand still stuck up like a robbery victim. 'Missus Bonnie says no.' And he lifted his face to Bonnie and gave her a smile, for all the world as if it was his decision to make and he was only indulging her.

Fuck you. Bonnie put out her arm. 'Come on, Louie.'

'No,' said Louie, and pulled at Doug. 'Let's go in the workshop, Douggie.'

'No, come on, Lou-Lou.' Bonnie shook her hand in the air, opened and closed her fingers as if she could drag Louie to her by force of will.

'No!'

Doug stood with Louie rattling at him. He was looking straight at her, still with that smile on his face.

Louie started to wail. 'But I want to go in the workshop!'

'Come on, Lou-Lou. I'm sorry — I forgot to tell Doug about the new rule. Come on, possum.' Bonnie walked over and tried to pick him up.

'No-oooo!' went Louie. 'I want to go in the workshop!'

'Come on, darling.' She bent and grabbed him, pulling his hand out of Doug's. Doug didn't move.

'But — I — Want — To!' shouted Louie.

'I know, I know. Come on, possum, let's go in and you can listen to any talking book you like. Which one will you choose, do you think?' And she hobbled back up the path and up the steps and in the door with Louie struggling, hanging from her arms the whole way.

And just before she kicked the kitchen door shut, she couldn't believe it but she heard herself call, breathlessly, over her shoulder and over Louie's wailing, 'Sorry, Doug!'

'And now we're going to read another book about pigs,' said the librarian into her headset, her voice booming through the speakers. She leaned forward to pick up the book, and there was the muffled thumping of the mic hitting her chest.

'What's with the microphone?' Mel whispered.

'God knows.' Bonnie put her chin in her hand and her fingers over her mouth. *Don't laugh.*

The librarian held up the book to show the cover. 'Can anyone guess what this book is called?' The speakers crackled, and there was a faint whine of feedback.

'Why is it so loud?' whispered Mel.

Bonnie couldn't answer. She was trying to hold it back, but the laugh was coming over her like something involuntary. *Don't laugh, don't laugh.* But it was like a sneeze, a building urge, tickling up between her ribs and towards her throat.

'That's right!' boomed the librarian. 'It's *The Three Little Pigs!*'

On the hiss at the end of *pigs* the feedback took off properly, in a slashing shriek that sent one little girl crying to her mother. The rest of the children sat as though stunned.

'Jesus,' muttered Mel.

Bonnie, tears in her eyes, tried to clear her throat, but it didn't work — the laugh took hold. She tried to disguise it as a cough, but it broke through, shook its way out in a series of breathy, strangled sounds. 'Excuse me.' She got up and shuffled, bent over, past the row of other parents perched on tiny chairs, to the shelter of the nearest shelves, where she turned her back and tried to smother with both hands great shuddering gusts of laughter that racked her like sobs.

'*Once upon a time …*' thundered the voice behind her. Bonnie buried her face in the crook of her arm and braced her other hand on her knees. She hadn't laughed like this since the last time she was stoned, however long ago that was.

'You okay?' She felt Mel beside her, touching her arm.

'Yeah,' she said, straightening and wiping her eyes. 'Sorry. I just couldn't stop laughing.' She peered between the shelves. 'The kids okay?'

'Yeah,' said Mel, peering too. 'I'm so paranoid now at this library.'

'Me too.' Bonnie watched Edie and Louie sitting together, mouths agape, eyes scanning as the librarian turned the pages. She felt the last of the laugh go out of her like the final zip of air from a let-go balloon. 'How long ago was that now?'

'I don't know,' said Mel. 'Must be a while. A year?'

'Yeah. Still freaks me out though.' She glanced from the twins to the pram parked behind the row of parents. The mound of blankets was peacefully still, one tiny hand just visible, loosely curled. 'Was it … was it actually a … rape?' Her stomach twisted as she said the word. 'Or was it just an … assault?'

'I think it was a rape. Well, that's what was in the papers anyway.'

'God. That poor child. And her parents. I mean, obviously it would be just completely devastating for something like that to happen anywhere, but I guess you think … well, the library's always felt like such a safe place.'

'I know. I used to leave Freddie in the kids' area while I went off to get my own books.' Mel made a face. 'Josh'd kill me if he knew.' She sighed. 'Oh well. Not any more.'

'No way.'

'And now,' the librarian was saying, disentangling herself at last from the headset, 'we're going to make some pigs of our own. We're each going to get one paper plate …'

'Do you think we're too paranoid?' Bonnie said, as she and Mel went back over to the children.

'I don't know.'

'Nobody worried about stuff like that when we were kids. I can remember sitting in the car for ages outside the shops waiting for my dad. And I reckon I was going to the milk bar by myself when I was not much older than these guys. Okay, maybe more like seven — but still, I can't imagine letting Edie or Lou, even in another couple of years …'

'Yeah, but …' Mel looked up from where she was crouched beside Freddie, a pink pipe-cleaner between her fingers. 'Just because our parents didn't worry about it doesn't mean bad things didn't happen. It's just not worth the risk, is it? That's what it comes down to.'

Outside the cafe around the corner Bonnie opened her coat, lifted her jumper and latched Jess on. Her exposed skin tightened with the cold. 'God,' she said, 'it's freezing.'

'Sure is. Here.' Mel scooted her seat closer and grabbed the edge of Bonnie's coat, pulling it around and tucking it into the top of her jeans. 'How's that?'

'Better. Thanks.'

'No worries.' Mel glanced over to the three older children, who were on a bench with their paper-plate pigs. 'Freddie,' she called, 'if you sit like that you're very likely to fall over backwards.' She resettled in her seat. 'So, what else is news?'

'Nothing much. Doug's back.'

'Pete's friend?'

'Yeah. You remember — you met him at that barbeque that time. You said you thought he had, you know, personality border whatsit.'

'Oh yeah, him. I thought they had a falling-out.'

'God, I don't know.' Bonnie looked down at Jess. 'I mean, they did. But now he's back. I think that's what Doug does — he goes from friend to friend, sort of insinuating himself, and then because he's so hard to be around eventually there's a fight of some sort and he goes off in a huff. And moves on to the next person, I guess.'

'Yeah, right. Must be annoying.'

'The problem is ... Well, it's what you said, really: the boundaries aren't clear. He's Pete's friend but he's also working for Pete. And Pete's kind of giving him the work as a favour. I mean, I don't think he's really qualified to do what he's doing. God, he annoys me. He does —' She found herself glancing around, leaning forward, lowering her voice. 'He does all this really annoying kind of powerplay stuff, acting like he's the lackey and we're high and mighty — you know, calls me Missus Bonnie and stuff like that. Like it's a joke but sort of actually having a go at me. Know what I mean? And then he'll have a go at Pete in front of me, I don't know, criticise his haircut or something, like that's funny.'

'That sounds really irritating.'

The man from the cafe came out with a tray.

'Kids!' called Mel. 'Babycinos!'

Bonnie lifted her glass carefully over Jess and sipped. 'It wasn't so bad,' she hissed, as the children ran over and started clambering onto chairs, 'before we moved, when Pete had his old workshop. But now, because they're right there in the backyard, Doug's — well, he's always hanging around the house, playing with the kids, and — look, I'm sure he's totally harmless, not, you know, pervey or anything, but I feel like I have to, you know, supervise.'

'Where's my coffee?' said Edie.

'I don't know, darling,' said Bonnie, lifting Jess to her shoulder and fixing her own clothes. 'They must've forgotten it.'

'But I don't have a coffee.'

'Hang on, darling.' She got up. 'I'll go and see what's happened to it.' She stood for a moment looking at Mel. 'I mean the whole thing's just really stressful.'

Back at the house the twins started up again at the sight of Doug's van.

'Douggie! Douggie! Douggie!'

Bonnie parked the car and swung around in her seat. 'Listen,' she said. 'Doug is here to do some work for Dad, okay? He's not here to play with you guys. I want you to leave him alone, okay?'

'Douggie! Douggie!'

'Edie! Louie!' They both had that same little knot of resistance between their brows. She raised her own eyebrows. 'Okay?'

'Okay,' said Louie.

'But he plays with us,' said Edie. 'And he reads us books.'

'I know he does. But the thing is … Look. Doug — he gets distracted. You know, like when I ask you guys to do something, like put your shoes on. And you go to put your shoes on but then you get distracted — you see a book or a toy and you start playing.' She kept shifting her eyes from Edie's face to Louie's and back again. 'And I know you mean to put your shoes on, it's just —'

'Can I have my library books?' said Edie.

Bonnie sighed.

'Can I have mine too?' said Louie.

'Please, Mum?'

'Please, Mum?'

She turned back in her seat, pulled the keys out of the ignition, started gathering up the bags. 'Just please try to leave Doug alone, you guys, okay?'

'Can we have our library books? Please?'

'When we get inside.' She opened the car door and tried to heave herself out holding all the bags and a bundle of coats. The nappy bag slid off her shoulder and onto the road. 'Shit.'

'Oh, can't we just hold them now?'

'Please, Mum?'

'When we get inside.' She bent to pick up the nappy bag. The string handles of the two library bags were cutting into her forearm.

'Just one book then.'

'Edie! Louie!' Bonnie rearranged everything she was holding and leaned back into the car. 'Sorry, guys, it's just that your books are inside your library bags and look how much I'm carrying — I just can't get a book out for you right now, but when we're inside I'll get them all out and we'll read some of them, okay?' She looked from face to face, the two knotted frowns. 'Okay?'

Edie sighed. 'All right then.'

'Let's go outside,' said Louie to Edie. 'Let's play Teacher, Teacher on the trampoline.'

'Have you finished your lunch?'

'Yes.'

'Yes.'

'Okay. Hang on a sec and I'll help you put on some jumpers.'

Bonnie scraped the plates and stacked them, poured Edie's half-finished milk into the cup with the rest of Louie's and put it in the fridge for later.

She found jumpers and made the twins put them on. Wiped Louie's nose. Looked out and checked that the workshop doors were shut. Machine noises came from in there, and Doug's voice, raised in some exclamation or punchline.

Out the twins ran, overstuffed figures in their warm clothes. She shut the door behind them and stood at the glass pane, nose to the top of Jess's head. She watched them bounce on the trampoline, round and round in some game of their own invention. 'Teacher, teacher,' they chanted. A plastic spade, faded red, lay in the middle of the black mat, bobbling and flipping. There was a moment's pause while Edie made some adjustment to it, and then they resumed.

Bonnie let her gaze drift past them, down the side of the workshop to the bare limbs of the back-fence wisteria vine, its knobby grey joints and snaking fingers, and then higher, to the roof of the neighbours' house with its usual fat pigeon shapes, and the cold sky behind. She breathed Jess's smell again. Tears came to her eyes. What was wrong with her? Maybe she was going to get her period. She turned and scanned the kitchen. She should do a proper tidy-up before dinner. Finish off the breakfast dishes. And go to the supermarket. She went to the bench and looked at the shopping list. Most of it was in Pete's writing. She picked up the pen, dashed her eyes around the room, saw the fruit bowl with its two pallid oranges and scribbled *fruit*. Then she let the pen slip from her fingers, hitched Jess to her shoulder and wandered further into the house.

She settled Jess on her play mat and opened the laptop. There was an email from Mickey. *Recording?* read the subject line. Bonnie felt a fizz of happiness, pure and straight. She opened the email.

Hey Bon, hope all's well. Got some recording coming up, mid August. Couple of tracks I'd love you to play on if you can. Let me know, Mickey xx

She felt her face split into a grin. She read the email again. Hope twirled through her. August. A month away. Jess would be just about six months, starting solids, not needing so many breastfeeds. Only a couple of tracks — she could knock it over in an afternoon, if Mickey gave her demos so she could prepare. She shut the computer and got up. Went past Jess kicking on the floor and to the mantelpiece mirror. Lifted her hair, bundled it into a topknot. Let it fall. Tried to close her mouth over that grin. Shook her head. *This is nothing*, she said to herself. *A titbit, a morsel*. One little recording session, and she was all atremble. She ducked her head from her own eager reflection.

But she could feel it still, like it hadn't been — what? — almost a year. Stepping into the overdub booth and putting on the headphones, her heart in her throat every time. The song beginning, that choking feeling as she laid her fingers on the strings, before the first note sounded. Doubt and nerves always almost swamping her, but then that blank moment of launching into it, the strange lost second as her brain slid into some kind of neutral gear and her hands just took over. The riffs in her headphones merging with the drums and bass and rhythm guitar tracks, moving amongst them and then detaching, rising up and then swooping back down again.

'Mum!' came a yell from the back door. 'Louie's stuck in the apricot tree! And he keeps kicking me when I want to climb!'

Jess was beginning to whinge. 'Coming,' called Bonnie. She picked the baby up and headed for the kitchen.

At five-thirty Pete came in with Doug. Bonnie, rocking Jess in the pram in the living room, heard the jingle of the back-door bells, and Doug finishing a story.

'... worked with it all his life, and you know what he died of? Heart attack. Must've been eighty at least. Strong as an ox.'

'Yeah, right,' came Pete's voice, benignly uninterested.

Doug went on. She could picture him, the way he hovered, talking at you, head angled, as if aiming the words. 'Anyway, I reckon it's all a big fucken beat-up by the media. You wait, next they'll be trying to tell us what sort of paint we can and can't use —'

'Bon?' called Pete, talking right over him.

'In here.'

Pete came into the living room. 'Hi.'

'Hi.' She nodded at the pram and rolled her eyes. 'I'm just trying to get her to sleep. She's been up all afternoon.'

'Where're the others?'

'In the bath.'

Pete slung an arm around her neck, kissed her cheek. 'Had a good day?'

She made a groaning sound. 'Okay,' she said, leaning into him. 'I'm tired. Got up too early. Jess's been a bit nuts. And the others've just been fighting all day. I tried to take them to the shops on their scooters, but Louie fell over and hurt his knee so we came straight back.'

'Is he okay?'

'Yeah, yeah, he's fine — just a scrape. And then I sent them out the back to play, and Edie figured out how to turn the tap on so they got themselves soaked.' She gave a dry little laugh. 'I was wondering why they were being so quiet.'

Pete laughed with her. 'Little buggers.'

'What's that?' It was Doug standing in the doorway. He was drinking one of Pete's Coronas.

18

'Oh, nothing,' said Pete. 'Just the kids getting into trouble.'

'Well, I remember when we were kids, growing up in Ballarat,' said Doug, moving into the room. 'On Sat'dy afternoons me gran used to give me and me brothers and sisters twenty cents each and say, "Go on — bugger off till teatime."'

Pete didn't answer.

'Really?' said Bonnie unwillingly. She looked down at Jess. The baby's eyes were closed. She slowed her rocking, then stopped it. Jess's eyes opened and she squirmed and gave a squawk. 'God,' said Bonnie, and started rocking again. The pram creaked rhythmically.

'What's that you're doing there?' Doug stepped closer and craned over the pram. 'Trying to give the kid brain damage?'

'I'm just trying to get her to go to sleep.' She felt herself shrinking away from him, lowering her gaze. Pete's arm still lay across her shoulders. It felt heavy. He was staring into space, she could tell, not listening to either her or Doug. How did he manage to just switch off like that? She kept her eyes fixed on the pram, on Jess. 'She seems to like quite big rocking movements.' Irritation quivered in her throat, tickled her palms. She gripped the handle harder. *Just shut up. Stop explaining.*

'What's wrong with a bit of brandy in the milk, eh?' Doug threw out his elbows and laughed.

She made a wan 'Ha' sound and bent further over Jess to hide how mean and pinched her put-on smile was. 'Pete?' She tried to speak as if Doug wasn't there. 'Would you mind checking on Edie and Lou?'

'Sure.' He gave her shoulder a squeeze and went out of the room.

'Ahh,' said Doug, draining the beer. He tapped himself on the chest with a fist and held the empty bottle up to the light. 'I do like a beer at the end of a hard day's work. Especially when it's someone else's nice fancy beer.'

Bonnie looked at him. He gave an exaggerated wink. The irritation rose again. Her fingers felt numb, swollen with it. *Tell him to buy his own bloody beer.* But all she did was make that stupid little 'Ha' sound again, smile that uptight smile.

Doug continued to hold the bottle level with his face. 'I notice you're all out of limes though. To stick in the neck, you know. Like a real wanker.' He kept his eyes on the bottle.

Something cold clenched in her stomach. *He hates me,* she thought. She watched Jess and slowed her rocking. *Please don't wake up.* Jess stirred, eyelids fluttering. Bonnie gave the pram a couple of last, slow rocks and then stopped. The baby turned her head to the other side. Her eyelids settled. Carefully Bonnie started wheeling the pram to the doorway. 'I might just put her in the bedroom,' she heard herself say to Doug, as if he'd give a fuck. 'It's quieter in there.'

Back in the kitchen Pete was looking in the fridge. He shut the door and turned as she came in.

'Oh god, sorry,' she said, stopping and putting her hands on the back of a chair. 'I meant to do the shopping. But Louie hurt his knee and then I kept thinking Jess would go to sleep ...' For the third time that day tears threatened. She rubbed her face, swallowed them back down. 'Sorry, Pete.' *I think I'm getting my period*, she would have said, but she was aware of Doug there somewhere, listening, in the living room still, or in the hallway behind her.

'It's okay.' Pete opened the freezer. 'Maybe there's something in here.' He pulled out a plastic tub and read the label. 'Minestrone.'

'I'll do it.' She took the icy package from him. 'If you do the kids I'll do this.'

'Okay.'

'I'm sorry,' she said again.

'It's okay.' He smiled, bent to kiss her. He looked tired. 'I know it's hard. I'll go later and get some milk and bread and stuff.'

'Thanks.'

He left the room.

She got the big saucepan and a knife, and started prising the giant block of frozen soup from its container. Blunt bone-coloured ends of pasta stuck out the top of it, and bits of vegetable lurked mistily in its depths. She wedged the knife in one side and levered. Once it was in the pot she left it to melt and went to bring the clothes in from the line.

Out in the sharp night she tried to savour the minute of quiet, the peace of the clear cold, the stretch of the sky above. Tried to move slowly, to let her shoulders drop, to stand straight but not tense, the way the teacher had described in the yoga classes she'd been to before the children were born. She'd always loved being outside a house at night. The light from windows, the muffled sounds inside — the safe world you'd only stepped away from, that you would go back into soon.

She breathed to accompany the movements of her arms and body as she reached and dropped, stepped to the side and reached again. She thought of Pete's tired face, the touch of his kiss on her cheek. She stopped for a moment and looked up into the sky, the blue-black that comes just before the real dark. *You're lucky, really*, she told herself.

When the soup was heated to bubbling she ladled out the kids' first to let it cool. She made toast from a loaf that was also in the freezer. Spread the pieces with butter and put them on a plate. Ran out again into the cold and picked some parsley. Chopped it and put it in a little dish and set it on the table with parmesan cheese and bowls and spoons. Then she stood over the spare place, hesitating.

'Doug?' she called, trying to make her voice light. 'Would you like to stay for some soup?'

No answer.

She went into the living room. Pete was in the far corner, doing something on the computer. Doug was on the couch in front of the gas heater with Edie and Louie squashed together into his lap, pyjama-ed legs dangling. He was reading to them. Bonnie watched his work-battered hand turn the page, his eyebrows go up as he put on a silly voice. She saw the open-mouthed focus of her children, the clean glow of their freshly bathed faces. The way their heads rested against his jumper.

'*Little pig, little pig,*' growled Doug, '*let me come in.*'

The poor man, Bonnie thought. *He must be so lonely.* The image came to her of Doug as a child, lining up with his raggedy brothers and sisters to take their twenty-cent pieces. Heading out into the cold streets of the country town. Doug running, young and lithe, eyebrows not yet grizzled nor face cragged and pitted with the life that was to come.

She waited for a break in his reading. 'Excuse me.'

'Yes, Missus Bonnie?' Cracking that sly grin.

'Would you like some soup?'

'Yes, please, Missus Bonnie.' Bobbing his head.

'Well, it's ready now.'

Louie tapped the page. 'Read, Douggie.'

Doug looked at Bonnie. There was a pause, just the burr of the heater.

'Read, Douggie,' said Louie.

'As soon as you've finished your story.' Bonnie went out and back down the hallway.

'I got an email from Mickey.'

Pete turned from the washing-up. 'Yeah?'

'She wants me to do some recording with her. Must be

doing a new album.'

'That's great.'

'Yeah.' Bonnie picked up a missed glass and took it over, slipped it into the sink. 'It is, isn't it. I should do it.'

'What do you mean?' Pete rinsed the glass and put it down on the folded tea towel. 'Of course you should do it.'

'It's just …' She sighed. 'Yeah, of course I should, it's just that I don't know how easy it'll be to leave Jess. It should only be a couple of days' work but, you know, I'll need to feed her. I could take her in with me, but what if she cries? And she'll distract me.'

'You could leave her with me. Couldn't you express? How many feeds is she having?'

Bonnie took the dishcloth and wiped down the table. Her earlier excitement was gone. She thought of expressing milk, the whole tedious business, endless boiling of pots of equipment, waiting for a chance to sit down with the pump, trying to time it right so there was still enough for the actual feeds. 'I don't know, Pete,' she said. 'It all seems too hard.'

'Bon.' He pulled out the plug, turned towards her. 'You should do it. It's an opportunity. People need to know you're still out there. Available.' He pulled down the sleeves of his shirt. 'I think it would be really good for you. Worth the effort.'

'Yeah, I know.' She tossed the cloth on the bench. The tension of the dinner, of putting up with Doug and his yammering and gesticulations, of riding the alternating waves of pity and irritation — it all sat in her, dragged at her, pulled her down.

'Did you reply? Did you say yes?'

'Not yet.'

'Well, I think you should. Get the dates and then we'll work out how to deal with the kids.'

'Okay.' She went to him, leaned into his chest. His arms were warm. She could hear his heart beating. Behind him the last of the water gurgled out of the sink and then there was nothing, the precious quiet of one of their short evenings.

She ran herself a bath. As it filled she moved in and out of the bathroom, tidying, doing things now because she knew that afterwards, her body warmed and loosened by the hot water, all she'd want to do was crawl into bed. She kicked the scatters of dirty kids' clothes into a pile, bundled them into her arms and took them to the laundry. She picked up all the bath toys and stuffed them in their net bag and tried unsuccessfully to stick its exhausted suction cups onto the tiles. She flossed and brushed her teeth. She looked in the mirror. Stood for a moment. Twisted off the bath taps and went to find Pete.

He was on the computer. She sat down behind him, on the arm of the couch. 'Pete.'

'Mm?'

'Doug doesn't need to turn up so early in the mornings.'

'I think he likes to.'

'Yeah, I know. But …' She was trying to speak slowly, to keep it a normal conversation. 'If he doesn't actually start until eight-thirty or nine, he doesn't really need to turn up at seven, does he?'

Pete tapped something on the keyboard. 'No. But I think he likes to. I think he's staying somewhere pretty miserable — some friend of a friend's place. He calls it a bungalow, but it sounds like it's pretty much a glorified shed. It's probably freezing.'

'Really?' She pulled her arms around herself. She got a glimpse again of that boy running, his clear, undamaged face. 'Poor guy. That sounds terrible.' She stood up. 'Still, though,' she said. 'It kind of makes it hard for me, having him hanging around. This morning I had to stop him from taking Louie out to the workshop.'

'Really?' He tapped the keys again, resettled his hand on the mouse.

She refolded her arms. 'I know you're in the middle of something, but I feel like we should talk about this.' Her voice was creeping upwards, getting thin. 'Before ... well, before he's back again in the morning and I have to deal with it all again.'

Pete turned to her. 'He's harmless, Bonnie. He's great with the kids. They love him. And so what if he comes a bit early? We're up, aren't we?'

'What, so you're okay with him taking them out to the workshop? Without you?' She tried to bring her voice back down. 'Because I'm not. It's not safe out there, there's dangerous stuff, and I don't think the kids should be in there with anybody other than you or me.'

There was a pause. 'Fair enough,' he said. 'You're right.'

Another pause. 'Well, thanks. Good.' Bonnie felt out of breath. She glanced down at the rug. It needed vacuuming. *Just leave it now*, she thought. But she couldn't help going on. 'So ... um, will you, you know ... say something to him then?'

He turned back to the computer. She heard him puff out his cheeks, as if dealing with a pestering child. 'Okay.'

She stood behind him, watching him move the mouse, the line of his shoulders. *Leave him alone.* But still she kept talking. 'Well, I hope you will, Pete, because I think this is important.'

'Look, Bon.' He turned again, his voice louder this time, and short. 'I'll try, okay? But it's not easy — he's fragile, you know? I don't want to upset him.'

'Upset him?' The anger came rushing, ready. 'Upset *him*?' Her voice was stretched, strained. 'He's working for you, Pete. You've got to be clear about where the two of you — where all of us — stand. I mean we can't be held to ransom by this person who turns up at our house whenever he feels like it to take our kids off to play with the bloody saws and helps himself to beer from the fridge because we're worried that we might upset him if we — I don't know — demand a bit of respect?' A faltering laugh broke from her lips. 'I mean, can't you see how ridiculous this situation is?'

Pete didn't move. His hands lay in his lap.

'Can't you?' She tried to unfold herself, open her arms and reach to him, but she was stuck there, unbending, a pillar.

'I've got to do these emails.' Pete went back to the screen.

In the bath Bonnie looked down at her body. Heavy breasts half afloat. The slack flesh of her thighs. The rack of her hips. Her stomach with its web of stretch marks, with the trench-like hollow that showed if she went to sit up, where the muscles hadn't fully joined together again. She put her head back and stared up at the ceiling.

Doug was Pete's friend. An old friend. What did she want to be: one of those women who gradually took over, made their partner cut ties with everyone from the life they had prior to the relationship? A ball-breaker? Or was she a brat? A princess, who couldn't stand having her territory invaded, who wanted everything her way?

She sat up and pulled out the plug. Got out and dried herself, put on her pyjamas and went into the kitchen. Took down the bottle of gin from the top of the fridge and poured a slug into one of the kids' plastic cups that was sitting in the draining rack. Knocked it back in two gulps, like medicine. Rinsed the cup and returned it to the rack. Switched off the light.

By the time she'd checked on the kids and made her way down the hall to the bedroom the alcohol had started to warm her, bring her partway unclenched. She fell into bed without even putting on the light. She almost wished she'd said goodnight to Pete, apologised. She thought about getting up again, going out to him. Thought about him coming back into bed with her, them both saying sorry, their bodies pulling close in the darkness. She fell asleep thinking about it.

Next morning she was up early again. She did try to return to bed after feeding Jess, but it was no good. She lay alongside Pete, eyes scratchy, that faint pain in her throat that always came with tiredness, but every time she dipped towards actual sleep she'd start awake again, checking the clock. Five-thirty. Five forty-five. Six a.m. At six-fifteen she got up. Crept down to the bathroom. Shut the door carefully. Ran the shower. At least she'd be up and dressed when Doug arrived, and not caught in her pyjamas again.

He came at seven-thirty. Everyone was in the kitchen. Edie and Louie eating porridge at the table, Jess kicking in her baby chair, Pete filling the coffee maker at the bench. Doug's face appeared in the glass pane of the back door, and Bonnie was the only one to see at first. He fixed her with that grin of his; down his head went, and up, like a cockatoo's.

'There's Doug,' she said, and hated herself for the sinking in her stomach, the forced awful smile that seemed to be all she could give him. *Just be nice. It's not that hard. He doesn't mean any harm.*

'G'day Douggie,' said Pete, opening the door.

'Mornin', Boss.' Doug strode in. 'Mornin', Missus Bonnie. Mornin', kids.' He settled himself in a chair and stuck his face out towards the children. 'Porridge!' he said. 'What a treat! You kids don't know how lucky you are.'

Louie and Edie giggled into their bowls.

'There's some left,' said Pete. 'Do you want it, Douggie?'

'Oh-ho-ho,' went Doug, flapping his elbows. 'I feel like all me Christmases have come at once. I haven't had porridge for years.' He stretched his features in a look of delirious joy and leaned back in his chair.

Pete took a bowl over to him. 'Sugar?'

'Yes, please, Boss.'

She stood by the sink and watched as Pete got the jar of brown sugar down from the high cupboard and took it over to the table. She saw the craning of the twins' necks. She steeled herself for what was coming.

'Can I have sugar on my porridge?'

'Can I have sugar on my porridge too?'

'Please?'

'Please?'

'What?' said Doug, heaping spoonfuls from the jar. 'Haven't you got some already?'

She opened her mouth, moved forward, but Pete was there.

'Just a tiny bit,' he said. 'Special treat.' And he took Louie's spoon and dug out some sugar with it.

'Pete.' Bonnie's voice, tight and mean, rang in her own ears. *You're a nag*, she thought. 'Pete, you know we don't usually —'

'It's just a tiny bit, Bonnie, come on.' Pete moved on to Edie's bowl. 'And a little bit for you, Edie-Pedie.'

'Yeah, but you know we don't give them sugar. They've already got honey on there. And there's sultanas in it. It's sweet enough.'

'Bonnie.' Pete gave her a look. 'It's just this once.'

Just leave it. You're making things worse. But she couldn't help it. She began stacking dishes by the sink. Her hands were shaking. 'There's no such thing as just this once,' she heard herself say, in that pinched voice.

'Watch out!' said Doug behind her. 'Have I got everyone in trouble?'

Bonnie didn't need to see. She knew he'd have that grin on again, his head waggling, spoon raised. She was rigid with anger. All she could feel, in the whole room, was him, his presence, taking up all the space. She dropped a fistful of cutlery in the sink, turned and walked with her eyes on the floor to Jess in her chair. She scooped up the baby into her arms and then continued stiffly past the table and out of the room.

'Hurry up, Edie and Lou,' she managed to call back once she was safely in the hallway. 'Swimming this morning.'

'Yay! Swimming lessons!' came the yells, and there was a clatter of spoons and a scraping of chairs.

She stood in the living room holding Jess. She looked at herself in the mirror, her tense face, the lines either side of her mouth. At the sound of Edie and Louie thudding down the hall she lifted her chin and a smile broke over that reflected face — a grim smile of victory.

Bonnie pulled down her goggles and pushed off the edge. She stroked and kicked, feeling the extra flesh on her legs and arms wobble. She was slow and heavy, but it felt good. On she churned without stopping, at each end turning without pause, ducking again, pushing into the new lap. Twisting her head to take in air and then letting it go in a controlled rush. In, out. In, out. Arms, legs, head, breath, all working, busy, occupied. Thoughts coming and going as if washing through with the water. Images: just-born Jess being passed between her legs by the midwife, little thighs closed coyly like a cherub's, cord trailing, smears of blood and vernix; a camp site with Pete, long ago, big white trees like ghosts, a wallaby in the dawn, lowering its head to the ashes of their fire; the balcony of a hotel room somewhere once, drinking vodka with Mickey and the others after a sold-out show, listening to Bowie, feeling that this was it, this was the best and happiest she'd ever get; the twins bouncing round and round the spade in their bundled-on clothes; Pete turning away from her to the computer; Doug at the back door, his grin and eyebrows and cockatoo nod.

She stopped at the shallow end, crouched neck-deep, panting.

The din of the enormous room broke over her. She pulled off her goggles and glanced up at the clock and across to the kids' pool, where Edie and Louie and three other children were bobbing on foam noodles around the teacher. Beyond them Bonnie's mother sat on a bench, rocking Jess in the pram.

She pushed off again, breaststroke this time, old-lady style, goggles off, head held high. Why couldn't she be nice? Be generous to Doug? Like Pete — open-hearted, easygoing. That was what she wanted to be. She concentrated on squeezing the muscles in her thighs and bum. Another swimmer overtook, sending a patter of water into her face. Bonnie shook it off, steadied herself and swam on.

'Great swimming!' The teacher held up her hand, and each child in turn jumped to do a high five.

Louie and Edie came floundering over to the edge. 'Can we play for a bit?' called Edie.

'Sure. We'll be watching.' Bonnie waved to them and went back to the bench. She rewrapped her towel and sat down beside Suzanne. 'Is that okay with you, Mum?'

Suzanne glanced at her watch. 'Should be fine,' she said. 'If it's only a few minutes. I'll need to get going pretty soon though, so if you want me to help get them showered and everything ...'

'Yeah, okay, I'll get them out in a sec.' She watched Edie and Louie splashing in their goggles and breathed slowly, trying to ease the annoyance that squeezed her chest. *For fuck's sake. It's one hour a week and she can't wait to get away.*

'And how was your swim?' said Suzanne.

'All right.' She kept her eyes on the children in the water. 'I've got a way to go.'

'You'll get there. You managed to bounce back after those whopping great twins — you'll be fine. And Jess is only — what? — five months now?'

'Nearly.'

'Well, five months isn't really all that long, in terms of your recovery. So don't worry too much just yet.'

There was a silence.

Suzanne sat up straighter, crossed her legs. 'Let them play a bit longer,' she said. 'I can hang around an extra ten minutes. I just wanted to get to that boutique in Clifton Hill before I had to head back in time for bridge, that's all.'

Bonnie tugged at her towel. The annoyed feeling was still there, and showed in her voice, its chilly formality. 'Are you sure?'

'Yes, yes — really, it's all right. No hurry.'

There was another silence.

Come on. She's trying.

Suzanne settled back on the bench. 'So what else is news?'

Bonnie took a breath, smoothed her voice, made it friendly. 'Not much. Pete's got his old friend Doug working for him again. Remember — you would've met him at that barbeque we had, you know, at the old house, when Pete got that bar fit-out?'

'Doug.' Suzanne frowned. 'Don't remember him.'

'Yes, you do. Skinny guy, bit manic, little bit older. Talks all the time. Calls me Missus Bonnie.'

'Oh, him. Mad as a snake, that feller.'

'Well, he's driving me crazy. He turns up at seven-thirty, sits around the kitchen eating porridge that Pete makes for him. And I'm trying to get the kids organised and he just keeps playing with them and — Oh, it doesn't sound that bad when I say it, but ...' She pushed back her hair. 'It's not what he does, it's just him — he's really intrusive. You know, watches everything you do and has some comment ready. Makes these jokes that are actually jibes at me, and ... or, I don't know, maybe I'm just paranoid. Maybe I'm sensitive to everything he says now, 'cause I've tuned into it.'

'So what's he doing for Pete, exactly?'

'Just odd jobs in the workshop. I don't know really.'

'Well, is he a carpenter or anything?'

'I don't think so. I think he just does easy stuff — you know, sanding or whatever.' She half stood. 'Louie! Edie! Over this way, please, where I can see you.' She waited until they came closer.

'Hold on,' said Suzanne. 'Hasn't there already been an issue with this Doug feller? Didn't he make a big mistake last time, get an order wrong or something?'

'Yeah.'

'What happened again?'

'Well. These people rang up and changed their order. Pete had gone off somewhere and left his phone.' Bonnie rolled her eyes. 'So Doug took it upon himself to answer Pete's phone and underquoted them by, like, fifteen hundred dollars. Pete didn't find out until he went to make the delivery. So what could he do? He had to just give it to them for the cheaper price.'

'Yes, well, that's no good. You can't have someone like that working for you.'

'But, Mum, the thing was that Doug wouldn't admit it was his fault. When Pete asked him he swore black and blue he quoted them the right price. Even though he'd written the wrong price down in the book. He even tried to say it was just his messy writing — that Pete couldn't read the numbers properly.'

'Did Pete blame Doug?'

'Yeah, of course. But I don't think he pushed it. I think he just let it go. But Doug was offended anyway.'

'And feeling guilty too, I imagine.'

'I don't know about that. He's a pretty weird guy. I wouldn't be surprised if he convinced himself it really wasn't his fault.' She stood up. 'Anyway, that was the last we heard of him —

until now. Come on, we'd better get these kids in the showers.' She went to the edge of the pool. 'Edie! Louie! Time to get out.'

Edie looked up at her, flashed a smile and blithely splashed off in the other direction.

'Right.' Bonnie went along the edge a bit, closer to where they were. 'Edie! Louie! Out now or there'll be no hot chocolates!'

'The thing is, Mum,' she said, as they herded the kids out to the car park, 'with this whole Doug business — I mean, one of the things I love so much about Pete, and really admire in him, is his generosity. He really is one of the kindest people I know. And I wish I was more like that myself. You know?' She stopped at the car, felt in her bag for the keys. 'I mean, poor Doug — he's got troubles, obviously. He never has any money. He doesn't own any property or assets.'

'What's he spend all his money on then?'

'I don't know. Gambling, I think. He's into the horses.'

'Then he's only got himself to blame for that.'

'Yeah, well. But, you know what I mean — he's on his own. I've never heard of him being in any sort of relationship — a girlfriend, or anything. And I don't think he's got much support in terms of family or whatever, and he doesn't seem to have many friends.' Bonnie pulled out the keys, unlocked the car. 'He really is a lost soul. And we've got — you know, it's no skin off my nose if someone else eats a bit of our porridge in the mornings — why should I begrudge him that? And the kids do really love him.' She looked across at Edie and Louie, who were swinging on a rail. 'He reads them stories and all that, and, you know, it probably means a lot to him, that contact, if he's as lonely as he seems —'

'Yes, but, Bonnie, this is business we're talking about. That bloke sounds like a liability.' Suzanne leaned over to kiss her cheek. 'You need to put a stop to it.'

Doug's van wasn't out the front when they got home.

'Where's Douggie?' said Louie.

'Don't know, darling. Maybe he's gone out to get something.'

'Some wood?'

'Yeah. Maybe some wood.'

All afternoon she found herself listening out. Glancing towards the hallway, the front door. Doug didn't return though. She saw Pete go down along the side of the workshop to the outside toilet at some point, but he didn't come up to the house.

When he did come in, at five-thirty, she was at the stove stirring a cobbled-together pasta sauce of canned tuna and tomatoes.

'Smells good.' He put his arms around her.

'The only part of it not to come out of a can is the onion.'

'Well, it still smells good. I'm hungry. I'll just go and get cleaned up.'

'Wait.' Bonnie turned and reached up to him. She kissed him, his face and neck. 'I'm sorry I've been so horrible.'

'That's okay.' He gave her a quick smile and went to move away.

'Wait.' She pulled him close again, kissed him on the lips this time, breathed his sweet wood smell. She reached under his shirt and put her hands to his skin. 'I missed you today. Sometimes I feel like I hardly see you, even though you're just out there.'

Pete kissed her back. She could feel him leaning into her, responding. 'Where're the kids?' he whispered.

'Listening to talking books.'

'Oh, really?' He grinned and pulled her top untucked, slid his hand up to her breast. The two of them shuffled, still kissing, until Bonnie was pressed up against the bench. She could feel him getting hard, pushing against her thigh.

There was a wail from the other side of the room. Pete let go and straightened up. 'Who's that? Is that Jess?'

'Oh god.' Bonnie gave a defeated laugh. 'Yeah, it's Jess. I forgot about her. She's in her chair.'

'Bugger.' He worked his hands back under her clothes. 'Maybe she'll stop,' he whispered.

'I don't know about that.'

Jess wailed again. Pete sighed and tucked his shirt in. 'I'll just wash my hands and stuff and then I'll get her.'

'Okay.' Bonnie turned back to the stove.

'So guess what?' said Pete at dinner.

'What?'

'No, Mum — you have to guess,' said Edie.

'Um ... You're secretly a woman,' said Bonnie.

'Bonnie!' Pete frowned and jerked his head at the kids. 'You'll confuse them.'

'Dad's not a woman!' Louie laughed, mouth full of pasta.

'He's a man,' said Edie. 'You're a woman, Mum.'

'And I'm a boy and Edie's a girl,' said Louie. 'And Jess is just a baby.'

Pete stabbed more pasta on his fork. 'So does anyone want to actually hear my news?'

'Yes.'

'Yes, *please*, Mum.'

'Yes, please, Pete.' She smiled across at him.

'Well, you remember Grant, who owns Juno?'

'Yeah.'

'He's opening another bar. And he wants me to do the fit-out again.'

'Pete, that's fantastic.' Bonnie got up and went around the table, put her arms round his shoulders and kissed him. 'That's such good news.'

'What's happened?' said Edie.

'What's a sit-out?' said Louie.

'Fit-out,' said Pete. 'A fit-out is when someone builds all the furniture in a place, like a shop or a restaurant. You know how I make furniture — table and chairs and things? Well, this guy wants me to make lots of furniture for him.'

'It means Dad's got lots of work to do,' said Bonnie.

'It means we don't have to worry about money for a while,' said Pete, and squeezed her hand.

Pete sat down on the edge of the bed to unlace his shoes. 'We should go out for dinner sometime,' he said. 'To celebrate.'

She looked up from her book. 'Yeah. We should.'

His voice was muffled as he bent over. 'Well, let's actually do it this time.'

'Yeah, I know. But it's just so hard, organising someone to babysit, and worrying about if Jess needs to be fed and all that.'

He sat up again. 'What about your mum?'

She sighed.

'Just ask her.' Pete stood and unbuttoned his shirt. 'I mean, she's their grandmother. You'd think she'd want to spend the time with them.' He tossed the shirt over a chair. 'Or at least do it to help you out.'

Bonnie sank lower in the bed. She felt exhaustion drag at her, her limbs weighed down with it. 'I know. It's just — she's so hard to pin down. I just, I feel like it's not worth the effort.'

Pete undid his belt. 'Does she know she's not normal?'

She closed her eyes.

'Does she know that most people — all our friends, Greg and Kylie, and Mel and Josh, everyone — they've got parents who actually help out with the kids? Weren't you just telling me Mel's mum takes Freddie for whole weekends? Imagine that.'

She put her arm across her face. 'Yeah, but Freddie's an only child. One kid, that's easy — three's just, well, it feels like too much to ask. And anyway, Jess's too young. Maybe one day, when they're all a bit —'

'Yeah, right, like she'll just suddenly start helping one day, after doing nothing for five years.' There was the sound of him taking coins from his pocket and putting them on the bedside table. 'Hasn't she got friends who're grandparents? Doesn't she know that's what they're supposed to do?'

She opened her eyes again. 'Come on, Pete.'

'What? You think because she gave us that money she doesn't need to do any more?'

Bonnie didn't answer.

'We didn't ask for that money.'

'I know.'

'We would've been okay. Eventually.'

'Pete. It covered almost the whole deposit for this house.'

His voice softened. 'Why would you do that? It just seems really weird to me that someone would give away half of their dead husband's life insurance like that. She could've retired. Gone travelling.' He looked down at her. 'I mean — why?'

'I don't know. I guess she does want to help us out. But just — on her terms.' She put her fingers to her temples. 'And it's a bit unfair, all the pressure being on her. I mean, if she wasn't the only one — if Dad was still around, or if your parents lived in Melbourne …'

'They're too old now anyway. They'd probably try, but I doubt they'd be capable of much.'

There was a silence.

'The thing is … I just don't know why a grandmother wouldn't want to spend time with her grandchildren.' He threw his jeans on the chair. 'And why doesn't she do it just to help you out?'

'I don't know.' Bonnie yawned. 'I didn't ask her if she wanted to be a grandmother.' She pulled the covers further up. 'Anyway. It's not like it would've stopped us from having the kids —

if we'd known she wasn't going to be on board.'

'Yeah, I guess not.' He sat down and touched her hair. 'But we had no idea, did we? What it was going to be like.'

She smiled and shook her head. 'Absolutely no idea.'

He got into bed.

'So ...' She let her book slide to the floor. 'When did you find out?'

'Find out what?'

'About the new job for Grant?'

'Last night.'

She switched off her lamp and moved closer, rested her head on his shoulder. 'So why didn't you tell me then?'

'Well, you know, we had that fight.'

'Oh.'

'And then this morning you were in such a bad mood I thought I'd leave it for later.'

'I'm sorry. I feel like such a harpy.' She kissed his neck. 'You know I hate being like that. It's just ... I'm always tired, and I find it so stressful with Doug around and —'

'Let's not talk about Doug.' Pete turned towards her, slid down so their faces were level. He kissed her and moved closer.

Bonnie shut her eyes. She tried to let go, to lose herself in the kissing and the touching, to sink into that fluid place where there was no thinking, only their bodies together. But she couldn't. She had to keep pressing words back. *But where was Doug this afternoon? Will he be back in the morning?* Behind her eyelids came the vision of Doug at the door, the bob of his head, the solicitous grin. Pete put his mouth on her breast, and she couldn't help it, she squirmed, only just managed not to push him away.

'You okay?'

She nodded. 'That tickles.' She concentrated on his smell, the taste of his skin. In her head she took herself back to that camping trip, to looking out at the wallaby, silent in the grainy dawn light. The pale trunks of the trees towering, just visible, hanging like brushstrokes. Turning to Pete in the dark tent. The woodsmoke smell of him. Just the two of them there in all those miles of trees and scrub.

Pete was awake next morning when she came back to bed after feeding Jess. His eyes were closed, but Bonnie could tell by his breathing. 'Pete?' she whispered.

'Mm?'

'What're you thinking about?'

'Nothing. Trying to sleep.'

She rolled over to face him. 'Yesterday,' she said in a low voice. 'What happened to Doug?'

He didn't open his eyes. 'What do you mean?'

'Well, he wasn't here all afternoon.'

'Oh, I don't know.' He turned the other way. 'He went off somewhere, to meet a friend or something.'

She lay looking at Pete's back. She bit down on all the incredulous words that sprang to her mouth. *So he just comes and goes as he pleases? You have no formal arrangement? You don't even communicate about what's happening on a day-to-day level?*

'Hey, Bon?'

She shut her eyes. How unfair, that Pete could afford to be so casual when she was the one picking up the slack. The one trapped, politely listening, while Doug told his bullshit stories and Pete drifted off as if somehow exempt. Or popping up like some horrible ghoul to drag the kids away, spoil their fun, because she knew if she didn't Doug would just sit around reading stories all morning instead of working. The one tiptoeing, feeling watched and judged. Feeling she had to explain or justify herself, her behaviour, her parenting — in her own house.

'Bon?'

She managed a 'Hm?' noise.

Pete rolled onto his back. 'I need to get some timber. For this Grant job.'

'Okay.'

'Should we all go? Go away for a weekend? Family holiday?'

She opened her eyes. 'Really?'

'Why not? I think I'll go back to that same guy as last time, near Orbost. He was good. I was thinking we could see if we could stay at Jim's shack. It's not far from there. It'll be freezing, but could be fun. Get out of town.'

'When?'

'What about this weekend? Maybe we could even stay an extra day. Leave tomorrow morning. Do you think we could get organised that fast?' Pete moved closer to her. 'Be nice to spend some time together. And I wouldn't mind getting away from the workshop for a while. Doug's been driving me a bit crazy.'

Bonnie stared. She opened her mouth. A double layer of thought slid through her mind. The top layer was strident. It said: *You have to get out of your own workshop because this friend who you don't even know will turn up or if so for how long and has a history of fucking things up for you and your business is driving you crazy?* And the bottom layer, which resonated like a bass line, said: *Pete is kind and generous and tolerant and you, Bonnie, are not. Look at him, trying to help Doug and manage you at the same time. The poor man.*

'Bon?' Pete was watching her face.

She turned away and pushed her back into him, and he lifted his knees, fitted them to the backs of hers. She pulled the covers up over her ear. 'Sounds great,' she said.

Doug arrived while they were having breakfast.

'Croissants,' he warbled, tossing a bulging plastic bag into the middle of the table. 'Been up since half-past five this morning. Went out to see me mate Phil at Flemington.' He rubbed his hands together and stuck them in his armpits. 'Phew. Cold as a witch's tit out there.'

Bonnie cringed at the saying. Was he trying to get a rise out of her? She couldn't tell. She watched him bouncing up and down on his toes and grinning at the children. *Just ignore it. Whatever he's doing, look, he's brought us a gift. He's trying to be nice.* 'Thanks, Doug.' She picked up the bag. 'They're still hot.'

'From the Vietnamese bakery on Union Road.' Doug winked. 'Best croissants in the inner north-west.'

'I'll make some coffee,' said Pete.

She got out plates and knives and jam and put them on the table.

'I got to see lots of great big beautiful horses this morning,' Doug was saying to Louie and Edie.

'Did you ride on them?' said Edie, tearing the end off a croissant and stuffing it in her mouth.

'No, no. Normal people like me aren't allowed. But I got to pat one.'

Bonnie sat down next to Edie. She watched Doug's rough hands breaking apart the pastry, the way he wolfed down the bites with jerks of his head. She willed herself to look him in the eye. 'So is your friend a trainer then, Doug?'

'No, no — stablehand.'

'Did he give you any tips?' said Pete from over by the stove.

'Not today, no.'

'Been years since I had a bet,' said Pete. 'Hey, remember, Douggie?' He brought the coffee pot over. 'At McKean Street? We had all the money for the phone bill and we put it on that trifecta?'

41

Doug flung his head back and let out a wheezing laugh. 'And we cleaned up — made enough to pay all the bills plus that month's rent.' He wiped his fingers on his pants. 'We bought a bottle of champagne on the way back from the TAB.'

'And then we got stupid and put it all on another trifecta and lost it all.' Pete shook his head. 'God, we were idiots.'

'We were young,' said Doug. 'We thought we were gods.' He tossed the last bit of his croissant into his mouth and chewed. 'We were gods.'

Bonnie half filled her cup with coffee. 'I can't believe you put it all on another bet,' she said to Pete. 'Shouldn't you have at least hung on to half of it?'

'Like Douggie said — we were young,' said Pete with a shrug. He swung a look at her, and his eyes were bright and for a moment she saw him, the younger him, from before her time, unencumbered, full of swagger.

'We were gods!' Doug raised his mug and grinned round at them all.

'But still,' she said. 'You'd think …' But then she stopped. 'Oh, never mind. I can't believe I'm even bothering to reason with two people who'd think it was a good idea to put all their bill money on a horse.'

'Three horses,' said Pete.

'Well, even worse.' She shot him a smile, drained her coffee and stood up. 'Thanks for the croissants, Doug. They were delicious.'

'Pleasure, Missus Bonnie.'

'Come on, you kids.' She smoothed back Louie's hair. 'Kinder today.' Outside the yard was lit with thin winter sun. She could feel the caffeine, her heart picking up. Maybe after she'd dropped the twins she'd give herself a treat — go and look in some shops.

As she hustled Louie and Edie down the hallway she could

hear Pete and Doug still talking in the kitchen. 'What came second?' Pete was saying. 'It was Special that won, wasn't it?'

'Special first, Snippets second, then Redelva third,' came Doug's voice. 'And remember Deano didn't want to put Snippets in, 'cause he thought it was a weak name — he wanted to have another horse instead, with some macho name like Rock Hard or something, but we said ...' Their voices faded and the back door slammed.

They arrived at the childcare centre at the same time as Mel and Freddie. The kids brushed away their mothers' goodbye kisses and ran out to the sandpit. She and Mel took turns at the sign-in sheet, checked for notices, skimmed the lost-property box.

Outside they stood in the cold street, Bonnie with Jess on one hip, Mel with her heels and clean, unladdered stockings, the black oblong of her handbag tucked under one arm.

She glanced down at her worn jeans, a stain over one knee. 'I've been offered some work,' she said.

'That's great,' said Mel. 'Live shows, or ...?'

'No, recording.' She moved Jess to the other hip. 'Probably only a half-day. But' — she gave a sheepish grin — 'it still feels like a big deal to me.'

'Well, it is a big deal. You've got three kids, Bonnie. One only a tiny baby, really.' Mel reached to touch Jess's hair. 'I can't believe the amount of music you've done while your kids've been small. Remember you'd go off for those weekends when the twins were babies?'

'Yeah. But ... I don't know. It doesn't seem as easy this time.'

'Really?'

'No. It doesn't. It seems really hard actually.' Tears slid into her eyes. She swallowed. 'I guess it's just — well, Pete's got a whole lot more work on these days, and ...' She wiped dribble from Jess's chin. 'I mean, I can't complain really — I've got these

43

two days with the twins in childcare, and Jess, you know, it's easy to take a little baby along …' She could feel Mel watching her. She stared at the ground. 'I should be doing more really — I could, if …'

'Bonnie.' Mel took her arm. 'What do you mean, doing more? You're doing an amazing job just — well, getting through the days. If I had three kids I'd be rocking in a corner, seriously.'

Bonnie tried to laugh then shook her head. 'Sorry, I don't know where all this self-pity's coming from.'

'And do you know what else? There's no way I could manage work and Freddie without my mum. And Josh's parents too. No way. And your mum's … your family …' Mel released her grip. Her voice had softened, gone tentative. 'Well, you don't seem to be getting the same kind of …'

'My mum's crap.' Bonnie did laugh this time. 'When it comes to helping me with the kids she's just … crap.'

Mel laughed too; her lipstick shone. There was a pause. Mel took her car keys from her bag. 'What is it, do you think, that's stopping her? Is it just her work?'

'No, no — it's not work. She didn't have to keep working.' Jess started whining, and Bonnie jigged her up and down. 'After Dad died — I mean, she could've just lived on the money from the life insurance. But.' She shrugged. 'I don't know — she wanted to work. Which is fair enough. She enjoys it. She likes being busy. And with the kids — I think she just felt like she'd done her time, with me and Luke, and …' She sighed. 'It's complicated.'

A woman came out of the centre behind them, struggling with the security gate and a pusher in which a toddler cried, red-faced, snot streaming. Mel stepped over and held the gate. The three women exchanged smiles of removed, polite commiseration.

'Thanks,' the woman said, and walked away. The child's wailing receded.

Bonnie watched her go. 'My mum ...' she began. 'I don't think she enjoyed having young kids herself. She's always just talked about how she put us in crèche from six weeks and went straight back to work, and how when we were older we'd come home to an empty house and look after ourselves; how we took turns to cook dinner and stuff like that. Almost like she was proud of how much she, well, wasn't there.'

'Right,' said Mel. 'But couldn't you ... If you just straight-up asked her to help with your kids, don't you think ... she wouldn't say no, would she? Couldn't she make time?'

'Yeah, I guess. I mean, yes, of course. But it's like — she's never offered. Her heart's not in it. Her house is totally not kid-friendly. She's had the kids for a sleepover once, when Jess was born. It's just, you know, it's just obvious that it's something she's not interested in, and also, because it's always been like that — I mean, if she'd been involved from the beginning then the kids would've developed a relationship with her. But they haven't. And that makes it harder as time goes on. Leaving them with her now would be almost like leaving them with a stranger.'

'That sucks, Bonnie.' Mel made a face. 'And it's not like you've got anyone else, with Pete's parents — where do they live again?'

'Perth. And they wouldn't be much help anyway. They're old, you know — in their seventies. And Pete's brother's a kind of weird itinerant ageing hippie. We might see him once every two years. And my brother ... I'd be surprised if he ever came back now. He's been in London since he finished school.' She shrugged. 'It really is just pretty much the two of us, me and Pete.'

'That must be so hard.' Mel flicked the blade of her car key out and then back in again.

'Oh well. At least I don't have to put up with my mum all the time. Sometimes I imagine what it would be like if she was one of those, you know, full-on grandparents — always visiting, giving unwanted advice and all that.'

'It'd drive you crazy. Josh's mum moved in with us for two weeks after Freddie was born.' Mel rolled her eyes. 'I was just about ready to kill her by the end. She kept saying I was tired and offering to give him bottles of formula during the night, and that it wouldn't make any difference to the breastfeeding, blah blah blah. And of course Josh wouldn't say anything.'

Bonnie smiled.

Mel pressed the stubby black key, and her car made a demure bipping noise. 'Still,' she said, 'it was pretty nice having an extra adult there sharing the cooking and cleaning. Even if it was Josh's mum. I guess it's like the work thing: it's a toss-up whether it's worth it, in terms of sanity. Everything seems to require some sort of compromise.' She lifted her head. 'Hey, did you see that thing in the paper — I think it was in one of those Sunday magazines a couple of weeks ago — about that kind of inner-suburban community?'

Bonnie shook her head.

'It's in Northcote, or Thornbury maybe, and there's, I think, about five houses, and the people've taken down the fences between them, and they sort of — it's not a commune, they don't share everything — but they do share the care of their children to some extent, and they all have this group meal together once a week, and they have a shared vegie garden, stuff like that.'

'Really?' Jess was notching up her whingeing. Bonnie pulled out her own keys and dangled them in front of her. 'I don't know,' she said. 'I don't know if I could do something like that.' She watched Jess grab at the keys. 'I think I like my privacy too much. I mean, what if you just really didn't get along with one of the other people?'

'Yeah. I think I'm with you on that one.' Mel spread her hands and smiled a rueful smile. 'What can you do? You can't win.'

Bonnie wandered up and down the rows of shelves in the bookshop, Jess strapped to her in the sling. She lingered by the art section, sliding out the heavy books, turning the glossy pages. There was one about twentieth-century furniture: big, hard cover, with full-colour illustrations. She looked at the price sticker and bit her lip. It was beautiful though. Pete would love it. And he had the new job coming. Maybe she could put it on lay-by, save up and pay for it before Christmas.

'Excuse me?'

She jumped, pushed the book back into the shelf.

'Sorry.' It was a man — a boy, almost — younger than her. Glasses and a cool haircut. 'Um, are you — did I see you playing guitar in Mickey Meyers' band? It would've been a while ago now. Start of last year?' He was nervous; his eyes flicked on and off her face. 'At the Forum?'

Bonnie felt her ears go hot. She wished she was wearing better clothes. She felt bulky and squat in her flat boots, Jess bound to her like a clumsy extra layer. 'Yeah,' she said, trying to smile that modest-yet-assured smile she'd seen Mickey do so many times. 'That sounds right.'

'I just wanted to say I love your playing,' said the boy. 'I think you're a really amazing guitarist.'

'Oh, well, thanks.' She shifted her weight and looked down at his narrow shoes.

'So do you still play with Mickey?'

'I've been on a bit of a break. You know, maternity leave.' She indicated the sling.

'Right. Yeah.' The boy didn't even glance at Jess. 'She always seems to have a new band, every time I see her play. What's the story? Is she, like, hard to get along with or something?'

Bonnie pushed her hair back off her face. 'Oh, no. She's very easy to get along with. I think that's just the way she works. She likes to change things around — you know, keep herself interested.'

'You're a bit of a regular though.'

She shrugged. 'Yeah … she does get other guitarists though, sometimes.'

'Right.' There was a pause. He kept looking down at his hands and then back up again. 'So. You playing any music at all?'

'Not really, no. But I think Mickey's working on a new album. So, who knows?'

'New album? Great.' He adjusted the bag on his shoulder. 'Well, I hope you'll be on it.' He dipped his head and swivelled on his toes, ducking away. 'See you.'

'Bye.' Bonnie went back to the books, bumping her fingers over the spines, angling her head to read the titles, but she wasn't concentrating. She waited an appropriate amount of time and then, trying not to be obvious, scanned the shop. There was no sign of him.

Acting casual, but feeling like a clunking robot, she went over to the music section. Hovered along to the 'M's. Flipped through and pulled out a CD. The photo on the back showed the inside of a tour van. Soft, warm colours. Maybe they put some sort of effect on it: it looked like an old photo, those faded, seventies tones. Mickey leaning back in the middle of the seat, arms around Bonnie and that drummer — what was his name? She squinted down at his face. She couldn't remember. The photographer, whoever it was, must have used a special lens because Mickey's legs looked incredibly long, stretching from the centre-point at her crotch out to either side of the camera, where each blue-jeaned knee provided a frame. Guitar cases sticking up in the background. The schedule in thick black texta on three A4 pieces of paper gaffer-taped above the window on the non-door side. *Krefeld, Berlin, Dresden.*

She smiled. It didn't matter that she knew it was probably exhaustion and a hangover, the lighting and the luck of the moment that lent her face in this photograph — her hair falling in her eyes, her smile bright white and just a tiny bit blurred — that easy, dreamy quality you saw in those classic rock photos, like in old copies of *Rolling Stone*. The illusion worked even for her. A current of something like homesickness ran through her, tugged insistently. She replaced the CD.

She didn't put Pete's book on lay-by, or search out something affordable but special for the twins whose birthday was not far off. She left the shop and went across the road. Without trying them on she bought two dresses and two tops in the size she was before getting pregnant with Jess. When she got home she'd hang them in the wardrobe and not even look at them for at least another month. And she'd reply to Mickey's email, and say yes.

THEY LEFT EARLY FRIDAY MORNING.

At Sale they stopped for lunch and afterwards all the children fell asleep. It would have been a good time to talk, but they didn't. They sipped their bad takeaway coffees and drove in silence, not even playing music. Outside the car the landscape changed. Stretches of paddocks and stretches of bush. Towns at regular intervals, like stations on a train line. The sun moved over them.

On the outskirts of one town Bonnie saw a woman emptying a bucket outside a flat-fronted white house. The entrance was set in, but there was no veranda or porch or anything, only a boxy area the same width as the door, like the narrow opening of a fort or something, unwelcoming, defensive. There were no trees in the yard. She twisted in her seat as they passed but she couldn't catch the woman's face.

At the shack they unloaded into the dark room, shivering, talking just to send their voices into the undisturbed air. She set the esky on the floor by the bar fridge and something scurried away under the sink.

'Are there spiders here?' Edie stood close to Louie in the middle of the rug.

'Probably,' said Bonnie.

'Oh, oh — but I'm scared.' Edie pulled her arms in against her chest and hopped up and down.

'Me too.' Louie hopped as well.

'Don't worry. They don't like people. They'll keep away from us — we make too much noise.' Bonnie squatted and peered down the side of the fridge, looking for the switch to turn it on.

'God, it's cold.' Pete slung the last of the bags onto the low couch. 'Let's get the fire going.' He went to the wood-burning stove and clanged its door open, wiped his hands on his jeans. 'Who wants to help me find some kindling?'

But the twins went to perch on the edge of the couch.

'Is this Uncle Jim's house?' said Louie.

'Yes,' said Bonnie.

'Where is he then?'

'Well, he doesn't live here all the time. He just comes here for holidays sometimes.'

'Where will we sleep?' said Edie.

'Here, on the floor.'

'All of us?' said Louie. 'Even Jess?'

'We've got the port-a-cot for her.'

'Oh. Can we make our beds now?'

'No, because then we'd be stepping on them all afternoon.'

'Oh.'

'Come on,' said Pete from the doorway. 'Who's going to help me get the kindling?'

Silence from the twins.

'Let's all go,' said Bonnie. 'We can have a look around.' She went over to Pete and took his hand. 'Come on, you guys.' She stretched out her other hand and wiggled her fingers. Louie came first and took it. Edie took Pete's free hand, and like that, in a chain, they stepped out and off the narrow veranda, down the steps and past the parked car with Jess still sleeping in it, blankets tucked in and the windows down. Into the sparse trees they went, lifting their feet high over the tussocks of grass.

Pete cooked sausages in the electric frypan, boiled potatoes and broccoli over the little gas stove. They ate in front of the fire, Bonnie and Pete with their plates on their laps, the twins kneeling at the coffee table. Behind the blackened glass of the little door the fire burned, settled into a concentrated heat, red and liquid at its centre. They stared into it.

'When's our birthday?' said Louie.

'Soon,' said Bonnie. 'About a month away.'

'And who's coming again?'

'Oscar, Frankie, Tom …'

'Maya?' said Edie, licking tomato sauce from her fork.

'Yes, Maya. All your kinder friends.'

'Grandma?'

'Yes.'

'Nan and Pop?'

Bonnie looked at Pete.

'No,' he said, reaching forward to smooth Edie's hair. 'Nan and Pop live too far away. They can only come at Christmas-time.'

'Are Nan and Pop your mum and dad?' said Louie.

'Yes,' said Pete. 'My mum and dad.'

'And Grandma's my mum,' said Bonnie.

'And your dad's dead,' said Edie.

'Yes.' She reached to bounce Jess in her baby chair. 'You're getting tired, aren't you, possum?'

'I can't believe these guys are nearly five years old,' said Pete.

'I can't believe it either,' said Edie. She straightened her spine and put down her fork. 'Lovely dinner,' she said in an important voice. 'Very nice.'

Together Bonnie and Pete ducked their heads, slid sideways smiles at each other.

Louie speared a slice of sausage and collected a gob of sauce with it. 'Doug says when he was six he could drive a car.'

'I don't know about that,' said Pete.

'It's true,' said Louie, posting the sausage into his mouth.

'I don't think so,' said Pete. 'He must've been joking, Lou.'

'He wasn't joking.' Louie's brow knotted. He chomped furiously. 'He told me.'

Pete softened his voice. 'Well, maybe —'

'Actually,' said Bonnie, 'Doug did say that.' She looked at Louie. 'The world has changed a lot since Doug was a little boy,' she said, feeling her way. 'I'm not sure what the rules were back then. But now you have to be really quite grown up to drive a car.'

'You have to be sixteen,' said Pete. 'And then you can have lessons. Your mum or dad has to sit in the car with you and show you what to do.'

There was a pause. Louie kept up his chewing, eyes on his plate.

Pete stretched, reached his arms up, elbows out, hands behind his head. 'That'll be you one day, Louie and Edie.'

'One day,' said Bonnie, 'but not for a long, long time.'

Silence. Louie chewed on, his fork stuck upright in his fist.

Bonnie and Pete sat at the table with a bottle of wine. The children were two dark huddles on the camping mattresses in the middle of the rug, Jess quiet beyond them in the nylon travel cot. The glow of the fire threw the corners of the room into darkness. Over Pete's shoulder she could see her own face hanging in the black window.

'How could a six-year-old reach the pedals?' said Pete.

She shrugged. 'He must've made it up.' She poured herself more wine.

Pete sipped from his glass and leaned back in his chair. 'I feel like a cigarette.' He got up and started searching through the drawers of the single kitchen bench. 'Maybe Jim left some.'

She looked into her reflected face. 'I didn't know he smoked.'

'He doesn't really,' said Pete, rummaging. 'Only sometimes. Like me.' He shut the last drawer, scanned the room. 'No luck.' He came over and put his hands on her shoulders. 'You okay?'

'Yeah. Why?'

'You just seem a bit quiet.'

Bonnie dropped her eyes from the reflection. 'I'm fine,' she said, lifting one of Pete's hands and kissing it. 'Just quiet.'

He went back around the table and sat down. He drank more wine, glancing around the room. 'This place is great. Lucky Jim.'

'It is great. So peaceful.'

Pete tapped his foot, shuffled a rhythm with both feet and one hand. 'It's good to get away,' he said. Then he stopped his restless movement and sat straight in his chair. Picked up his glass and stared into it. 'There's something I haven't told you. About Doug.'

Her stomach went cold. 'Oh.' Her limbs were suddenly very heavy. She felt like she had when she got the phone call about her father, the accident — the suspended moments before the actual words were said; the not-yet-disclosed information looming, ready to crash down. That hopeless urge to stave it off, push it away.

Pete looked at her, gave a twitch of a smile. 'It's not that serious, don't worry,' he said quickly, but his face was strained. His hands lay either side of his glass, palms flat to the tabletop. 'It's just something I …' He swallowed, dropped his head again. 'This thing happened, when we were young. Me and Doug. Pretty young — like eighteen, nineteen. Well, I was eighteen or nineteen, so I guess he was in his twenties.' He glanced at Bonnie, who nodded. 'We were living together, in this share house, with a whole gang of friends. Peter Wilson, and Simon Wright, and Deano — I think you've met him?'

'Once, yeah.'

'Anyway.' Pete took his eyes off her again. 'We went to this party. Some people we knew invited us — some girls. We didn't know the people whose party it was.'

Across the room one of the children stirred, moaned. They waited and the child settled.

He continued. 'Anyway, we went, and the guys whose party it was really didn't want us there. And we were pretty messed up — stoned, and drunk.' He breathed slowly out through his nose. His voice was quiet. 'So we were out the back, and there was this laundry trough all filled with ice and beer. And I took a beer — you know, showing off, being a smart-arse in front of the girls. But as I did it I saw the guys, the hosts, walking up.' Pete paused, shook his head, swallowed. 'And I just gave the beer to Doug, shoved it in his hand.'

Bonnie sat still.

Pete's voice was thick. 'And then it all happened really fast, but, basically, the guys — and they were tough, you know, older than us; you wouldn't want to mess with them — well, they saw Doug with the beer and they were like "You took our beer" and I just stood there like a ...' He screwed up his nose and gave a short, hard laugh. 'Like a fucking *coward* and didn't say anything, and then the next thing you know they're ... they're just totally laying into Doug. Beating him up.'

She heard herself make a sound, a faint little groan.

'Everyone started screaming and carrying on, and trying to break it up, get them off him. I mean he didn't stand a chance — he wasn't even fighting back. But' — he breathed again, that long, controlled breath — 'I just stood there.'

'Was he okay?' The words came out in a croak. She cleared her throat. 'Doug?'

Pete kept his eyes on his feet. 'It was pretty bad. He went to hospital. Broken ribs, and his face was pretty smashed up.'

There was a silence.

Pete picked up the wine bottle, tipped more in his glass. He looked up. 'You know what I think about? Still?'

She waited.

He lifted the glass but didn't drink. 'There was this moment, when they first came up, the guys, when they said "You took our beer" and everything ... There was this moment, only a couple of seconds, before they started hitting him, and Doug, he did this thing, made this face, kind of' — Pete lifted his chin with a sudden, aggressive movement — 'kind of like "Fuck you" and he took a big swig out of the beer. And then he looked at me. He gave me this look, like, I don't know, like he was saying, "You owe me."' Pete shook his head. 'I don't know — I don't know how to explain it. It was weird.'

Silence. She touched her fingers to the base of her own glass.

'But you know what? What's really weird?'

'What?'

'He never said anything. I mean, we were living together — and he just came home from the hospital and he never said anything.'

She turned her glass on the tabletop. 'But didn't you?'

He shrugged. 'No.'

'But why not?' Her voice came out too loud, and she glanced at the children and lowered it. 'I mean — wouldn't you apologise straight away?'

'I know it sounds crazy but no — I didn't. Well, maybe I did try to say sorry and he wouldn't listen. It was a long time ago now, and I can't remember all that well ... But mostly, the way I do remember it, it was ... he came back and there was just this vibe, like — I don't know, it was like when he gave me that look he'd already said something, communicated something to me, and we both knew it, and we didn't need to talk about it.'

Bonnie got up. She went over to close the curtains. They were worn and limp, with irregular patterns. Sewn from old tablecloths maybe. Before she drew them she put her face right up to the glass but she couldn't see anything. It was too dark.

Pete left after breakfast. 'You'll be right, won't you?' he said, pulling on his jacket and opening the door. The morning glittered — you could almost see the warm air rolling out into it. He stepped onto the veranda, peered out and up. 'Looks like it should be a fine day. You could go for a walk.' He came back to the door, leaned in. 'Or do you want to come? Should we all go?'

'No.' Bonnie lay back on the low couch with Jess propped against her knees. 'We'll stay. It'll be nice. We'll see you later.'

'Okay then. I've got my phone.'

She wrapped Jess in a blanket and sat with her on the veranda, watching the twins playing.

'No,' said Edie, standing on a stump. 'I'm the princess and this is my house. Your house is over there. And when it's morning time the rooster will go cock-a-doodle-doo and then you can get up.'

Obediently, Louie went to his own stump and draped himself over it, pillowing his head with his arms.

She tipped her head back and looked up into the crowns of the trees, the bunches of foliage so high up, the skinny branches like pointing arms. Somewhere down on the road a truck went past, its brakes a thin, far-off sound. She thought of Pete in the car. That thing happened, where she tried not to but couldn't help her mind snaking into the wrong places. She saw Pete take a corner, a truck coming the other way. Metal hitting, smashing, their car hurled off the side of the road, crushed and broken. Rolling, bouncing back off a tree. Panicked birds shooting upwards. Gravel dust in a cloud. All the noises — the screeching, the bang, the thudding tumble — happening in such a tight succession and then over. And then the moments when things settled. Upturned wheels spinning, slowing, stopping. A wrenched side-mirror swinging into stillness. Some last bits of glass tinkling, detaching, pattering into the dirt. Silence. Until the door of the truck opened and the driver climbed down and went over.

How long before she got worried and tried to call him? Or before the truck driver or someone else — police probably — used Pete's phone and called her? Answering to the foreign voice, that dropping-away feeling, her arms and legs getting heavy.

Or what if there were no mobile phones? How long would they wait here at the house before she took the kids and walked all the way down to the roadside to flag down a car? What if it got dark? If she kept thinking he'd come, kept looking for his headlights in the falling dusk until it was too late? Waiting longer, sitting by the stove. And then what? Would she put the children to bed? Sit up and wait by herself? Fall asleep and wake in the middle of the night, the fire died down, the chill creeping in? Getting up to put on more wood. Going to stand by the window, staring out into nothing while the kids slept behind her.

Or would she go down sooner? That night, that evening. Knowing something must have happened. Finding a torch in a drawer. Rugging the children up, strapping Jess to her in the sling. Tottering down the unmade road with the twins clinging, fighting over who got to hold the hand without the torch. The weak beam of light giving them only a wavering little circle directly in front, the black dark pressing in on it, on them. The awful thought of the battery running out.

The road. A car. Waving the torch.

'Cock-a-doodle-doo,' went Edie.

Bonnie blinked and looked around, and up rose Louie off his stump.

They walked behind the shack this time, uphill. Jess in the sling blowing bubbles and grabbing at Bonnie's hair, her cheeks bright with the cold. Edie tramping ahead, gumboots swishing, beanie bobbling. Louie dragging a fallen branch that collected ribbons of bark in a jiggling pile. It was easy walking, the spaces wide between the trees, the ground uncluttered, the grass tussocks scattered evenly as if sown by hand.

Up they went in a serious procession. 'Here?' she said, and Edie looked around and shook her head. 'Here?' she said a bit later, and Edie shook her head again. 'What's wrong with here? There's a nice flat spot, and we can look back down at the house and watch the smoke come out the chimney.'

'Not quite right.' And Edie stamped on. Up and up between the trees, until behind them enough of the spare bush was aligned to screen the house and it became just a darker blob amongst all the other dark blobs.

'Oh.' Edie stopped. It was the fence. Drooping wire and leaning posts, a wattle sapling thrusting through it — but a fence still.

'Well,' said Bonnie. 'That's it. That's the end of Jim's land.'

'But whose land is on the other side?' said Louie, poking the wires with his branch.

'I don't know. Somebody else's.'

'But what's their name?'

'I don't know. Jim might know.'

'But who are they? Is it a boy or a girl?'

'I don't know, Lou. I don't know everyone in the world.'

'Can we go and visit them?' said Edie.

'No. I don't even know if there's a house on that land. It might just be bush.'

'But where do the people live?'

'Well, there might not be anyone living there. It might just be bush — trees and stuff, and animals and birds. But the land still belongs to somebody and we don't know that person and that's why we can't go on it.' She turned back to where the smoke from their fire rose in a string above the treetops. 'So,' she said, 'where shall we have our picnic then?'

Edie sighed. 'I s'pose it'll have to be here,' she said in a world-weary tone.

Bonnie plonked down the bag. She spread the canvas-backed picnic rug in a clear spot and knelt on it. She took Jess out of the sling and put her down on her tummy on the rug. She set out plastic plates and the bottle of water. Sandwiches in a Tupperware container. Apples and pears. A little tub of dried apricots and sultanas. Everything tilting on the grass tufts and sticks underneath.

They ate and looked back down at the scrub and the string of smoke. The sun came out and warmed them. She stretched out her legs. A bird hopped nearby, angled its eye at them, sprang into the air and away.

'What if there are people on that land?' said Edie. 'If there are people, can we visit them?'

Bonnie put her head back, her face to the sun. She closed her eyes. 'No. You can't visit people you don't know.'

'But what if they came down here, to the fence, and invited us?'

She sat up and reached for the water. 'Well, then it would be okay.' She drank. The water from Jim's tank was sweet, with a slight taste of ti-tree.

Pete came back in the late afternoon.

'I found some good timber.' He sat down at the table. 'Eastern mahogany. Two big fallen trees — be almost enough for the whole job.'

'Great.' She filled the kettle and switched it on.

Edie climbed onto Pete's lap. 'We had a picnic, Daddy.'

'Did you?' Pete kissed her, but Bonnie who was watching from the bench could see him gazing off, out the window. 'It's beautiful wood,' he said, resting his cheek against the top of Edie's head. 'Should work really well with just a bit of Vic ash as trim.'

'Great,' she said again, opening the tea canister. 'Good on you.'

'And it's quite cheap too. He's ready to mill it on Monday and he can deliver, maybe even on Tuesday, so I could get started this week.'

'That's so good.' She took mugs from the drying rack. 'Will it all fit in the workshop?'

'Just. I'll have to move some things around.'

'We found a fence,' said Edie to Pete. 'It was nearly falling down, but Mum said we couldn't go on the other side because we didn't know the people.'

'Yeah,' said Pete. 'Best not to climb over fences when you're in the country.'

Edie reached up and took hold of one of Pete's ears. 'And do you know what it looked like, on the other side?'

'No.'

Edie made a face of theatrical bemusement. 'Just the same. It even had the same birds.'

That night when the kids were asleep they sat down on the couch with Pete's laptop and a pile of DVDs.

'What's this?' Pete held one up. '*Cockatoo Island.*'

'Oh, you know — that music festival I did with Mickey, ages ago. Someone made a documentary about it. Mickey sent me a copy.'

Pete slid it into the computer. 'Let's have a look.'

'Oh, do we have to? It'll probably be really boring.'

'Come on. You might be in it.'

'That's what I'm worried about.'

'Just quickly.'

The opening credits rolled. Aerial views of Sydney Harbour, beautiful, blue water and lush green land. Scruffy-looking musos dressed in black and wearing sunglasses loading equipment onto ferries. Windblown hair. Laminated passes around necks. A view from side of stage — some young indie-rock band in full swing, heads bowed to guitars, legs jerking and kicking as if independently. A drummer bent forward, eyes closed. People in the crowd, faces upturned, rapt. A group of girls laughing, arms around each other.

Fade to black. Then the opening scene. A young guy with a goatee, sitting on a leather couch, arms spread along the back of it. 'It's always just so amazing when something like this all comes together,' he said. 'It's such a pleasure and a privilege to be a part of an event like this.'

'Who's he?' said Pete.

'Oh, you know, the guy from — what're they called again? Anyway, some band. He's boring.'

The goatee guy was still talking.

'... really appreciate how much hard work goes into ...'

'Yeah, okay, he's boring.' Pete went back to the main menu. 'Here we go — live performances.' He scrolled through. 'Mickey Meyers.' He ran the cursor over Mickey's name and it lit up.

An outdoor stage. Half in shadow. Mickey in the sunny bit, saying something into the mic. A burst of laughter from the crowd, and cheering. Mickey turning to the rest of the band, looking to the drummer for the count-in, lifting her arm high before bringing it down to her guitar. Doing one of her funny little dances, shuffling, dipping her knees. Swinging back around to the mic stand, leaning in, starting to sing.

'Where're you?' Pete put his face closer to the screen. 'I can't see you.'

'There, next to the keyboards.'

'You're in the shadows. I can't even tell it's you.'

'Oh well.' She watched the little silhouette of herself sway, arms working, head down. 'I'm not very interesting.'

The camera zoomed in on Mickey's face, her bright red lipstick, the yellow scarf knotted around her hair, the way she made funny faces as she sang, rolling her eyes, shaking her head. The sight of it brought that feeling again in Bonnie, the one that had come over her in the bookshop. A lost, desolate pang that almost hurt, lunging through her.

'That's a good look Mickey's got going on,' said Pete. 'Looks like a cartoon character. Like Minnie Mouse or something.'

'She looks great.' Bonnie watched as Mickey finished the first chorus and turned from the mic again to dance over towards the drum kit, dropping first one shoulder and then the other. The camera followed, and as Mickey skipped into the dark part of the stage the rest of the band came properly into view. The camera panned across them. First the bass player: Will, the tall, beardy one Mickey used on that album that time, who only drank Coopers beer because it was vegan and who tended sometimes just a little bit too far towards funk for Bonnie's taste. Then the drummer: another one whose name she had forgotten; Mickey seemed to change drummers the most. This guy was small and thin, and very good; he actually somehow lifted up off his stool sometimes when he got really into it. Then a woman on the keys, blonde hair, pale skin. 'Kristen,' she said aloud. 'God, I'd forgotten about her. She was lovely.'

She stared into the screen at Kristen bouncing on her toes behind the keyboard, head nodding. The camera went right in close and Kristen's eyes moved sideways and she smiled, and then the camera followed the smile and there was Bonnie smiling back. The camera pulled out again and showed just her and Kristen, holding that smile between them for a moment longer and then letting it drop as together they launched into the bridge. Bonnie watched her own fingers move over the strings, her head bent, hair hanging in her face now. Like a spider her left hand ran up and down, limber, fluid. The right hand went from picking to strumming and back to picking again. Incredible, that those were her hands, that that was her.

'Sound's not too good,' said Pete.

'No. It's terrible.' But she could hear it anyway, perfectly, each run of notes as they flew from her fingers, each riff uncurling, opening out and moving through its cycle, bringing itself back to the beginning and then starting again, living out its own small, perfect life.

'Bye, house!' called the twins, twisting in their booster seats as the car bumped down the track to the main road. 'Bye, trees! Bye, birds!'

She waited until they were on the bitumen before opening the thermos. The coffee steamed as she poured it carefully into the little round cup. She sipped and then passed the cup to Pete. She watched him drive one-handed, elbow braced against the inside ledge of the car window, fingers at the top of the steering wheel, lips pulling back to sip, his throat moving as he swallowed.

Overhead the limbs of the giant trees almost met. Leaves hung down, greenish grey, swirling like floating masses of seaweed. And the flashes of white bark — the undersides of branches exposed like something else belonging to the sea, the pale legs of swimmers seen from below, or the bellies of fish. In the murky shade beneath they drove on.

She looked back at the children. Louie and Edie on either side, heads tilted to the windows, eyes flicking, catching at passing sight after sight, holding and letting go. And the top of

Jess's head just visible in the rear-facing capsule. The soft hair. The curve of that small skull.

Bonnie turned to the front again. Pete passed her the cup, and she fitted it to the thermos and wound it tightly, feeling the seal take hold.

It was late afternoon when they got home. The twins went running through the rooms, snatching up toys as if everything was new. She and Pete carried loads in from the car and dumped them on the floors of the laundry and kitchen. They slumped at the table. Bonnie rubbed her eyes. She felt dirty and tired.

'What shall we do for dinner?' said Pete, and exhaustion overwhelmed her — that paralysing inertia that always descended at the thought of having to cook, to prepare food and serve it, to tidy everything away afterwards, save leftovers, wash dishes, wipe down the table, sweep the floor. Only to go through the whole bloody thing the next morning, afternoon, evening. Again and again, over and over.

'Takeaway?'

'Sounds good.'

Pete rang the Thai place and at six went to pick it up. Bonnie put on a load of washing and got the twins in the bath. She began to lay the table. There was a newspaper folded on it, the form guide on top. She picked it up and looked at the date — Saturday. Yesterday. She refolded it. Put it on the bench. Stepped into the middle of the room and turned slowly around. In the dish rack were plates, cutlery, wineglasses. The dishes she'd washed and left to dry on Friday morning were in a stack on the bench. She went to the laundry door and checked the recycling box, which she'd emptied on Thursday night. A champagne bottle and four Coronas.

Jess was crying from her chair in the kitchen. Bonnie picked her up and walked into the living room. Nothing that she could see. The cushions were flattened on the couch, one of them on the floor, but that could have been how they'd left things, or done by the twins since. She stood with the baby in front of the unlit gas heater. She wasn't sure but she thought she could smell something — a trace of cigarette smoke, and something else, perfume maybe. Very faint, but unpleasant, sharp, one of those perfumes that actually hurt her nostrils, that made her think of cheap clothes and bad make-up.

The front door opened and footsteps went down the hall.

'Dinner,' called Pete. 'Hello?'

She went back to the kitchen. 'Pete.'

'Yeah?'

'Someone's been here. In the house.'

'Really?' Pete was taking the lids off the plastic tubs. 'Oh yeah,' he said, in a light voice. 'That'd be Douggie.'

'What?'

'Yeah, I gave him a key. I asked him to drop in both days and give that table a coat of oil. I really wanted to get it all finished so I could deliver it this week and get on with the Grant job.'

She watched him putting out plates and forks, glasses of milk for the kids. 'But why did you give him a key to the house?'

Pete took a spoon and started heaping rice onto the plates. 'Well, you know, I thought he might like to come inside. Take a break, make himself a cup of tea.'

'But he can make himself tea in the workshop.'

'Bonnie. Come on. Don't kick up a big stink about this. It's no big deal. I asked him to come and work on that table over the weekend — do me a favour — and I gave him a key to the house so he could take a break. Get warm in front of the heater. Maybe watch a bit of telly. The races were on.' He put down the spoon. 'I don't think he's got telly at that place he's staying. And it's cold, you know — I mean, the poor bugger —'

There was a yell from the bathroom. 'Mum!'

66

'Coming.' She tried to put Jess down in her chair, but the baby protested, so she picked her up again. 'Well, I think he had someone over here. Like a woman or something.'

'What makes you think that?'

'They used wineglasses. They're in the dish rack.'

He looked over at the sink. 'How do you know it was Douggie? Maybe we left them. Didn't we have some wine the other night?'

'Mu-um!'

'Coming.' She put Jess in the chair, and the baby immediately started to cry again. Bonnie gave the chair a little rock and straightened up. 'Sorry, possum,' she said, 'I've got to get the big kids out of the bath.' At the doorway she turned back to Pete. 'There's an empty bottle of cheap champagne and some beers in the recycling.' No answer. Bonnie glanced at the table, the plates of food. 'That's too much for the kids,' she said, raising her voice over the crying. 'They'll never eat all that. It's just a waste.'

'What're you doing?'

She didn't look up from the bed. 'Changing the sheets.'

'Didn't we put clean ones on the other day?'

Bonnie didn't answer. She threw the last pillowcase into the pile on the floor, started tugging at the mattress, lifting the corner of it out of the frame and pulling off the fitted sheet.

Pete came over to her. 'Hang on,' he said. 'I'm supposed to help you with that.'

She kept pulling at the sheet. She got one corner up and went to do the next.

'Bon,' said Pete, and put his hand on her shoulder. 'Come on. Didn't the physio say you still shouldn't lift too much?'

'Yeah, right.' She shrugged him off and went round to the other side of the bed. 'And of course I never lift anything, like

Jess all the time, and the other kids, and all the bloody bags when we go to swimming and the library and kinder ...' She was choking with anger. Her back was hurting, and her throat. She sank down on the mattress, the sheet in a tangle beside her. Pete came and tried to put his arm around her. Bonnie glared up at him. 'Don't you think I have enough to deal with, without bloody Doug? I mean, what's going on with him? He's — he's using our house now? To entertain his friends?'

'Shh.' He glanced towards the door. 'You'll wake up the kids.'

She pulled her shoulders forward, away from his touch. Her hands were fists in her lap. She lowered her voice to a hiss. 'This is creeping me out, Pete. I wish you'd told me you were giving him a key to the house. I had a pair of dirty undies lying right here on the floor.'

Pete took his arm back. 'Look, Bonnie. I feel weird about him coming in the house too. Especially if he did bring someone else here. I just thought he'd —'

'We don't know what he's been doing! For all we know he's been shagging some woman in our bed!'

'Come on, he wouldn't do that.'

Bonnie stared down at her hands. She shook her head. 'I don't know. I don't know what he's capable of. I don't understand him. I don't understand why a grown man would still be living the way he does, hand to mouth, staying with friends, doing shit work ...'

'He's depressed,' said Pete. 'He hates working for me, I can tell. And I don't blame him — it's really fucking boring. I'm sure he'd rather be doing something else. But I guess he's ... well, he's getting older, and he doesn't have any skills really, and I guess he's not all that employable. And' — Pete sighed — 'he's hard to get along with. You know, I think he's got the sack from his last few jobs.'

'I know. I know all this!' Bonnie threw her head back and squeezed her eyes shut. 'God, I'm sick of having this conversation.' She took a breath. 'If you want to be Doug's friend and show him some support because he's depressed then go out and have a beer with him, or go to the races, or go out for dinner. Or invite him over here for dinner. Be his friend. Don't try to solve his problems for him by finding work for him to do. I mean, he's a grown-up — he needs to solve his own problems. You said yourself he hates the work. Do you really think it's helping?'

'Yeah. You're probably right. But, you know, it's been really good for me having someone around to do odd jobs this past week, and I'll need extra help with the Grant job. And it's easy for you to say that I should just cut him off and leave him to solve his own problems, but …' He looked down at his hands. 'You know, when I say I think he's depressed — well, a couple of times he's said stuff, kind of like he's joking, but really, you know, I think it's true …'

'What stuff?'

'That he feels, you know … suicidal.'

'Look, Pete. This is all just so messy. And I don't want to keep fighting with you. I'm not saying you should cut him off. I just don't think you should mix business with friendship. It's as simple as that.'

'Yeah, but it's happened now.' He rubbed his hands over his face. 'I don't feel good about it either but I don't know what I can do.'

Bonnie carried the sheets to the laundry. She stuffed them into the hamper on top of the rest of the clothes from the weekend. Then she pulled one of the pillowcases back out. Holding it by a corner she put it up near her face. Breathed in. Nothing. She was pretty sure anyway. She dropped it back on the pile.

She went into the kitchen, to the cupboard where she'd put the two glasses from the dish rack away with the rest. Opened the door. Took down the first glass. Held it by the stem, up to the light, turned it slowly, running her eyes along the rim. *What are you doing?* She put the glass back and shut the door. Stood by the bench with her cardigan pulled tight around her. An image came to her: Friday, the glimpse from the car window, the woman with the bucket. Her hidden face; the house with its mean, barricaded look. Bonnie stood up straight. 'So what?' she said out loud, into the empty room. 'So what? Doesn't matter.'

She walked back into the laundry and took the wet load from the machine. Then she went into the living room, opened out the clotheshorse in front of the heater and started hanging the clothes on it.

'Mornin', Boss. Missus Bonnie. Kids.' Doug came in the back door, saluting them each in turn. He swiped at the mat with his boots, and flapped his arms against his sides. 'Cold out there.'

'Hi, Doug.' Bonnie got up from the table, moved over to the compost bin and scraped out her bowl.

'No porridge left this morning, sorry, Douggie,' said Pete. 'But there's Weeties or toast.'

'I'll have Weeties, thanks, Boss,' said Doug. 'You're too good to me.'

Bonnie stood at the sink. She couldn't look around. The skin on her back felt cold, even under her clothes. She neatened the stack of dirty dishes and listened.

'So when're we off to get the timber?' said Doug.

'I don't have to pick it up,' said Pete. 'The guy's delivering.'

Doug spoke through mouthfuls of cereal. 'Oh. Well. I actually feel a bit disappointed. I was looking forward to a trip to the country.'

Bonnie grabbed the cloth and wiped the bench. *What makes you think you'd be going?* Her teeth were clenched.

Pete stood up. 'I'm going to make a start,' he said. 'Got a meeting with Grant later, so better try to get a bit done this morning. Bye, you guys.' He kissed the twins, and went over to her. 'Bye, Bon.' Bonnie raised her face to kiss him back, and he met her eyes. She thought she saw something there, some acknowledgement, a flicker of shared feeling, but then he said, 'Have a great day,' the way he always did and she wasn't sure.

Pete went to the door. 'See you out there, Douggie.'

'I'll hold the fort then,' called Doug as the door swung shut. 'This arvo. I'll be able to actually get some work done, without you getting in me way.'

'What's the fort?' said Edie.

'It's a saying, darling,' she said, going over to her and touching her hair. 'It means that someone will look after a house or a place while another person's away.'

'Is Douggie looking after us? Where're you going, Mum?'

'Oh, no — I'm not going anywhere. Just Dad's got a meeting later today. But you guys'll be at kinder anyway. And I'll take care of Jess. And Doug' — she kept her eyes on Edie's face — 'Doug'll be doing some things in the workshop.'

Across the table Louie put down his spoon. 'Does Douggie make furniture too?'

'Well ...' She turned to Louie. Doug's shape throbbed at the corner of her eye. It was as if her gaze was pushed away from him, repelled by some force field. 'Well, what Doug does,' she said slowly, as the Doug shape continued to spoon up cereal in her peripheral vision, 'is he ... he helps Dad make the furniture.'

Doug slurped a last gulp, put the spoon in the bowl and carried it to the sink. At last Bonnie looked at him, at his back. 'That's me,' he said, putting the things down with a flourish. 'Chief bottlewasher and general dogsbody.' He took a mug from the pile of dirty dishes and swished it under the tap. Then he came back to the table and poured tea into it, lifting the teapot high so the brown stream went long and thin. Louie and Edie stared. Doug slitted one eye in a slow wink. 'You don't mind, do you, Missus Bonnie?' he said. 'I like your tea better than those teabags the boss's got out there.'

'Pete gave him a key,' said Bonnie.

'Why?' said Mel.

'I don't know. He was doing some stuff in the workshop — Pete asked him to; this table needed a couple of coats of oil or something — and Pete said he thought he might want to come inside to warm up, take a break or whatever.'

'So he had someone over, you think?'

'Well, there was an empty champagne bottle, cheap, and some beers — Pete's beer, from our fridge, and —'

'Really? He took beer from the fridge?'

'Yep.'

'Did he replace what he drank?'

'No.' Bonnie spooned up froth from her coffee. 'I don't know, I feel like I'm being really uptight or something, but I just feel sort of … invaded. And don't you think it's weird that he didn't say anything? I mean, I could understand — he's staying at this miserable place apparently, a bungalow in someone's backyard, and it's probably cold and no TV or whatever. And we weren't around, and Doug's an old friend of Pete's and … It's just, it's really hard to put your finger on why it feels so weird.'

'But if it was someone else — like an old friend of yours, say, visiting from out of town, or with some other reason for needing to use your house — they'd have probably called you and checked it was okay to host a dinner there. And if they couldn't get onto you then they would definitely say something as soon as they saw you again.' Mel frowned. 'But the thing is, there's no real reason he'd need to use your house. He's not staying with you guys. He's just working out the back with Pete. The house is your territory.'

Bonnie shifted Jess on her lap. 'You know, that's exactly what it feels like — like an invasion of my territory. But the thing is, another person could do all the same things he does — you know, hang around and have dinner, or a beer, or a cup of tea in the morning — but somehow when he does it it feels weird.'

Mel looked at her watch. 'I'd better go soon. I've got a client at eleven.'

'Thanks for talking about this.' Bonnie felt in her bag for her purse. 'I just — I feel like I've lost perspective. You know, the way my whole life's sort of shrunk … It's like it's just me and Pete and the kids, this little world, and I don't know, maybe I've lost the ability to recognise what's normal behaviour. And, honestly, sometimes I don't know how much of this stuff with Doug is him and how much it's me.'

'I'd say most of it's him.' Mel put some coins down on the table and stood up. 'That's definitely not normal, using your house without permission or explanation. Drinking your beer without replacing it.'

'Well, he did have permission, sort of. Pete gave him the key.'

'So you think Doug took that to mean he had free use of the house, day and night?'

'I don't know.'

'How much do you think they communicate?'

'Not much. I don't get it. It's like this weird super-casual relationship where nothing ever seems to be actually spoken about or agreed on.'

'Well, there's your problem. I reckon anyway.' Mel slipped the straps of her bag up her shoulder. 'It's all about communication.'

She reached to stroke Jess's head. 'And boundaries, with people like that.'

Back at the house Bonnie pulled up behind Doug's van. She sat looking at it, its yellow rust-spotted doors and bald tyres, and tried to rein in the surge of irritation, and something more, some deeper feeling that she didn't really want to own up to — something childish she'd long been conditioned to bury. *You're lucky*, she told herself. *You've got so much — why can't you be more generous?* She sighed and got out of the car.

'Hello, darling.'

She jumped and turned. It was Grace from down the road, all dressed up in her boxy green coat and thick beige stockings. She had her stick — the one the twins were so fascinated by, that branched out at the bottom into four little black stoppers. 'Oh. Hi, Grace. How are you?'

'Ah, you know.' The old woman gave a shrug, blinked behind her big, thick glasses. 'I have a bad leg, but apart from that I am all right.' She peered at Bonnie. 'Where are the children?'

'The twins are at kinder today. And the baby's just in the car there. Hold on, I'll get her.' She opened the back door and lifted Jess out.

Grace bent to the baby. 'Beautiful, beautiful.' She straightened up. 'Can I give her a kiss?'

'Of course.'

Grace put the backs of her knobbly fingers to her mouth and then gently lowered them to Jess's cheek. 'Beautiful,' she said again, and then, still with her eyes on the baby, she added, 'I met your husband's business partner on Saturday.'

'Sorry?' Bonnie looked at her.

'He is very nice.' Grace curled her fingers around one of Jess's feet. 'I hope you are warm enough in this weather, my little one,' she said. She turned to Bonnie. 'What is his name again?'

'Do you mean Doug?' said Bonnie. 'The guy who's been working for Pete? He's not actually —'

'Yes, Doug, that's right. The partner in the business. He came over, and we had a cup of tea. We had a long talk. He is very nice. He says they have a lot of work, very busy.'

Bonnie felt that cold shrinking in her stomach. 'Oh,' she heard herself say.

'And it's so nice that he is like a part of your family. Like an uncle to the children. That is nice.'

Bonnie stared.

Grace let go of Jess's foot and leaned on her stick. 'Good to see you, darling. I'm glad to hear they are busy. That is good.'

She was feeding Jess on the living-room couch when she heard the back door.

'Bon?' called Pete.

'In here.'

He stuck his head in the door. 'I'm going to get some Turkish pizza. Want some? Spinach pie?'

'Yes, please.'

'Won't be long.' He paused, glanced down at Jess, at Bonnie's pulled-up top. 'Doug's in the kitchen.'

'Okay.'

Jess finished, and Bonnie took her time changing her nappy and settling her to sleep, all the while listening out. She didn't go into the kitchen until she heard Pete come back.

Doug was sitting at the table with the newspaper. Pete had got some plates and was unwrapping the bundle of pizzas.

'Isn't it nice and quiet without the two terrors around,' said Doug.

'Yes, it is.' She tried to look at him. *Say something. Why can't you just be straight with him? Ask about the empty bottles. Make it light — just say, 'So did you have a bit of a party?'* She unfolded the paper from her spinach pie. Her hands were shaking.

'So where are they?' said Doug. 'Child care?'

'It's a long day-care place, but they have an integrated kinder program.' She cringed at how prim she sounded.

'Integrated program, eh?' said Doug. He picked up a meat pizza and folded it in half. Looked at it for a moment, then back at her. 'So do you reckon your kids'll be grateful for all this — what do you call it? — all this *hot-housing* they're getting?'

Ignore it. She tried to take a bite of the pie, but it was too hot. Her eyes stung.

Doug went on. 'I mean, look at me: I got nothing. We played in the streets, or in the backyard if me gran and me mum weren't using it. Or we went and worked for Dad at the shop, for twenty cents a day, on weekends and holidays. Sunday school, that was our *extra-curricular activity*.' He said the words with an exaggerated posh accent, eyebrows jerking, grin cracking.

'Oh.' Bonnie broke off a bit of pastry and blew on it. She snuck a glance at Pete, but he'd taken the paper and was reading it.

'Miss Spensley, in the church hall. She had a bung eye.' Doug gave a tittering sort of laugh. 'She'd stand there' — he got up, one hand with the half-moon of pizza in it, the other thrust out in front of him, sweeping his pointed finger wildly back and forth and squinting up his face — 'and she'd go, "Stop talking! You know who I mean! You know who I mean!"'

'Oh,' went Bonnie again, and tried to smile.

Doug sank back down in his chair. 'But your kids,' he said through a mouthful of pizza, 'they'll be thanking you when they're geniuses won't they? Or' — he swallowed loudly — 'or they'll be blaming you when they turn out as hopeless as me, despite it all!' He gave a sort of wide-mouthed hoot, exposing his broken teeth, wagging his head and slapping his knee.

She stared at the piece of pie in her fingers. A muted,

embarrassed rage swelled in her, and still she couldn't seem to wipe the pathetic smile from her face. *Just get up and walk out. You don't have to listen to this.*

'So I've got this meeting with Grant,' said Pete without looking up from the paper. 'In Fitzroy. Can I take the car, Bon, or will you need it? It's just that it's easier to park than the van. I'll be back by three.'

She put her uneaten pie down and watched Pete sitting there in such untouchable peace. Her eyes pricked at the injustice of it. 'Take it, that's fine,' she said.

'I'll need some money for parking.' Pete leaned back and felt through his pockets. Then he got up and went over to the pottery dish that sat on the windowsill. 'Did you take all the coins from here, Bon?'

'No.'

There was a pause. 'Funny. I just put a whole lot of gold coins in here last week.' He checked the dish again. 'At least I thought I did. Never mind, maybe it was the kids.'

'How much was it?' She was keenly aware of Doug across from her, hunched over his pizza.

Pete was rustling through the piles of papers on the bench. 'Nothing here.' He glanced at the clock. 'I'd better get going. I'll have to stop and get some change from somewhere.' He came back past the table, pausing to kiss her. 'See you later.'

She stood up. 'I'll check if I've got any change in my bag.'

'See you later, Douggie,' said Pete.

Still chewing, Doug bobbed his head. 'Bye, Boss,' he said. 'Knock 'em dead.'

Bonnie followed Pete down the hallway. He opened the front door and waited on the step as she got her bag from the table and dug through it. She found two twenty-cent pieces and a one-dollar coin, and held them out to him. 'Pete,' she said in a low voice.

'What?'

'Shh.' She glanced behind her, moved closer, reached up to murmur right in his ear. 'Those coins. I don't think the kids took them.'

Pete's eyes flicked over her shoulder, and he lowered his voice as well. 'How do you know?'

'I'd know if they did. They never keep a secret for long.'

'So, what're you saying?' he whispered. 'Douggie did it?'

'Well?' She lifted her shoulders. 'What else could've happened to them?'

Pete looked down the hallway again. 'I've got to go. Let's talk about this later.' He started towards the street.

'Pete, wait.' Bonnie held out the money.

He shook his head. 'It's not enough. I'll just stop and get change somewhere.'

Bonnie watched him get in the car and drive off. She closed the door and stood in the dark hallway.

She hid in the bedroom, fiddling on her acoustic guitar, and when Jess woke she went straight out with the pram, walked aimlessly up and down the shops, buying milk and bread and a slab of parmesan cheese. It was cold. Jess got sick of being in the pram and cried. Bonnie tried to ring Mel but got her message bank. She couldn't think what to say so she hung up.

At a quarter past three she went back home. The car was there. The kitchen still, the wrappers from the lunch scattered on the table. The back door shut.

She looked in the pottery dish. One lonely ten-cent piece, some rubber bands and a broken fridge magnet. She went to the twins' room and checked under their pillows, searched through the open bookshelves that served as bedside tables, opening every little treasure and trinket box. No coins.

She sat on Louie's bed. The next-door neighbours' dog

yapped frantically. A machine drone came from the workshop. She rubbed her thumb along the tips of her fingers, where her skin with its long-gone calluses was tender from the guitar strings. She tried to remember a song, a whole song, in progression — intro, verse, change, verse, bridge, chorus — but her mind slipped, drifted, couldn't hold it.

'So.' Bonnie took a glass from the dish rack and dried it. 'I checked the kids' room today.'

Pete glanced up. 'For the money?'

'Yeah.' She went to the cupboard, put the glass in it, picked up the next one. 'Didn't find it.'

'So, maybe they hid it somewhere.'

'I don't think it was them, Pete.'

He looked at the plate in his hands. 'Neither do I,' he said. 'It was quite a lot of money — maybe twenty bucks. I bought some stuff from the hardware and they'd run out of notes so they gave me a whole handful of gold coins. So I put it there because I thought it might be handy, you know, for the milk bar, or parking meters or whatever.'

'Do you think Doug took it, on the weekend?'

'Guess so.' Pete scrubbed at the plate. 'I know he's really hard up.'

'But that's ... I mean, he's stealing from us. And he had a chance to say something today, you know, if he meant just to borrow it — was planning on paying us back. But he didn't. He just sat there.'

Pete said nothing.

'Pete?'

'What?'

'Well, don't you have a problem with this?'

He put the plate in the rack.

'Pete?'

'Yeah, of course I do.'

'So what are we going to do?' Bonnie heard her voice crack. She saw Pete close his eyes for a moment, draw in breath as if bracing himself. 'I'm sorry,' she said. She took up the plate and wiped it. 'I know you're in a hard situation with this but … but Pete he's really driving me crazy. I mean, when you went out this afternoon I was *hiding* from him. I had to hide in the bedroom while Jess had a sleep, because I didn't want to get stuck out here with him.'

'Really? He's not that bad, is he? I mean, you're not … scared of him or anything, are you?'

'No.' She put the plate down and took the next one. 'No, I'm not scared of him. But I get really tense when he's around. I feel like he's always picking at me — making these kind of backhanded insults, you know? Like all that stuff today about hot-housing our kids —'

'Hot-housing?'

'You know, like accelerated learning. Like those parents you hear about who're always driving their kids around to all these extra activities: music lessons, and sport, and dance or whatever.'

'But we don't do that.'

'I know! That's the thing! I mean, it's such a stupid thing to say. We don't do that at all. I guess he just thinks we're these super-careful, over-protective, you know, precious parents, who wrap our kids in bubble wrap and —'

'But we're not like that either. Are we?'

'Well, Doug obviously thinks we are. Or he thinks I am anyway.'

Pete put the last pot in the rack. 'You know, I think he just shoots his mouth off. He doesn't think about what he's saying at all. He's always been like that. You just have to not take it seriously, whatever he says.'

Bonnie sighed. 'I don't know. I feel like I'm … tuned in to

him now. I can't switch off the way you can. I feel like —' She stopped, put her hand to her mouth. 'Oh my god!'

'What?'

'I forgot to tell you. I saw Grace this morning.'

'Grace?'

'Yeah, you know, the old woman who lives down the road. Walks with a stick. Remember the day we moved in, she came and said, "Hello, my name is Grace, and I am Maltese"? She's quite sweet. Bit lonely, I think. You know, she always tries to get me to go and have a cup of tea at her house, and I always have to make excuses.'

'Oh yeah.'

'Well, I was getting out of the car and she was walking past, and anyway she told me Doug went over there on the weekend — had a cup of tea with her.'

'So?' He looked at her uncertainly. 'That's nice, isn't it?'

She frowned. 'I don't know about that. I actually feel like it's just another way he's sort of inappropriately moving in on us and our lives —'

'Oh, come on, Bonnie.'

'Well, anyway, that's not the point. The thing is, he told her he's your business partner.'

'Really?'

She nodded.

'Maybe she got it wrong.'

'I don't think so.'

'What did she say exactly?'

'I can't remember exactly, but, well, the way she said it — it sounded to me like Doug had actually given her that impression. Not just her getting it wrong.'

'I don't know, Bon. All this stuff — the money, and this thing with the neighbour. I mean, it's not anything we can ... It's not anything concrete.'

'Well, what are we going to do?'

Pete rubbed his eyes. 'Wait.' He exhaled, puffing out his lips. 'Wait till this Grant job's over and then just not offer him any more work. He won't hang around if there's no work.'

'Let's just try to keep things low-key,' Bonnie said to Pete, the morning of the party. 'These guys are exhausted already — they weren't asleep until nine-thirty last night, and they've been up since six.'

'Yeah, good idea.' Pete opened a packet of corn chips and tipped them into a bowl.

The table was spread with dips, bread, bowls of olives, cut-up fruit, and biscuits and cheese. A jug of very weak cordial sat next to a stack of plastic cups. Streamers hung from the light fitting and over the doorways.

She went to the bench and lifted a corner of the tea towel that was draped over the cake. 'Bugger,' she said.

'What?' Pete came over, and Bonnie held the tea towel up so he could see. 'Looks okay,' he said. 'Just a bit saggy in the middle.'

'Saggy? It looks like a patch of quicksand.'

'Can't you just put more icing on it?'

'It's got about half a kilo on there already. I think it might be making it worse — weighing it down.' He laughed. 'Pete!' She slapped his arm. 'I was up till midnight making this stupid cake.'

'It'll be fine.' He put his arm around her. 'I'm sure it'll taste just fine, and the kids won't care.'

She lowered the tea towel. 'That's the last time I make a cake. Next time I'm just going to bloody well buy one.'

The doorbell rang, and there was the sound of Edie and Louie exploding out of the living room and running down the hall, some screeching and then the sound of them running back again. They burst into the kitchen.

'Someone's here — quick, hide!' said Louie, and the two of them crammed under the table.

'The first guest, how exciting,' said Pete.

'Hide, hide!' went the twins.

There was a silence.

'Did you open the door?' said Pete.

Silence.

'Come on,' said Pete. 'It's your party, you guys — you won't have much fun if you spend it under the table.'

'Hide, hide!'

'All right.' Pete laughed and went to the doorway. 'I'll get it then.'

People came, just a few at first and then all in a rush, and the party took over. Bonnie poured drinks, tried to supervise the unwrapping of gifts, made tea, picked up squashed pieces of mandarin from the floor, moved in and out of a series of fragmented conversations. The room filled with hectic noise. Children ran in and out.

'Hi, Bonnie.' A woman smiled. 'Kylie. Greg's wife.'

'Oh, Kylie, yes, of course. Sorry.' Bonnie did remember. A lunch once, across town. A couple of years ago. Pete kept saying they should all get together again, but it never happened. Bonnie glanced over at him standing with Greg by the door, talking, hands in pockets. He must have invited them. She felt a small pulse of that pleased surprise that came whenever she caught a glimpse of Pete as a separate social entity, making his own efforts. Bonnie smiled back at the woman. 'You've cut your hair.'

'Yeah.' She lifted her hand to it.

'Mum?' A blonde girl popped up next to Kylie.

'Yes?'

'Can we go now?'

'Meg. No. Can you not be so rude, please? Go and see what Dad's doing. Maybe there'll be a game.'

The girl groaned and flounced off.

'Sorry,' said Kylie. 'She's a terrible brat. Can I do anything to help?'

'Um,' said Bonnie, as Kylie slid the tray of party pies along the bench and capably transferred them to a platter. 'Oh ... thanks.'

'No worries. Sauce in the fridge?'

'God, sauce. I forgot. I don't actually know if we've —'

But Kylie had already opened the fridge door and found it, and a small bowl in the cupboard.

'You don't have to ...' but Bonnie trailed off. She stood behind the bench and let her arms drop, felt a wash of guilty relief go through her as Kylie neatly ferried the platter of party pies to the table and came back with a stack of dirty plates and cups.

'I'll just pile these up by the sink, shall I?' she said.

'Thank you,' said Bonnie in a murmur.

Suzanne appeared. 'How's it all going over here?'

Bonnie moved forward as Kylie passed behind her with more party pies. 'Um,' she said.

'I thought I'd come and see if you needed any help,' said Suzanne. 'But it looks like you've got it all under control.' She drifted away, adjusting the floaty scarf around her shoulders.

Across the room Pete clapped his hands. 'Piñata!' he called. 'Everyone outside!'

Out they all rushed. Bonnie followed but stopped at the door.

'This might just be entertaining enough for her royal highness,' said Kylie beside her.

Sure enough, there was Meg in the line, arms folded, a good

head taller than the rest of the children.

'Poor thing,' she said. 'It must be pretty boring for her, a little-kids' party.'

Kylie rolled her eyes. 'Pretty much everything's boring for her these days, unless it involves a screen or a console. Honestly' — she gave Bonnie a sidelong glance — 'I had no idea all this would happen so quickly, this *tween* bullshit.' She looked back out at Edie whacking at the hanging papier-mache fish with a stick. 'Enjoy this while it lasts.'

Bonnie watched her daughter swing the stick, and then she watched her son do the same. She saw their faces in profile, their animal focus. She noticed aspects to them, to their features, that she never had before — for a moment it seemed they could be someone else's children, just two children playing the game along with all the others. She saw Pete standing, his hand on the shoulder of the next child in line, the nod of his head, the child walking forward. The stick being passed on. The order of it all. 'I guess I should ...' she said, more to herself than to Kylie, but she didn't step out there to help or cheer, and she didn't go to get the cake ready, or check on Jess, who was asleep in her room. She just stayed where she was, watching emptily, the way someone sitting in a cafe window watches passers-by.

The back door stood open, letting in a stream of cold air. The remains of the cake lay in the middle of the table. The children ate standing up, stuffed last mouthfuls in and then raced outside again. The adults nibbled and talked.

Bonnie stood at the bench in a slipstream of quiet. For a minute nobody spoke to her. Nobody cried or tugged at her clothes or demanded anything. She picked up a mug of tea she thought might be hers. She sipped from it. It was cold, but she sipped again anyway, tasted the tannin, felt it on her teeth.

Kylie came over. 'So Greg says you've got Doug hanging

around.' She raised her eyebrows.

'Yeah.' Bonnie wasn't sure how much to say.

'He driving you mad yet?'

She felt her face dissolve into a grateful smile. 'Yeah.'

Kylie laughed. 'You know he did some work on our place when we were renovating. About four years ago. He actually lived with us.'

'Oh god, how long for? How did you cope?'

'About three months it ended up being. The actual reno took about six, but Doug nicked off well before the work was finished. Got his nose out of joint about something — had a disagreement with one of the builders, I think.'

Bonnie watched Kylie, the way she held her slim body, the gleam of her smooth hair and the expensive-looking little earrings she was wearing. She had a sudden flash of memory from the lunch that time: the shining, clear surfaces of the kitchen, Kylie effortlessly trotting out dish after dish, stuffed peppers, fish baked in the oven. Prawns. All the things Bonnie had never been brave or organised enough to try cooking herself. 'How did you cope?' she said again.

'Oh, I just tuned out.' Kylie waved a hand. 'I just ignored him.'

'Really?' Bonnie ran her fingers through her hair. 'But how? I mean I can't tune out. I'm always tuned in. I feel like he's …' She glanced at Kylie's still, listening face and faltered. 'I mean, I just find it really hard.'

There was a pause.

'Well,' said Kylie. 'You just don't engage too much with people like Doug. That's the trick.'

Bonnie looked down at her piece of cake, which was mostly icing.

'So what's he doing?' said Kylie. 'Jobs around the house?'

'No. He's helping Pete in the workshop.'

'Oh well, at least he's out there. Out of your way.'

Bonnie pushed the curve of her spoon into the slab of wet icing so it bulged up around the metal. The little buoy of solidarity or hope or whatever it was that had bobbed there so briefly let out its last breath and sank back under. 'Yeah,' she said weakly. 'I guess so.'

'I'm exhausted.' Pete lay down heavily and pulled up the covers.

'Me too.' She slid across and put her head on his chest. 'It's pretty hard work. I think they had a good time though.'

'They had a great time.' He yawned. 'Nice that Greg and Kylie came.'

'Yeah. I didn't know you invited them.'

'I always invite them. It's just that they usually don't come. I think they're pretty busy.' Pete put his hand up the sleeve of her pyjama top and stroked her arm. 'It's been ages since Greg and me last got together. We figured it out. Two years. Since Deano had that party at the bowls club.' He yawned again. 'Time just seems to pass so quickly now, with the kids and everything.'

'I know.' Her eyes were closed. At the edge of her consciousness swam the image of Kylie, her trim figure, the wave of her hand. Her words. *I just tuned out. You just don't engage too much.* As if Doug was simply another thing to be managed, to be dealt with in the way you were supposed to deal with everything — with competence, without fuss. Bonnie concentrated on slowing her breathing, on slipping further into warm darkness.

'I feel a bit sad about it sometimes,' said Pete. 'I feel like I don't have friends any more.'

She reached up to kiss him and then moved away, turned onto her other side. 'You have to call people. You know, organise to see them. Do stuff. It doesn't just happen.'

'So what's she actually like?' said Mel the next morning as they sat outside the cafe with Jess in the pram. 'Mickey Meyers? You must know her pretty well.'

Bonnie tried to think. 'It's funny. I've known her for ages, but I still don't feel like … Well, she's sort of … she kind of holds something back.'

'What do you mean, holds something back?'

'She's so nice,' said Bonnie quickly. 'She's one of the most generous people I know. She'll do stuff like send me a postcard from Mexico just completely out of the blue, saying something like: *Dear Bonnie. Riding horses on the beach. You would love it.* And she gives me stuff, like brings back little presents from exotic places — really thoughtful things like that. And she does that for everyone, you know — she has this way of making everyone feel special …'

Mel nodded.

'But …' She hesitated. 'I don't know. She just … it's all kind of one-way. It's like, I couldn't make those gestures towards her. If I bought her a present, or sent her a postcard — not that I'd ever know where she actually lives — it would feel weird. Like I was intruding or something.'

'I think I know what you mean.' Mel sipped her coffee.

'It's almost like charisma's one of her tools, you know. What she uses in her work, on stage, and all that. But it's also like it's a part of her, of who she is. Her identity or something. She sort of — I don't know how to say this without it sounding like a criticism, but it's not; I don't think this is a negative thing about her, it's just the way she is — it's like she sort of, well, plays people. Not in a bad way. Just — she's aware of herself, of the effect she has on people.'

'She does have that quality, doesn't she?' said Mel. 'She's not what you'd call a classic beauty, but she kind of … glows.'

'Yeah, she's luminous.' Bonnie pushed back her hair. 'I don't know though. I mean, I love Mickey, and I admire her so much. And, you know' — she rolled her eyes — 'I'm the same as everyone else: I respond to her; I'm like a squirming puppy whenever she pays me any attention. But ...' She looked up at the grey sky. 'It would be hard, I reckon, knowing you have that kind of an effect on people. I wonder if it would feel a bit like — well, a burden, or a responsibility, or something.'

'Yeah.' Mel smiled. 'The burden of talent and beauty.'

'But it kind of would be, don't you think? There must be a pressure that goes along with that drive to be special. To make a mark or whatever.' She raised an edge of the rug that covered the hood of the pram, peeked in to check on Jess sleeping. 'And the other thing, you know: I really feel sorry for her sometimes.' She screwed up her face. 'But then again, this is all pure speculation. I'm only judging her by my own definition of happiness ... But I don't think she really has relationships. There's always men floating around — lots of them — but I've never known her to have a real, long-term relationship with anyone.'

Mel turned her glass in its saucer. 'Does she want kids, do you know?'

'No idea. She's never shown much interest in mine. And she did stuff like ask me to play a show only about three weeks after the twins were born.' She shook her head. 'She doesn't have a *clue* what it's like, to have kids.'

'Yeah, let alone newborn twins. But, in a way, that's kind of great, don't you think — that she didn't just give up on you.'

'Yeah, of course. It is, it's actually really cool. And she's — she always has been — so encouraging of me, just in the most practical way, by, well, offering me work.'

There was a pause. Bonnie shrugged. 'I think she's just — probably because she is so talented and beautiful — she's just got really good at keeping her distance. As a way of protecting herself, because so many people want a bit of her. And maybe there are special people she chooses to let in. But I'm not one of them.'

'Oh well.' Mel raised her glass. 'Here's to being ordinary.'

Bonnie stood in front of the bathroom mirror and turned from side to side. It was no good. She could get into her old jeans but she looked ridiculous. Her thighs like sausages in their casings. She went back to the bedroom and found tights and a skirt. Her old boots with the heels that she never wore any more. Returned to the mirror. Searched through the cabinet for earrings and a necklace, eyeliner, mascara.

'What're you doing, Mum?' It was Louie.

'Getting ready.'

'What for?'

She used her fingertips to remove a clump of mascara and stepped back. She had a last look in the mirror. She squatted down next to Louie and put her arms around him. 'I'm going to work today.'

'With Dad?'

'No. With Mickey. Remember Mickey? Who I used to play music with?'

Louie nodded but seemed uncomprehending.

'Well, anyway, a long time ago — before Jess was born, and even before you were born too — I used to play my guitar with Mickey in her band. And now she's asked me to play with her again. So today I'm going to a recording studio.'

'Who's going to look after us?'

'Dad. He's taken the day off.' She kissed Louie's cheek and stood up. 'So you've got the whole day with Dad — what a treat.'

Still he stood uncertainly. 'But what about Jess?'

'Dad's going to look after her too.'

Louie frowned. 'Does he know how to look after babies?'

She turned back to the mirror. 'Yes, he does know how to look after babies. He looked after you when you were a baby. Lots of times.'

'But how will he feed her?'

'He's got some milk in a bottle for her. You know how I've been using that special pump to get the milk out of my boobs?'

'Yeah.'

'Well, I've been saving the milk up so Jess can have it from a bottle while I'm not here.' She smoothed Louie's hair. 'We used to do the same thing for you and Edie when you were babies, sometimes.'

'Can I have some of that milk?'

Bonnie laughed. 'If there's some left you can. Ask Dad. But it doesn't taste very nice.'

'Oh.' Louie took her hand. Then, in a happy voice he said, 'I've got an idea. I'll just taste a little bit. And if it's not nice I can spit it out.'

Bonnie parked around the corner from the studio. She sat for a moment and ran her fingers through her hair. Straightened her tights and fixed her top. She got out of the car and opened the boot. Slid out the guitar case and her gear bag. Reached in and gripped the handles of the amp, eased it down over the lip of the boot, one thigh up to take some of the weight. Then she braced her arms and, guiltily, what was left of her stomach muscles, swung it out and set it on its wheels on the ground. Stacked the guitar and gear bag on top.

It was almost a relief to have something heavy to push. Without the amp she imagined she'd feel light, weird, unburdened. Like she'd forgotten something. *Don't think about it*, said a voice in her head, but it was too late, the telltale shooting sensation went through her nipples and she felt in the cold air the milk soaking through her bra and top. She stopped and looked down. Two dark circular wet patches. She'd forgotten breast pads. She did her jacket up and kept pushing.

A man came to the door of the office.

'I'm here for Mickey?' She felt her face flush in the heated building, sweat break out under her arms.

'Studio Two,' said the man, pointing down the hall.

'Thanks.' Bonnie set off, trundling her load. Her heart was thumping. This was ridiculous. How many times had she done this before? She passed all the posters of various glammed-up singers posturing with microphones or guitars and the framed platinum and gold records with scribbled autographs, the shelves of gleaming trophies. Everything looked so hard and shiny. Her feet and the wheels of her amp made no noise on the plush carpet.

The door was ajar. She pushed it open. The bright control room, the engineer's back, the spread of the desk with its rows and rows of faders and knobs and buttons. The expensive leather couch.

'Hi!' Mickey jumped up and hugged her.

'Hi.' She accepted the hug awkwardly, trying to wipe the sweat from her upper lip.

'How you doing?' Mickey let go of her and stood back.

'Good, thanks. Yeah, good.'

'Well.' Mickey plopped back onto the couch. 'Let's get down to business.'

Bonnie sat in the half-dark. The room was small. Her amp took up most of the space. There was one overhead light that shone in a pool on the microphone and her feet on the rung of the chair. She shrugged off her jacket at last and threw it into the corner. Settled the guitar in her lap.

'And loud again, please,' came the engineer's voice through the headphones. She reached down with her foot, clicked on the overdrive pedal and hit a few chords. She looked through the window at the engineer bent over the desk. Behind him she could see the top of Mickey's head, the back of the low-slung couch. 'And now just some picking,' came the voice.

She moved her fingers over the strings, flicked the plectrum up and down. She fumbled some notes. She hated hearing just the guitar with no other instruments — imagining it blaring out into the control room, loud and bare through the big speakers.

'Okay,' said the engineer. 'I think we're ready. You've got a volume control there but if you want to change the mix you'll need to tell me, okay?'

'Okay.' She heard her own voice, choking, too clear, coming back through the headphones.

'So let me know if you want to stop and change anything, but I might as well roll from the beginning, okay?'

'Okay.'

There was a moment of silence, and she heard her own indrawn breath, through her nose, a slight whistle. *Come on.* Another breath, another whistle, and then there it was. Just the tiniest whisper of white noise at first — amp hiss, cables, connections, microphones, the sound of everything ready to make sound — and then a stray voice, Mickey's, faint, spill from a guitar amp maybe — 'We rolling?' — and a count-in, and Mickey's rhythm guitar strumming, rolling through the chords, warm and open and regular. It was a bit slower than the demo version. Bonnie listened for a few seconds, nodding to get the feel of it. Then she hit a couple of notes to test the two guitars together, picked a little chain of melody that snaked itself across the spaces between three of Mickey's strums. She fiddled with the volume knob on the console next to her chair, pulled one side of the headphones half off so she could have some of the real sound of her amp in the room. The drums kicked in, and the bass, and Bonnie looked down at the worn neck of her guitar, the shine on the frets from where her fingers had touched so many times, and she dropped her shoulders and slid into the song and away.

She did two takes of the first song: one with more picking during the verses and one with less. She didn't make any mistakes. Then they moved on to the second song. She swooped through it, note perfect. The third song she had an idea to use a different sound: ultra-distorted with lots of reverb, but not too loud, so it washed through the other instruments at times and at others hovered in the background. She tried to explain it through the mic, hesitatingly, cringing again at her amplified voice. 'What do you reckon?' she said, squinting up at the window.

Mickey's face popped up behind the engineer's shoulder. 'Do it,' she said, and waved. 'Sounding like a million bucks in here.' Making a big thumbs-up.

Bonnie smiled and reached to her amp. 'I'll just get this sound.'

'She's good,' she heard the engineer say to Mickey, before he took his finger off the talk button.

They did the third song and stopped for lunch. Someone had ordered sandwiches. They sat at a big table in the room adjoining the kitchen. There was a feeling of space after the boxy studio rooms. A long window opened onto a courtyard full of clumps of plants with big, fleshy leaves that swayed in the wind.

Bonnie felt like she was floating, disconnected. Like this was a dream, another world, her sitting in this uncluttered room, eating food prepared by someone else. The gently hissing coffee machine. The rows of cups somebody was paid to wash up.

'It's sounding so good,' said Mickey. She squeezed Bonnie's

arm. 'I'm so glad you could do it.'

'Yeah, it's great,' said the engineer. 'The sound you got for that last track was amazing.'

She smiled back at both of them. She couldn't remember his name, but it didn't matter. There was a pleasant tiredness in her body, and she was incredibly hungry. She took a bite of sandwich.

'So,' said Mickey, leaning on her elbows and pushing her row of clunky bangles up and down one forearm. 'Want to play some shows? I've got an east-coast tour coming up in a couple of weeks. Haven't decided yet about a lead guitarist.'

Bonnie looked out at the slow bending and dipping of the plants. Inside her head she put herself on those planes and in those hotels and vans and backstage rooms. And on those stages, under the hot lights. Feeling the bass and the kick drum beneath her, cymbals cutting through bright and high, the crack of the snare. Her amp at her back, Mickey's over on the other side of the drum kit, the swell of the two guitars like a tide they all rode on. Keyboards rippling.

'Bon?' Mickey was watching her. 'Or is it too soon?'

She kept her eyes on the window. Right then she wanted to do it so badly it was like an urge, like wanting to have sex when she was ovulating, or needing to push the baby out in labour. She bit her lip. Wrenched her eyes away from the plants and glanced at her chest. The milk had dried, leaving two very faint marks. She folded her arms. 'Yeah,' she said. 'It is too soon. God, I really want to. But. I just can't — Jess is still so little. I mean, I have to feed her all the time. And Pete's got lots of work on.' She met Mickey's eyes. 'But it's not just that. Even if I could go I don't think I — I'm just not ready to leave Jess.'

Mickey smiled. She picked up her pack of cigarettes and tapped one out. 'That's fine. Just let me know when you are ready.'

'Okay.'

Mickey went to the courtyard door. She stopped, flicking her lighter. 'You know,' she said. 'You could just do a couple of shows. You could bring Jess — couldn't you get a babysitter? At the hotel?'

'I don't know.' She pressed her arms close to her breasts. The mention of Jess had set them off again.

'Think about it.' Mickey winked, stuck the cigarette between her lips and slipped out into the wind.

She opened the front door. 'Mummy!' she heard the twins call, and then their thudding footsteps. She set down her guitar and bags and knelt, put her arms out.

'Hi, you guys.' She kissed their faces, their hair, breathed their wild, sweet smell. 'How's it going?'

'Good.' Edie started playing with the latches on the guitar case. 'Dad took us to the park. And he gave us chocolates.'

'Did he?' Bonnie could hear Jess in the kitchen, whingeing. She had to get to her. 'Come on,' she said, taking the twins' hands. 'Let's go and see what Dad and Jess are doing.'

Pete was washing vegetables at the sink. Jess was in her baby chair, kicking and grizzling. Bonnie picked her up. 'You're hungry,' she said, and sat down. 'And I really need to feed you.' She pulled up her top, unclipped her bra and latched Jess on to one of her hard, over-full breasts. 'That's better.' Bonnie leaned back. She watched Edie and Louie, who were putting stickers onto the blank pages of a scrapbook and drawing around them with crayons.

'How'd you go?' Pete came over and kissed her, touched her neck with his damp hand.

'So good. I was so nervous, but then it just … came back.' She stroked Jess's head. 'I forgot how much I love it.'

'That's great.' Pete returned to the sink. 'See? I told you.'

'Yeah.' Bonnie smiled and rolled her eyes at him. 'You were right.'

'Well, we had a good day,' said Pete. 'We went to the park, and we took some snacks, a picnic —'

'And we had chocolates,' said Edie.

'Chocolates!' said Louie.

'Yeah.' Pete made a sheepish face. 'I gave these guys some chocolate as a special treat because they were so good at the park.'

'Right.' She shook her head. 'They're going to want you to look after them every day.'

'Yes!' said Edie. 'Dad can look after us every day, and we can have chocolates every day, and go to the park and then have another chocolate.'

'Chocolates!' said Louie.

Bonnie laughed.

'And these guys made a cubby,' said Pete. 'In the living room.'

'Yes, yes — come and see our cubby.' Louie and Edie jumped up and down.

'I'll come when I've finished feeding Jess, okay?'

'Okay.' Louie turned to Edie. 'Let's go and make sure the cubby hasn't fallen down,' he said, and they ran out.

She looked down at Jess. 'I missed you, little possum.'

'Sorry about the chocolates,' said Pete. 'I just couldn't resist giving them a treat — they were so good. They walked all the way to the park, and when I said it was time to leave they didn't even make a fuss.'

'That's all right.' She changed Jess to the other side. 'I guess you just confirmed your status as Mr Nice Guy, and tomorrow they'll be stuck with me again — the ogre.'

'Oh, come on — they love you.' Pete piled carrots on the chopping board. 'All day it was, "This drawing's for Mum," and, "Let's save this and show it to Mum when she gets home."'

'Well, that's nice to hear.'

Pete sighed. 'I'm absolutely buggered though. I don't know how you do it.'

'Yeah, I don't know either sometimes. Oh well. I'm the one who wanted to have all these children.' She glanced at the back door. 'So did Doug turn up?'

'No,' said Pete. 'Not sure what's happened to him. He hasn't been around for a while.'

'Yeah. Weird.'

There was a silence.

'Come on, Mum!' yelled Louie from the next room.

'Actually,' said Pete. 'I think he might be a bit upset that we didn't invite him to the kids' birthday party.'

She looked at him. 'What do you mean?'

'Well, what I said. I think he might be offended that we didn't invite him.'

'But of course we didn't invite him. It was just friends and family.'

'He's a friend.'

'The kids' friends, I meant. We didn't invite any of our friends — except Greg and Kylie, and I didn't even know you'd invited them. Other than that it was all kinder people, and Mel and Josh and Freddie, and Mum.' She sat Jess up on her lap and fixed her own bra and top. 'And that was it.'

'Yeah, but you know,' said Pete, 'he's been around here a lot, and I think he really enjoys seeing the kids and playing with them, and he's on his own really —'

'But hang on. How did he find out anyway?'

'What do you mean?'

'About the party? How did he even know it was on? Did you tell him?'

'No. I didn't. He — I think he actually drove past on the day. Saw the balloons.'

She stood up, sat Jess on her hip. 'Really? What would he be doing driving past here on a weekend? Where's he living again? I thought it was over in Flemington or something.'

'Yeah, it is — Flemington.'

'Well, why would he be driving around here?'

'I don't know. I didn't ask.' Pete was keeping his back to her, stirring the food on the stove.

She went closer, stood behind him. She could feel her voice creeping up, getting tense. 'So he actually said he drove past and saw the balloons?'

'Yeah.'

'He just happened to be driving past?'

'Yeah.'

'And you don't find that weird?'

Pete turned to face her. 'You obviously do.'

'Well, it's not as if we're on a main road. I mean, this is a tiny street — we don't get much through traffic. It's not on the way to anywhere. I find it hard to believe he would have a reason to drive past here other than to — I don't know — check up on us.'

Pete sighed. He put the wooden spoon down on the bench.

She kept looking at him. 'Come on,' she said. 'You've got to admit it seems a bit weird.'

'Okay.' He spread his hands. 'Yes, it does seem weird. Okay? Happy?'

'Mum?' It was Louie in the doorway.

'Yes, darling?'

'Come on. Come and see our cubby.'

'Okay. Okay. I just need to … Hang on just one sec.' Bonnie lifted Jess sideways and pulled her pants halfway down. 'Yuck. How long has this poo been in here?'

'I don't know.' Pete turned back to the stove. 'I've been busy doing everything else.'

'Come on, Mum,' said Louie.

'Well, it's gone all over her singlet.' She went towards the hallway, holding Jess out in front of her. 'Hang on, Lou-Lou. I'll just change this nappy and then I'll come, okay?'

'Come on, Mum!' Louie pulled at her skirt. 'Come and see the cubby!'

'Just wait, please, Louie — I have to change this nappy.' She tried to push past him.

'No — come now!'

'Louie!' Bonnie stuck out one knee and tried to dislodge him. 'Let go. I'll come in a minute, all right?'

Louie gave the skirt a last, ferocious tug and shoved himself away, head down, shoulders drooping. 'You never come.'

'Oh, Lou, I'm sorry, it's just …'

But he was gone, stomping away.

'Bloody hell,' she muttered. She got a better grip on the baby, who was starting to complain, and turned back to Pete. 'Well, I think it's weird, him driving past here on the weekend. I think it's weird and creepy.'

Pete swung around. 'What do you want me to do? Do you want me to fire him? How about you fire him? Go on. You can ring him up now and fire him, and tell him it's because he drove past our house and because he might've taken some coins and because he might've had someone over here for dinner when I gave him the key, and because you don't like him being around here and because you just don't like him.'

Anger shivered through her. 'I'm not the one who hired him!' she yelled. 'I would never have hired him because I think it's a fucking stupid fucking idea!' Jess began to wail. Bonnie carried her out into the hallway. But then she stopped and went back. She took a deep breath and held her voice in, kept it calm and even. 'And actually, Pete, I don't not like Doug. I think he's a good guy underneath it all. I think he's pretty weird but, you know, he's probably harmless. But I've been put in this situation where I can't just — I don't know — be kind and generous, and tolerant, and all the things I'd like to be, because he's — he's bloody well in my face all the time. And I'm worn out by it. And you — you are the one who's put me in this situation.' She felt her voice tremble, but she kept it low. 'It's you. You've done this.'

Doug didn't turn up the next morning. Bonnie, showered and dressed early just in case, kept glancing at the door as she made breakfast for the kids and then sat down to eat her own. She shovelled in mouthfuls of muesli, her eyes on the pane of glass, the bare wind-beaten arms of the apricot tree, the waving tendrils of the wisteria vine, dun-coloured, dead-looking. She kept expecting his face to come bobbing into view.

The children got down from the table and ran off somewhere.

Pete came in, hair still wet from the shower, pulling on his jumper. 'Coffee?' He stood behind her, massaged her shoulders.

She leaned back. 'Yes, please.'

'You still pissed off with me?' He bent to kiss her neck.

'No.'

'I'm sorry.'

'I'm sorry too. I understand how hard it must be for you. You're sort of … stuck in the middle.'

Pete went over to the sink. 'Hey, I was thinking,' he said.

'Yeah?'

'I'll get my first lot of payment from Grant this week.'

'Yeah?'

'So.' Pete lifted down the coffee canister. 'Let's put some of it aside. Like four thousand. And let's — like at the start of next year maybe, when Jess is old enough to leave with your mum for a while, but before the twins start school — let's go away for a week. Just the two of us. Thailand or Vietnam, or something.' He glanced over at her. 'Give ourselves a bit of a reward for this hard year.'

Bonnie sat up straighter in her chair. She felt it all dissolve, the cramped irritation, the tiredness and strain.

'Although … I don't know what season it'll be. We could save it till winter next year. Or would that be too long a wait?'

She smiled.

He came over and picked up the milk from the table. 'Or Bali? Just lie on a beach somewhere for a week and eat nice food.'

She reached out her arms. 'Come here.'

'What?' Pete went closer. She put her arms around his waist and pulled him down, tried to make him sit on her knee. He wobbled, splayed his legs, gripped the edge of the table, laughing. 'What're you doing?'

She kissed him, his face, his neck. 'God I love you,' she said. 'I love you so much.'

Pete laughed again. 'So you want to do it?'

'It sounds like the best idea ever in the whole world.'

'Where should we go? When?'

'Oh god, anywhere. Whenever.'

'And do you think your mum'll be okay with the kids?'

'Well, she'll just bloody well have to be.'

'What're you two doing?' It was Edie, in the doorway.

Pete tried to get up, but Bonnie pulled him down again. 'I'm cuddling Dad,' she said. 'Because I love him so much.'

'Oh.' Edie kept watching. She wiped her nose on the sleeve of her pyjama top.

'Yuck, Edie,' said Pete.

'You're squashing Mum,' said Edie.

'She seems to want to be squashed,' said Pete.

Bonnie kept her arms around him, felt his solid weight on

her thighs, his body pushing hers against the chair-back. She tightened her hold. 'I do.'

Mel rang. 'Did you do the recording?' she said. 'How did it go?'

'It was great.' Bonnie stood at the clothesline with the phone tucked between her ear and shoulder. 'I was so nervous but it was fine — it went really well.'

'That's great.'

'Yeah.' She unpegged clothes and dropped them into the basket at her feet. 'And it was so nice to go to work! To this place where no one hassles you, where you can focus on a task and finish it, and then you can just make a cup of tea and sit down and finish that!'

Mel laughed. 'I know. It's amazing, isn't it? I couldn't believe how easy work was when I went back, compared to being at home with Freddie.'

'I can imagine.' Bonnie moved to the other end of the line, pushing the basket over the grass with her foot. The back of her neck was cold. She pulled at her scarf. 'Mickey wants me to play some shows with her.'

'Really? Will you do it?'

'I don't know — it's all a bit hard.'

'You must miss it though? Touring? You did so much of it. You were always off on the road somewhere.'

'I don't know.' Bonnie dropped the last piece of clothing into the basket, straightened, took the phone in her hand, uncrooked her neck. 'Sometimes, yeah. There were lots of good things about it.'

'I bet.'

'But, you know, when I was doing it, when I'd been doing it for ages and it was my life and took up all my time ... I was sick of it then. I hated it. It's — I don't know — it's kind of an empty way of life. You're always moving, you have all these weird superficial relationships.' She lifted the basket and went towards the porch steps. 'You meet so many great people, interesting people, but you never really get to know them — you see them once every six months or whatever, and you just go out somewhere, get drunk, have the same old conversations, and say goodbye.'

'Right.'

Bonnie set the basket of clothes down on the kitchen table. She stood looking at the fridge, its bristle of papers, the twins' drawings and paintings, notices from the childcare centre. 'I remember, when I met Pete, when I went back to his place and everything was just so calm, and settled. I mean, it was just a scungy share house, with crappy furniture and everything, but — well, he's a bit older, so it was more organised, I guess.' Bonnie moved closer to the fridge. 'Anyway, there was this moment, the next morning, sitting at the kitchen table. There was just something so straight about him. He wasn't trying to play any games or anything, act cool. I said, "I have to go, I have to catch a plane." And he just looked at me and said "Oh! I wish you could stay."'

'That's very sweet.'

Bonnie smiled. 'Yeah. It was. And only Pete could get away with something like that. Anyone else and I reckon I would've run a mile. But I remember thinking, Wow, I really like this guy, and feeling like all I wanted to do was race back into his bedroom and jump under the covers and never come out.'

'I remember the two of you,' said Mel. 'You were so in love.'

The sound of Jess crying came from down the hallway. In the middle of the fridge door, half hidden by a magnet, was a photo of Bonnie and Pete, from their early days. Their faces, younger, fuller. Arms around each other.

'It's funny, isn't it?' said Mel. 'How our lives seem to fall into these two time periods — before and after.'

'Yeah.' She looked at the photo. Pete unshaven, wearing that old brown jumper. The mottled bark of a tree behind, the soft grey-green leaves, filtered sunlight.

'And they seem so distinct, so separate from each other.'

'Yeah.' The dappled light on her skin. Her cheek against Pete's chest. 'But … towards the end, with the touring, it was like I knew something was going to change. I remember I had this … loneliness.' She laughed. 'I was surrounded by people, I couldn't get a moment to myself, and I was so, so lonely. Like the worst kind of homesickness, except I didn't really have a home — I just had that room at your place with all my stuff in it, remember?' Jess's crying was getting louder. Bonnie pushed the magnet higher so the top of Pete's head was visible, his sticking-up hair. 'It was like I was homesick for Pete, and I hadn't even met him yet. And then when I did, it was like suddenly that homesick feeling had a — I don't know — a reason or something, a target — and then it really kicked in. Every tour. And I just knew I was going to stop. It was only a matter of time.'

'Mum.' It was Louie.

'Yes, Lou?'

'Jess is crying.'

'Yeah — thanks, Lou. I'll get her in a minute.' She turned away from the fridge. 'Sorry, Mel,' she said into the phone. 'I'd better go.'

'Okay, you guys. Got your bathers on?' Bonnie sifted through the piles of clean laundry on the couch, pulling out towels and stuffing them in a bag. 'Oh, Jess, it's okay,' she said to the baby whingeing on her mat. 'We'll go in a minute.'

'Let's make another cubby,' said Edie to Louie, and started to pull one of the cushions out from under the laundry pile.

'Not now, you guys. Come on. We've got swimming.' She rescued the toppling mountain of clothes and shoved the cushion back in. 'Edie, come on — you're making everything fall down on the floor.'

'But we want to make a cubby,' wailed Edie.

'Look.' Bonnie zipped the swimming bag and swept Jess up into her arms. She stood with her leg pressed against the couch, holding the cushion in. 'Do you want to go to swimming or not?'

'I do.' Edie tugged at the cushion. 'But I just want to make a cubby first.'

'Edie, listen.' Bonnie reached down, tried to take her hand, but Edie pulled away. 'If we want to get there in time for the class we have to go now. The class doesn't just start when we get there. If we're not on time we'll miss it.'

Edie folded her arms and bared her teeth. 'But I want to make a cubby *now*.'

'When we get home from swimming you can make cubbies for as long as you want.' She went over to the door. 'Come on, let's get in the car. Grandma'll be waiting.'

'Let's go, Edie,' said Louie and followed Bonnie.

They paused in the doorway. Edie glowered. And then — 'All *right*' — she stomped after them.

Bonnie strapped Jess into her capsule and the twins in their booster seats. 'Oh, bugger — I forgot the snacks. Hang on one sec, you guys.'

She shut the door, cutting off Jess's crying. She dashed back into the house, down the hallway and into the kitchen, where a packet of rice cakes and two apples sat on the bench with a bottle of water. Bonnie grabbed them and turned. Something — a difference, an absence — caught her eye and she stopped. Went over to the door. Put her face right up to the glass. Looked down at the blank bit of concrete to the left of where the steps went down. The pot plant was gone. Only a mark, a left-behind dark ring full of silvery snail tracks.

'What's ...?' she said aloud. But then she glanced at the clock. It was nearly ten-thirty. They were late.

'Funny.' Bonnie started the engine.

'What's funny?' said Louie, over Jess's crying.

'My pot plant.'

'What pot plant?'

She drove to the corner of the next street, put on the indicator, waited for another car to pass.

'You know, my special pot plant. My great-aunt Jean gave it to me. It was just a geranium, but it was in this beautiful ceramic pot, sort of glazed green.'

'What's grazed green?'

'Glazed. Glazing's a way of finishing off a piece of pottery or ceramic. It goes over the colour and makes it shiny. And sometimes it sort of gets all these tiny cracks in it that look really beautiful.'

'I'm hungry,' said Louie.

'Me too,' said Edie.

Bonnie grabbed the packet of rice cakes and opened them awkwardly against the steering wheel. She took four out and passed them back to Louie. 'Give two to Edie, please. And don't drop any on Jess.'

The twins munched. Drizzle spattered on the windscreen. Jess wound back down to a whinge and then went quiet.

She put on the windscreen wipers and turned onto the main road. 'I wonder what happened to it?'

'How's Pete's new job going?' Suzanne bounced Jess on her lap.

Bonnie sat, her breath still short from the swim, her eyes on Edie and Louie ducking for plastic rings thrown by the teacher. 'Oh, good, I think,' she said vaguely. 'Yeah, good.'

Suzanne looked at her sharply. 'Has he got rid of that feller yet? What's-his-name?'

'Doug?' She sighed. 'No.'

Suzanne gave a disapproving click with her tongue. 'Silly boy. He's too much of a soft touch, if you ask me.'

She didn't answer. She watched Edie's pale legs kick up out of the water, skinny and frog-like. Her own leg and arm muscles throbbed with satisfying weariness. She leaned back and breathed the dense, unnatural air of the overheated building.

Suzanne yawned. 'I always get drowsy in these places.'

'Me too.' Then Bonnie sat up straight. 'Oh, I forgot to tell you. Guess what?'

'What?'

'Pete got his first pay from the new job and we're putting a chunk of it aside so we can go on a holiday.'

'What a wonderful idea.' Suzanne bounced Jess again. 'When?'

'Oh, not for ages.' Bonnie noticed Louie duck under for longer than usual, and half stood to watch. But then he bobbed back up, chin barely above the surface, arms working, misted goggles like two milky reptile eyes. She put her hand to her chest. 'God — tell you what, I'll be relieved when these guys can actually swim.' She sat back down. 'We were thinking maybe even next winter.'

'That would be lovely,' said Suzanne. 'Escape the cold. And the children will love it.'

'Actually, we were thinking of not taking them.'

'Really?'

'Yeah.' Bonnie looked at Suzanne. 'I mean — Pete and I, we haven't had anything like that since the twins were born. I think we need it.'

'Yes, yes, of course, you do. It's important to keep your

relationship going — keep the spark.'

'So ...' She squeezed up her eyes. 'We were thinking maybe we could get you to look after the kids.'

'Me?' Suzanne's head went up.

'Well, yeah. You could come and stay at our place.'

Jess started to grizzle, arching her back in Suzanne's arms. Suzanne bounced her higher. 'How long for?'

'We were thinking maybe' — she squeezed up her eyes again — 'a week?'

Suzanne made a face. 'A week?'

Bonnie felt uncomfortably hot. She took a breath. *You can ask her. She's their grandmother, for god's sake.* 'Well,' she said, trying to keep her voice level, 'we're thinking of going overseas, and with the flight time and everything, I mean, a week's not actually all that long ...'

'Yes, of course.' Jess was throwing back her head, her small body stiff in Suzanne's arms. 'She's getting sick of me.' Suzanne handed the baby to Bonnie and settled back on the bench. 'Yes, of course I can look after them,' she said, and flashed Bonnie a smile that seemed almost nervous. 'You'll have to show me what to do though.'

Bonnie's irritation melted. 'Thanks, Mum.'

'That's all right.' Suzanne crossed her legs and smoothed her pants. 'But just make sure you consult with me when you set the date so I can get organised with work and bridge and things like that.'

'Yes, of course.' Bonnie kissed Jess's head, her eyes on the twins in the water. Her excitement at the thought of the holiday, the bravado she'd needed to summon in the face of Suzanne's unavailability — both were gone. She found herself dropping into unexpected panic. Visions tumbled through her mind: Jess falling off the change table; Jess drowning in the bath; one of the twins pulling the boiling kettle down onto themselves; one of them running out in front of a car. 'Anyway,' she said quietly, holding Jess's small, solid body closer. 'It won't be for ages.'

She strapped Jess in her capsule, checked Louie's seatbelt and shut the door.

On the other side of the car Suzanne leaned in, kissed her fingertips and dabbed them in the direction of each child. 'Bye, gorgeous children,' she sang, then straightened up and pushed the door closed.

'Bye, Mum.' Bonnie went round and met her at the back of the car. 'Thanks for your help today.'

'Bye, darling, lovely to see you.' Suzanne's kiss barely connected with her cheek. 'And that's wonderful news about your holiday.'

'Yeah, it is.' Bonnie ran her thumb over the ridge of the car key. 'I think we need it — me and Pete.'

Suzanne took a pair of sunglasses from her handbag and put them on. But instead of turning to her own car she just stood, gaze lowered, running the zip of the bag slowly back and forth along its track. 'You know,' she said in a breathy voice, 'we didn't do enough of that — your father and I. I thought ...' She lifted one hand and adjusted the glasses, pushed them further up her nose. 'I thought it was all still to come — ahead of us.'

Bonnie stood in silence. She could see the top of her mother's head, the evenly spaced highlights and the regrowth of grey at the roots.

Suzanne's fingers kept working at the bag, drawing the zip closed and then open again. 'I was so angry when he died. I felt like I'd been robbed. I was looking forward to those times ... once all the hard work was over.' She made a snuffling little sound, half laugh, half sob. 'All my life — for our whole marriage — I thought he was waiting, like me, that our life together hadn't really started.' She raised her head. In each lens of the glasses hung the tiny white circle of Bonnie's face. 'I was furious that he hadn't retired earlier — that he wanted to keep working.'

Bonnie didn't move. She pushed down with the pad of her thumb on the key.

'And the funny thing is,' said Suzanne, drawing herself up, 'I'm pretty sure he was happy the whole time. Content.' She pulled her lips back in a closed-mouth smile. 'You think you know someone.'

Bonnie drove out of the car park.

'My seatbelt's not on properly,' said Edie.

'What?'

'My seatbelt. It's all twisted and it's not done up.'

'Shit. Hang on.' She pulled the car over and got out. She went around and opened Edie's door.

'See?' Edie shook the tangled straps, the metal clip dangling above its empty plug.

She straightened the harness and clicked the belt in. 'I thought Grandma did it.'

'She did.' Edie's fingers went up to tangle in Bonnie's hair, which was drying in clumped locks. 'But she didn't do it properly.'

Pete stood in the middle of the kitchen, wiping his hands on his work pants. 'So I've got this reunion thing.'

'Oh, is that tonight? I forgot.'

'Yeah. Will you be okay? With dinner and everything?'

'Sure.' Bonnie opened the fridge and looked in. 'If I can think of something to cook. The shopping situation's getting dire again.'

Pete bent to kiss Jess in her baby chair. 'You'll get a chance tomorrow, won't you, with the twins at kinder?'

'I guess so.' She felt her usual wave of exhausted apathy at the idea of shopping. Pete didn't understand, she knew. He really couldn't see how she could go off with the list and manage to come back with only half the stuff and even then not enough of certain things, or anything for dinner that actual night. She didn't understand it herself. It was a sort of paralysis. Once she was in there, with all the bright lights and the towering shelves, the people and stacks of goods and signs and specials and god-awful music, all she wanted to do was get out as fast as possible.

'Well, I'll go and get ready then.' He went through to the bathroom and the shower started up.

She put some water on for pasta and got out a tin of tomatoes. She went out to pick some herbs. Stepped onto the porch and saw the empty spot again. Went over to it. Scanned the porch, the steps. Walked down and cast around in the half-dark. Along both sides of the workshop. Over to the back fence and the outside toilet. Nothing. She wrapped her cardigan closer around herself and went back in.

'Pete?'

'Yeah?' Through the shower curtain she could see his blurred outline, his hair wetted down, the water bouncing off his shoulders. She moved closer. Stood for a moment just watching him. The steam, the smell of his shampoo, the rushing water sounds, it felt like it was all soaking into her, through her skin, loosening her. All she wanted to do was strip off and get in there with him. Not make dinner. Not clean up again and wash the dishes. Not fight her way through the whole bedtime routine with the older kids. Not feed the baby, and bathe her, and do her nappy and put her to bed. She wanted to step out of all that, shrug it off and drop it to the floor. Be naked with Pete under the water, her eyes closed, her hair wet, the taste of him and the mineral taste of the water on him, his skin and his lips.

113

'Yeah?' he said again. 'Bon? You there?'

'Mu-um!' came a call from the living room. 'Louie keeps taking my train tracks!'

'Um. Oh yeah, did you do something with my pot plant?'

'What pot plant?'

'Mu-um!'

'Hang on, Edie — I'll be there in a sec.' She put her palm to the shower curtain, felt its thin fabric cleave to her skin. 'You know,' she said. 'The pot plant that was on the back porch. The one my great-aunt Jean gave me.'

'The geranium?'

'Yeah.'

'Mu-um!'

'Hold on, Edie! Yeah — the geranium. It's gone.'

'Really? Well, I didn't move it.'

'You sure?'

'Of course.' Pete turned the shower off. He stepped out and started drying himself. He bent towards the mirror, flicking his hair around with his fingers. 'I wonder what this thing'll be like tonight.'

She watched him. Behind her, in the kitchen, Jess started to complain. 'It's so weird — it just seems to have vanished,' she said.

'I mean, I haven't seen any of these guys for, what, sixteen years,' said Pete into the mirror. 'Except Deano. And Douggie of course.'

She looked at the beads of water on his shoulders. 'It couldn't've been the kids. It's actually quite heavy. I don't think they could carry it anywhere. They could maybe push it down the stairs, but I checked and it's not anywhere in the backyard that I can see. And anyway, they wouldn't do something like that.'

Pete opened the bathroom cabinet and took out his

toothbrush. 'I wonder if Douggie'll turn up,' he said. 'After not coming here at all yet this week. Maybe he's sick or something.'

'Pete.' She looked at his face in the mirror.

'Yeah?'

'Maybe Doug did something with the pot plant.'

'Yeah, maybe. Although I can't imagine why. I guess you'll have to ask him.'

'But ...' Bonnie paused. 'He hasn't been here since last week, and I'm sure I would've noticed it missing before now.' She tried to picture herself, her movements over the past few days. Up and down the back steps so many times a day. Now that she really thought about it she couldn't see the plant there — had no clear memory of the last time she had noticed it.

'Mm.' Pete stuck his toothbrush in his mouth. 'It's a mystery.'

'I'm sure I would've noticed,' she said. She was looking past him now in the mirror, at her own face.

'Mu-um!' Edie's voice shrilled out over the sound of Jess wailing from the kitchen.

She turned and stomped out into the hallway. 'Oh for god's sake, Edie,' she shouted. 'How many train tracks are there? Why do you need to have them all? Can't you guys just play quietly without constantly bothering me with these petty squabbles?'

Edie came to the living-room door. 'But he keeps taking the bridge ones,' she said in a whine. 'And I'm trying to make —'

'I'm not interested,' she snapped. 'You two can work it out.' She marched into the kitchen, scooped up Jess and turned the gas off under the frantic water. Opened the bread bin, pulled out two slices and dropped them in the toaster. 'Right,' she said. 'Change of plan. Baked beans for dinner.'

'Shh! Shh! You guys.' She reached out her arms as if she could physically smother the noise the twins were making. 'I've just put Jess to bed.'

'But we're having running races,' said Edie. 'Ready, Lou? No — here's the start. Here. And you put your foot there and then you —'

'No.' Bonnie spoke in a stern whisper. 'It's not time for running races — it's time to read a story. Have you chosen your books?'

'… and then the starter says, "On your marks!"'

'*Edie!*' Bonnie went over and took her arm. 'Did you hear what I said? It's not time for games now.'

Edie shook her off. 'Just one more, okay?'

She sighed. 'Okay.' She squatted down in front of them. 'One more race, but it has to be a tiptoe race, okay? You have to go on your tippy-toes and be as quiet as you can. And when you're finished I want you to choose your books and I'll meet you on the couch.'

'Okay.' Edie giggled and made a face of exaggerated caution. 'On your marks,' she whispered. 'Get set …'

Bonnie went into the kitchen. A cold draught hit her. The back door stood open, swinging slightly in the wind, the rope of bells stirring. Through the open space the sky over the workshop roof was velvety black, starless, moonless. It looked low and close. There was the faint scratching of the branches of the apricot tree. She shivered. She went over and shut the door, and turned the lock. She had to suppress an urge to do it quickly, to snap it locked and lean against it. And she had to suppress the silly image that came slinking into her mind, the scene from the horror movie where the woman rushes from door to door and window to window, slamming and locking them, only to discover the predator already inside.

'Edie? Louie?' She went back out into the hallway. The twins were rolling and wrestling near the front door. 'Edie? Louie?' She stood over them. 'Did either of you open the back door?'

'No.' Louie didn't even look at her.

'Edie?' She could hear herself getting shrill. 'Did you?'

Edie didn't answer. She rolled on top of Louie.

'*Edie!*' Bonnie knelt down beside them. She grabbed Edie's arms.

'What?' Edie rolled back and stared at her.

Louie sat up and stared too.

You're frightening them. 'Sorry.' Bonnie let go and sat back on her haunches. 'Sorry, guys — I just get sick of asking the same question a hundred times.' She made her voice light. 'I was just wondering if one of you opened the back door for any reason.'

'No.'

'No.'

'Are you sure? After the bath? When I was feeding Jess?'

They glanced at each other. 'We didn't do it,' said Edie.

She moved her eyes from face to face. 'You're not in trouble. I just want to know if you did it or not. I promise I won't be angry.' She reached out and picked up one each of their hands. 'I promise.'

They looked at each other again. Then Louie lowered his head. 'I just wanted to find my super bouncy ball,' he said.

Bonnie pulled them to her, an unwieldy bundle, all bones and trailing limbs. 'God, you guys are getting big,' she said. 'Thanks for being honest with me.' She kissed Louie on the head. 'Now. Which books are we going to read?'

After they were asleep though, she couldn't help creeping all through the silent house, checking each room. She peered behind doors. She pulled back the shower curtain, fright wriggling in her chest. Nothing of course. Drops of water on the tiles. Pete's razor on the high ledge. She eased open the door to Jess's room and stared into the shadows between the wardrobe and the wall, the cot and the change table. She looked in again at the twins in their beds, the jumbles of clothes on the floor, toys and books. She reached over Louie and behind the curtain, felt the lock on the window. *This is ridiculous*, she kept saying to herself. But still she did it, and as she did the silence seemed to thin, to grow taut with waiting.

She finished in the kitchen. Stood scanning all around — the table full of crumbs, the accusing pile of dirty dishes. She went over and opened the pantry door. *As if anyone could even fit in here.* Closed it again. Her heart beating hard enough for her to notice it. She turned off the light and went to the door. Checked again the cold lock. Looked out at the blanketing sky, the faint skeleton of the apricot tree, the hulk of the workshop. And then down, at the glimmering concrete porch, stark and empty where the pot should have been. She could feel the chill of the glass so close to her cheek. Her breath was fogging it.

She turned away. Went into the living room and switched on the light and the heater and the TV with the sound low. Lay on the couch with her acoustic. Picked out little sketches of notes and watched a documentary about arctic life. On the screen a polar bear lifted one of her cubs, the tiny back legs hanging toylike from the huge jaws.

She started awake. The guitar slid to the floor with a hollow bump.

There was a noise, a scrabbling.

She sat up. Fumbled for the control and turned off the TV.

The noise again, and she held her breath, frozen on the couch.

A thump, then silence.

She sat motionless, straining to hear.

Another scrabble, another thump, then a quiet voice saying, 'Shit.'

Quickly, she got up and went to the front door. There was the jingle of keys. She put her hand to the deadlock. 'Pete?'

'Yeah, it's me.'

She opened the door. 'You gave me a fright.'

'Sorry.' He smelled of booze. 'Couldn't get the key in the lock. It's dark out here.' He stepped in, past her.

She shut the door behind him and stood for a moment with her hand on her chest. She could feel her heart knocking.

'Bon?' Pete turned. 'You okay? Sorry — I didn't mean to scare you.' He put his arms around her. 'I mean, you knew I was coming.'

She leaned her head against him. 'Yeah, of course. Sorry. I'm just half asleep.' She lifted her head again. 'Yuck. You stink.'

'Yeah, sorry, I had a few cigarettes.' He went into the bedroom.

Bonnie followed. She kicked off her ugg boots and got in under the covers with her clothes on. She lay watching as he unlaced his shoes and took them off. She tried to picture him at the party, drinking, talking, shaking hands. Would they shake hands, his old mates? Weren't they mostly ex-punks? Probably no shaking hands. Maybe hugging. But not the initial greetings — only at the end of the night.

Pete yawned. 'Jeez, I'm tired.'

She reached out and put one hand flat in the middle of his back. He was warm. 'So how was it?'

'It was good.' He flopped down beside her. 'Yeah, it was good. Some people there I haven't seen for a really long time. But it's funny — everyone looks pretty much the same. Bit fatter. Couple of them bald.'

'Well, it's only been — what? — sixteen years.' She gave a short laugh. 'Right, yeah, I guess it has been a while.' She stared up at the ceiling. 'God. We're not young any more, Pete.'

He moved closer. 'You still are. And I'm not exactly old yet, either. Forty-two, that's not old, is it?'

'No. But ... The funny thing is I still feel like I'm the same.

I mean, I feel the same inside as I did when I was twenty, or even eighteen, or even younger. It's like I'm the same person inside and all this stuff's just happened to me and sometimes I sort of … forget. And then someone yells "Mum" and I think, Oh my god, that's me — I'm someone's mum. Or I look in the mirror. Or try on bathers.'

Pete kissed her neck. 'Oh, come on, you're as gorgeous as ever.'

'Ha. You have to say that.' She turned to him. 'Anyway, you know what my mother always said: *All cats are grey in the dark.*'

'What does that even mean?'

'I'm not actually sure.' She laughed. 'You know: who cares what a woman looks like if you're just after a one-night stand.'

'Really? That's what it means?'

'I think so.'

'Jeez. What sort of a mother teaches her daughter that particular saying?'

She laughed again. 'Well, she didn't really teach it to me. I mean, it was just one of the things she said.'

'God. Your mum's weird.' Pete yawned again. 'I should brush my teeth.'

Bonnie closed her eyes. 'I should do the dishes.'

They lay in silence for a while. Pete slipped his hand up her shirt, but then he stopped. She opened her eyes.

He was staring at nothing, into space. 'You know who's really aged though,' he said.

'Who?'

'Douggie. He looks shocking. I was looking at those guys tonight and, like I said, everyone's just got a bit fat or whatever — bald maybe — but Doug … He's looking really rough. He looks like he's got about ten years on everyone else, and it's really only — what? — four or five.'

She felt wide awake all of a sudden. The warm, sleepy desire gone. 'Oh, so Doug was there, was he?' she said carefully.

'No. He wasn't. I was just thinking about him. And of course some of the guys were asking about him, where he was, what he's been up to.'

'So maybe he has been sick then.'

'Yeah, maybe.' Pete kissed her absently. 'But he might've just decided to give it a miss. He was never really a part of that group. He was more of a kind of … hanger-on. We were all at uni, and he wasn't. And also, he's burned a few bridges with some of those blokes. And I think he's just not all that good at, you know, social things.' He gave another yawn. 'Anyway, I wonder when he's going to show up here again. I kind of need him. I've got so much work.'

Bonnie felt a prickle of irritation. 'Well, you could always call him.'

'Yeah, I should, I guess. Poor old Douggie. He's had a rough time of it. I mean, when you look at all those other guys tonight — everyone's got some sort of career, or at least a job. Relationships, kids. Except Doug. Nothing seems to have worked out for him.'

She sat up. 'I'm going to do the dishes.'

'What? Leave them.' He tried to pull her back down. 'It must be two o'clock in the morning.'

'Well, it sucks starting the day with a big mess in the kitchen.'

'Come on, Bon. Don't be ridiculous. Don't do them now.'

Her eyes were sore, and her throat. Fatigue ran through her, swamping, deep. 'Yeah. Okay.' She took her clothes off, shivering, staying half under the covers. Felt for her pyjamas on the floor, pulled them on and lay back down.

She curled on her side, facing away from him. He stroked her arm, pressed into her, kissed her neck. She lay still. After a while he sighed and let go of her.

Doug turned up the next morning. He sidled in the back door in a gust of freezing air and cigarette smoke, went to the table and set down a tall bottle of tomato juice. Kept his hand on it for a moment, head bent, then straightened and released it with a flourish. Took a seat between the twins and flashed his grin around the table.

'G'day, Douggie,' said Pete.

'Hi, Doug,' said Bonnie, trying to meet his eyes and failing.

'What's that?' said Louie.

'Well.' Doug settled in his chair. 'That's a present for your dad. When him and me were young devils and we'd been out the night before and weren't feeling too wonderful the next morning, we used to have a bit of something called hair of the dog.' Bonnie looked up, and Doug met her gaze, cracked his lips and slid his tongue across the lower one. 'Bloody Marys we used to have. But I'm not sure you'd be in possession of the necessary ingredients in this' — he winked — 'house of virtue.'

She dropped her eyes. *Fuck off*, she thought.

Pete took a bite of toast and stood up. 'Yeah, but that was when we had no responsibilities,' he said, ruffling Edie's hair. 'Too much work these days.' He rubbed one hand over his face. 'Anyway, I don't reckon I could, even if I wanted to. I feel shocking this morning and I reckon I only had three beers. But thanks anyway, Douggie. You decided to give it a miss?'

Doug didn't answer. He leaned back and gave a croaking laugh. 'Jesus, Peter. Whatever happened to your lust for life? Your vim and vigour?'

Pete kissed the twins and Bonnie. 'Better get started. See you later, guys. There's some toast there if you want it, Douggie. I'll be out the back.'

Bonnie stood up. 'Come on, you kids. Kinder today.'

'Can we taste some of that drink?' said Louie, looking at Doug.

'Why not? Don't think your dad wants any after all.'

She stood with her hands on the back of the chair. 'I really don't think you'll like it, Lou.'

'Can I have some too, Douggie?' said Edie.

'Guys,' she said. 'It's not like normal juice — it's not sweet at all. It just tastes like tomatoes.'

But Doug was shaking the bottle and clicking open the lid, smiling indulgently at the children. 'How can I say no to you two?'

Bonnie glanced up at the clock. 'Louie, Edie ...' She sighed.

Louie got down off his chair. 'I'll get some cups.'

'This'll put some colour in their cheeks,' said Doug, directing a lazy smile at Bonnie. 'All this *Slip Slop Slap* and *Don't go out in the sun* business. It's all very well, but kids these days, well, they're like a bunch of' — he gave that tittering giggle — 'little spooks. In my day, we'd be *sent out* to *play* in the sun. We all got burned, every year. Blisters. Peeling. I remember peeling the skin off me brother's back.' He held up his fingers. 'Carefully. If you were really careful you could peel off these great big bits.' Edie and Louie stared, open-mouthed. Doug dropped his hands. 'Only kids with something really *wrong* with them stayed inside all the time. Like Michael Feathers, who lived down the road, who'd had some disease and was always really sickly.'

Bonnie watched Edie and Louie, their fascinated faces. 'Well,' she said, and she couldn't help her voice sounding prim. *Fuck it*, she thought, *this is important*. 'These kids do play outside. We just — we're teaching them to take care in the sun, because now we know how much damage it can cause. We never used sunscreen either when I was a kid. I know what you mean, Doug.' She made an effort to look at him. 'It's hard to change habits like that, and ... perceptions too.' The children were staring at the bottle in Doug's hands. He was putting the lid back on it. *Nobody's listening. Why bother?* But still she went on, lamely, painfully aware of how formal she sounded. 'It's not about staying inside and never going out in the sun. It's about, well, you know, like with anything, it's about being aware, and, well, moderate in your approach ...'

'But, Douggie, how did you get the skin off your brother's back?' said Louie. 'Didn't it hurt?'

But Doug was busy. He tightened the lid back on the bottle of juice and made a great show of shaking it sideways. Then he opened it, took the two mugs Louie had brought and filled each to the brim with the frothy thick red stuff.

'Maybe not so —' Bonnie started to say, but bit her lip. *Bugger it. Let him learn.*

Louie and Edie lifted the mugs, both slopping juice over the table and down the front of their pyjamas. She felt a spark of bleak satisfaction as she watched the two faces, the two grimaces of disgust, the setting back down of the two mugs.

'I don't like it,' said Edie in astonishment.

'Me either,' said Louie, licking his lips as if to make sure.

'What do you mean? It's delicious!' Doug seized one of the mugs and gulped at it. 'Ahh,' he said, wiping his mouth with the back of his hand. 'Delicious! Although' — and he aimed that wink at Bonnie again — 'it's just not the same without the vodka and tabasco.'

She grabbed a tea towel from the oven door. 'Okay, guys,' she said, scrubbing at the front of first Louie's and then Edie's pyjamas. 'Let's get ready for kinder.' She hustled them out of the room.

'Have a nice day,' called Doug.

She glanced back and saw him reach over to Pete's plate, grab a crust of toast, tip back his head like a pelican and toss it in.

She dropped the twins at kinder and went to the supermarket with Jess. She got every single item on the list, wheeling up and down the aisles, forgetting things and going back for them, revisiting the same section two or three or even four times. The list somehow actually became worn and thin between her fingers. She imagined a map, an aerial view of her bumbling progress, a haphazard web of inefficiency.

In the car park she strapped Jess back into her capsule and piled the bags into the boot. Half trotted with the trolley to the bay, throwing anxious glances over her shoulder at the car with the unattended baby in it. Half ran back. Got in behind the steering wheel. Heaved a sigh of relief.

At the house she staggered in with Jess on one hip and three bags in the other hand to find Doug sitting at the kitchen table. She pulled up short, heard her own embarrassing startled gasp.

'Hullo, Missus Bonnie.' He lifted a thick and asymmetrical sandwich to his mouth, bit, chewed, then stopped. Spoke through the mouthful. 'Did I give you a fright?'

She bent her knees and lowered the shopping bags to the floor. She let go of their handles and worked her fingers open and closed a few times. Her heart was pounding. 'Oh, no,' she heard herself say in a breathy voice. 'Just — wasn't expecting anyone to be in here, that's all.'

'The boss's gone for a meeting with Grant,' said Doug, tearing off another hunk and chewing. 'Cold out there.'

'Haven't you got the heater on?'

'Yeah. It's not all that good though. And there's nowhere nice to sit. Not like in here.' He smiled, stretched his back and rolled his shoulders. 'It's nice to get away from all the sawdust. You know, have a bit of home comfort.'

Bonnie looked down at his plate, the sandwich. Then over at the bench, the cutting board, the knife, the butterdish and unwrapped block of cheese. She noticed he'd used the actual crust, all that was left of the loaf in the breadbin, and at the same moment realised she'd forgotten to buy more.

Jess blew a raspberry.

Doug wiggled his fingers at her. 'Hullo, princess. Been helping your mummy? Been a good girl, eh?'

Bonnie turned and went back out to the car. Without putting Jess down she brought in the rest of the groceries in three more one-handed trips, piling the bags on the kitchen floor. Doug sat stoically and ate, looking at the newspaper. When she'd finished Bonnie went and locked the car. She took her bag and keys, put Jess in the pram, shut the front door behind her and walked down the street.

She sat on a bench in the empty park and breastfed, shivering, staring in a cold, blank fury at the bare ground in front of her, the straddled legs of the picnic table, a broken beer bottle over near the barbeques. She tried to call Mel, who didn't answer. Then she tried her mother's number, but closed the phone before it connected. She put the phone away, settled Jess back in the pram with her blankets and beanie, and tucked her own clothes back in. Did up her jacket and rewrapped her scarf. Took her phone out again to check the time. Only one o'clock. The day yawned ahead. Her fingers on the pram handle were pale, bloodless with cold. She needed to go to the toilet. *Fuck this*, she thought. *This is just fucking ridiculous.*

The lights were on in the neighbourhood house. As she moved closer she could see crowds of people in the windows, hanging coloured lights, garlands of what looked like paper stars. A door opened, and a family came out. Indian — two women in saris bright like cut flowers in the grey afternoon; a gaggle of lithe dark children; four men wearing bulky parkas over white linen. Two of the men walked ahead with the women and children; behind came an older man and a younger one, a teenager. They passed her on the path. The older man was being helped by the boy. He was quite old, Bonnie saw as they came level with her, with white hair and a wizened face. But his posture was good, and he walked with confidence. It almost seemed a formality, the boy's arm linked through his. Bonnie heard his voice, sure, low, measured. She caught the listening face of the teenager, saw how he was shortening his stride to match the old man's. His parka rustled. There was a faint smell, although she couldn't tell if it came from the people or from the building they'd come out of. She breathed it again. Sweet. Some spice she knew but couldn't name.

The group went on through the park, and Bonnie kept going her own way, past the lit windows and the sounds of music and talking. She pushed the pram along the last stretch of path, through the thicket of banksia and out to the street.

She was nearly back at the house when, crossing a laneway, she glanced down it and saw the smashed pot. The broken pieces with their pinkish insides showing, clumps of dirt sticking to them, and the pale tendrils of roots. The exposed backbone of the main stem lying there with the curved ceramic in loose fragments around it like a ribcage busted open. Something dark was spread underneath it, a piece of fabric.

She froze, shock jolting through her. She took two steps back, swung the pram into the narrow mouth of the laneway and bumped closer. Went right up to the edge of the mess and stood there. The smell of the bruised leaves of the plant rose, sharp and strong. She bent and picked up a piece of the pot and turned it over. Angled it in the overcast light to see the depth of the glaze, the network of cracks, the colour that seemed to change, sometimes blue, sometimes green. One of the edges was pointy and she pressed the pad of her finger to it, watched the indent it made, felt its tip like a blunt needle. Then she dropped the piece again, and it landed on the cobblestones at her feet and broke into three.

'Shit,' she said. Then she saw what the dark thing was, lying underneath. A blue towel, dirt-covered and torn. The smudged white label stuck out at one end. *Sheridan*. One of the towels Pete's parents had sent as a housewarming gift. The only towels they owned that were soft and not frayed or threadbare.

She looked around. The laneway ended not too much further down, at a greying timber fence. It seemed darker in there, enclosed, trees crowding above the fence-lines. She could smell urine. Everything was very quiet. She turned the pram again and went back out, trying not to hurry, trying to contain the fright that was buzzing in her arms and legs and hammering in her chest.

She walked past the house, past Doug's van and the space where Pete's van still wasn't, and down to the main road. Spent the afternoon in a cafe, in shops. She even went to the library, feeling naked without the twins. Found herself standing aimlessly in the middle of the children's section, where a toddler kept throwing himself face down into the sagging vinyl beanbags and biting them. 'Come on, Charlie, shall we read a book?' the mother said, giving Bonnie a weak smile of embarrassment, but again and again the child launched himself, legs flailing, something too intimate in the way he pressed his face to the rubbery surface and then pulled back, teeth gripping. Bonnie moved away.

She sat and leafed through magazines. Jess slept. Twice she took out her phone and started to call Pete, but then she thought he might still be in the meeting and put it away again.

At three-thirty she walked back to the house. Pete's van was there, parked behind Doug's. She put Jess straight in the car, left the pram on the front porch and drove to the childcare centre.

She checked the sign-in book. Mel was due to pick up Freddie in fifteen minutes.

'Can we play for a bit longer?' said Louie.

'Yes. You can today.' Bonnie followed the twins out into the centre's yard and perched on the edge of the timber sandpit frame with Jess on her lap.

'Look at this, Mum!' Louie hung upside down from the monkey bars.

'Mum! Mum! Look at me!' called Edie from the mini-trampoline.

'Wow! Great!' The smile strained her face. Her skin felt numb, her whole body hollow and husk-like. She heard her voice go on responding to the twins with the kind of facile praise she'd always taken pains to avoid. It hardly felt like she was even opening her mouth, but there it went, echoing out of her, robotically insincere. She imagined a gust of wind or a blow from a passing child catching her, knocking her off her perch, breaking her apart, Jess tumbling back amongst the pieces into the sand.

'Hi.' Mel stood over her.

'Oh. Hi.'

'Everything all right?'

'Well, no, not really.'

'What's happened?' Mel sat down beside her and as she did Bonnie felt tears rising, the mask of her fake-smiling face cracking, the terrible, unstoppable crumbling of her composure. 'Bon?' Mel's arm drew around her shoulders.

'Oh, sorry, sorry — have you got a tissue?' She snuck a glance at the children, who were taking oblivious turns in some game on the climbing frame.

Mel handed her one, and Bonnie wiped her nose and eyes. 'Sorry, Mel,' she said.

'What's happened? Do you want me to hold Jess?'

'No. It's okay.' She held on to the baby, put her nose into the top of her little knitted beanie. 'Oh god, sorry about this. Hang on, I'll just pull myself together and then I can tell you.'

'It's all right. Take as long as you want.' Mel rubbed her back.

Out of the corner of her eye Bonnie saw one of the childcare workers approach, hesitate, move away again. She threw another glance at the children. Any moment one of them would come over, call out, want something. She needed to stop crying, to regain control. She closed her eyes and breathed slowly, in through her nose and out through her mouth, like she'd learned at birth preparation classes. Jess's beanie smelled of wool wash. *Calm down, calm down.*

All around the sounds of children went on, a busy tangle of noise.

'Okay,' she said after a while. 'Did I tell you about the pot plant?'

'No.'

'Okay. Well, I've got this pot plant. A geranium — in a beautiful old glazed ceramic pot that my great-aunt gave me years ago. It was on the back porch.'

'Yeah?'

'Well. Yesterday I noticed it was missing.' She took a deep, wavering breath. Another surge of crying threatened, but she pushed it down. 'It just vanished. Off the back porch. And then today I was out walking just down the street and I saw it in a laneway. All smashed up.' She turned to Mel. 'Someone came into our backyard and took it — I don't know when, in the middle of the night maybe — and carried it down the street, took it into that laneway and just' — she heard her voice wobble again — 'smashed it all up.'

'Mu-um!' called Freddie from the climbing frame.

'In a minute, Fred.' Mel kept her eyes on Bonnie's face. 'How awful,' she said. 'And it seems so much worse that it was out the back. I mean, even if it'd been out the front it would still be bad, but ...'

'I know,' said Bonnie. 'The thought of someone sneaking around the back of our house. I mean, we forget sometimes even to lock the —'

'Mummy.' Freddie ran to Mel, leaned into her knees. 'Mummy, I want to go home now.'

'Okay, Freddie. One minute.' Mel turned back to her. 'That's so creepy. I wonder who it was?'

'Come on, Mummy,' said Freddie, pushing at Mel's legs.

'Actually, we do have to get going.' Mel stood up. 'Sorry, Bonnie. Will you be okay? It's just that we've got my parents coming for dinner and I have to pick up some groceries on the way home and —'

'Yeah, of course.' She wiped her nose again and stood up too. 'I'll be fine. Sorry I had such a meltdown.'

'No, of course. I understand.'

'But the thing is ...' Bonnie put her hand on Mel's arm. 'Can I just tell you quickly?'

Mel nodded.

'It's not just the idea of some random creepy, I don't know, drunk kids or whatever, sneaking in and taking a pot and smashing it up for kicks or something. Even though that's not a great thought. And I can't really imagine why anyone would do that. But the thing is —'

'Mum!' Louie ran up. 'Edie says I can't be in her game.'

'Hang on, Lou.' She lowered her voice. 'The thing is, Mel, I think' — she dropped it to a whisper — 'I think it was Doug.'

'What?'

Bonnie kept whispering. 'I think it was Doug. He's been

acting weird. Apparently he was upset we didn't invite him to the kids' birthday party, which he found out about because he just happened to drive past our house on the day, which is weird and creepy in itself, because he'd have no reason to drive past on the weekend —'

'Mu-um!'

Bonnie edged away from Louie, closer to Mel. She had an image of herself, her bloodshot eyes staring wildly, her urgent whisper, her hand on Mel's arm, holding her there. *I must look crazy*, she thought. *She probably thinks I've gone mad, that it's all in my head.* But still she kept going, the tense words rapping out. 'And then he didn't turn up for work for a while, well, pretty much all of last week, since the party, and he didn't go to this reunion thing last night with Pete and his old mates from uni. And then yesterday I noticed the pot was gone, and then this morning he just turned up as if nothing had happened. Except ...' She wiped her nose. Wound her whisper even smaller, tighter. 'I don't know — I mean, I've always thought he had it in for me, that all his jokes were really just a way to get at me. But now I'm wondering. I mean, I could be imagining this whole thing, but I really feel like he's giving me these knowing looks, and —'

'Mu-UM!' Louie tugged at her hand. 'Edie says —'

'Let's GO, Mum!' said Freddie at the same time.

'I really have to go,' said Mel. She leaned over and hugged Bonnie, squeezed her arm. 'Sorry, Bon. I'll call you, okay? Later tonight.'

'Okay. Thanks, Mel. Sorry for ...'

'No, no. It's fine.' Mel waved as she followed Freddie back into the building.

Louie yanked her arm. 'Mum! Edie says she's the princess and I can't go in her castle unless I be a guard and I don't want to be a guard, I want ...' His voice twined on.

She stood in the middle of the tanbark, her arm limp as he pulled at it. She put her nose to Jess's hat again, but the smell of the wool brought the crying feeling back so she lifted her head instead, shook her hair out of her eyes, stared up into the leaves of the small gum tree that shaded the sandpit. The way they raked and shook, their neat, clean spear-like shapes.

In the car she called Pete. 'Hi,' she said, hearing her words come out weak and teary.

'What's wrong?' The concern in his voice almost made her cry again. She was overwhelmed by a desire to be lying in bed with him, between warm, clean sheets, everything else, all concerns and responsibilities, simply removed, eliminated, dissolved. She could feel the tension between her shoulder blades, and her throat hurt.

'Nothing,' she said, forcing her voice to sound stronger. 'I'm, ah, I'm in the car with the kids, so ...'

'Oh.'

'I just wanted to ask you: is Doug still there?'

She wasn't sure if she imagined it but she thought she heard a sigh.

'No,' he said. 'He actually left a bit early today. Think he had something on with his racing buddies.' There was a moment's pause, and then he added, 'Why do you ask?'

She slumped in shaky relief. 'I'll explain later.' She turned the key in the ignition. 'Okay, thanks. I'll see you soon.'

'Don't you dare say we can't prove it was him.' Bonnie put her palms flat on the surface of the kitchen bench.

Pete set a load of dirty plates beside the sink. She saw him pull back his shoulders before he spoke. 'But why would he do that, Bon?'

'Because he hates me?'

133

'Shh — you'll wake the kids.'

She lowered her voice. 'Well, I think he does. Sometimes I think he does. The things he says ...'

Pete came up beside her, put his arms around her. 'Come on. I really don't think he hates you. I mean, forget about the pot-plant thing for a moment. We really don't know anything about that. But the things he says, he's just — he needs to get a reaction out of people. That's just what he's like, you know. You shouldn't even listen to him.'

She leaned into him, breathed his smells of sweat and wood. 'But I can't help it.' She pulled back and looked up at his face. 'And it's not just what he says, it's what he does. Like today. When I got back from the supermarket, while you were at the meeting with Grant, I came in and he was sitting at the table here eating a sandwich he'd made with the last of our bread, and he didn't even say anything. He just sat there eating our food and reading the paper while I brought all the shopping in. It's like he — I don't know — he can tell I feel uncomfortable when he's around and he's rubbing my nose in it, in the fact that he's here, you know, invading my territory, and I can't do anything about it.'

Pete touched her hair. 'I don't know about that. He was probably just embarrassed that you caught him eating our food. He was probably hoping he'd get away with it. I mean, it's pretty sad — a grown man who can't even afford to buy his own lunch. That's the only reason he'd be doing it. I'm sure he hates eating our food. But he's — well, he's got a lot of pride, Doug. I've never heard him apologise for anything. Like when he fucked up with that quote that time. He'd lie rather than own up to something.' He frowned. 'Hang on a sec.' He turned, took the torch from the top of the fridge and went out the back door.

Bonnie followed. She watched as Pete went down the steps, out of reach of the light that spilled from the house, and switched on the torch. He moved it back and forth across the paving, slowly, then stopped and went forward. 'Here,' he said. 'Come and look.'

She went down and stood beside him.

Pete squatted. 'See?' He brushed his fingers over the ground and rubbed them together. 'Someone's swept up here. Looks like a while ago though, I'd say.'

She bent closer and saw the faint broom-marks on the paving stones, the fine dark earth in thread-like lines, scuffed and messed slightly in parts.

Pete cast around with the torch. 'And here you go.' He reached down and picked something up, held out his hand. A sliver of ceramic, pinky-pale on its inner curve, glossy green-blue on the outer.

She took it and held it, closed her fingers over it.

'You know what I reckon?' Pete sat down on the steps. The torch played over his feet, his Explorer socks, old and pilled.

Bonnie stayed standing. 'What?'

'I reckon it was him.'

'Who?' Bonnie found herself whispering. 'Doug?'

'Yeah. I reckon he broke it by accident, and took it and dumped it to cover up.'

She glanced behind her at the clothesline. 'Took the towel off the line, you think?'

'Yep. Swept it all up, used the towel to carry it, stuck it in the back of his van and chucked it in the laneway.' He switched off the torch, and his feet disappeared. 'You know why I think that?'

'Why?'

'Because he sits up here to smoke. What he does — well, what he used to do — is kind of lie back, leaning on the railing, and rest his foot on the edge of the pot plant. And he'd kind of rock it, tip it up.'

She looked up at the back porch, the faint glow of the

concrete in the light from the half-open door. In her head she saw Doug, his scrawny body reclined, one leg bent, decrepit boot on the rim of the pot. The scrape of ceramic on concrete. Cigarette smoke in the cold air.

'I guess he was doing that, one time — I must've been inside the workshop with the door shut, or maybe out somewhere. And he must've tipped it too far and it fell down the stairs.'

Bonnie saw the cigarette between Doug's battered fingers, him leaning back on his elbow, head sunk between his shoulders. She saw the boot tipping the pot and then easing off, letting it fall back. Tipping it again but further this time. The cigarette lifting to his thin lips. One last tip, the pot teetering, swinging for a moment, balanced, poised, ready to fall.

'But …' She was still whispering. 'But why wouldn't he say something? I mean, if it was an accident?'

Pete's face was in darkness, but she saw his shoulders rise and fall in a shrug. 'Like I said. He's proud. Won't admit to a mistake.'

'But, Pete, why would you put up with someone like that?' She sank down beside him, put her elbows on her knees and her head in her hands. 'Why do you? I just don't get it.'

There was a pause, and then he said in a tired voice. 'I don't know. I guess I just want to give him a chance. He's a smart bloke — he's really smart, you know, and …' She could hear him rubbing his eyes. 'Shit, he drives me crazy too. Every time I spend any amount of time with him I find myself thinking, God, Pete, what have you done? But, I don't know … And then there was that whole thing at the party that time, when we were young.' He sighed. 'I guess I feel like I owe him.'

'But,' she said, and put her hand on his arm. 'Even if that hadn't happened that night, all that time ago — I mean, if you hadn't given him the beer, if he hadn't got beaten up — do you think it would've really made a difference? To his life, the way it's turned out?'

He put his hand over hers. 'Of course not. No. But look at me. Look how things turned out for me. I got lucky.' He rubbed Bonnie's hand. 'I guess I just feel like it would be, well, bad karma or something, to shut him out of my … good fortune.'

All the love she'd ever felt came swooping down on her. She lifted his hand and kissed it, the backs of his rough fingers.

For a moment there was quiet.

'Okay. So.' She let go of his hand, stood, and started up the steps. 'We'll just stick with our original plan?'

'What plan?'

She turned. 'You know. Wait until the Grant job's done and then just not offer Doug any more work.'

Pete glanced up at her. In the light from the kitchen the corners of his eyes were soft with relief. He smiled. 'Sounds good.'

Mel sent a text message at ten o'clock. *U still awake? Shld I call?*

Bonnie, in her pyjamas, stood at the kitchen bench with the phone in her hand. *Thanks anyway but just going to bed*, she keyed in. *Sorry again about today.* She clicked *Send*. Put the phone down.

Outside the back door something stirred, a shiver of wind through the dark yard, or a possum or a cat. Bonnie pulled her robe tighter. She felt exposed with the light on, the impenetrable black of the back-door glass showing only her stricken reflection. She had a vision of herself from the outside, standing in the middle of the lit room, eyes halted at the pane, seeing no further, like a creature in one of those zoo enclosures with the one-way glass walls. She went over and turned off the light. Now the sky appeared outside, high and cold, with weak stars and a sickle moon. Over on the bench the phone buzzed. She picked it up. Mel again. *Ok but call if u want tmrw. Can make time 2 talk. Quite serious if u do think was D.*

She closed the phone. Stood for a moment looking down

at it. Opened it again and deleted Mel's message.

As she left the room she couldn't help rushing the last few steps in a tiptoed half-run, the way she did as a very small child when going back to bed after using the toilet in the night, when the hallway with the light left on had always seemed so still and empty in the strange quiet of the house. The somehow frightening idea of her parents asleep in their room, off-guard, inactive, having laid themselves down, she always imagined, the way oversized animals did — with a slow, effortful lowering of bodies, a final folding and settling of heavy limbs.

Pete was at the computer desk in the living room.

She went over, bent to put her arms around his shoulders. 'How's it going?'

'Okay. Got orders for two new tables. And one sideboard.' He yawned. 'Don't know how I'm going to get all this done, plus the Grant job.'

'Pete?'

'Yeah?'

'Would you ever ask Doug? About the pot-plant thing?'

He didn't answer. Bonnie waited.

He closed the computer and rubbed his eyes. 'No,' he said at last, without turning around.

There was more silence. She was uncomfortable bending over but she didn't want to move, to take her arms away from him. She didn't want to break the mood, in case he was going to say more.

'Look, Bon,' he said after a while. 'I don't like the idea of him lying to us either. And sneaking around, you know, covering up like that. But ...'

Through her palms she could hear the vibration in his chest as he spoke.

He shook his head. When he spoke again his voice was different, louder. 'Look. Doug. He's just — he's so fragile. You

really have no idea how fragile he is, and it's just, it's not worth
— I know you think we need to do all this … boundary stuff,
and, you know, communicate clearly and all that. But, honestly,
I really think our best plan is to, like we said, just wait until this
work's over and, well, hope he moves on.' He put his hands over
hers.

Bonnie saw that foot again, the pot teetering. She bit her lip.
'Yeah.' She took Pete's hands. 'Okay.'

DOUG CAME AND WENT. SOME MORNINGS HE'D BE THERE, EDGING himself in through the back door, flapping and stamping, cursing the cold. Seating himself at the table, grinning round, drinking tea, eating porridge, talking relentlessly.

Bonnie couldn't ignore him. Everything he said she heard with excruciating clarity, and she was racked with the effort it took not to respond.

'Went to see me mate Vinnie yesterday,' Doug might say, tipping his chair onto its back legs. 'He's bought a new car. Had a big win. Splashed out.' Lowering the chair, placing his hands flat on the table, sticking his face forward and letting each word drop with theatrical importance. 'B ... M ... W ... nineteen ... eighty ... five ... Seven ... Series.' Leaning back again, eyes half closed, a wise nod. 'The classic — you know, the sports sedan — the cute one with the squared-off shape and the sunroof?' Forward again, hands on table, voice lowered. 'He wanted to get a Merc. Late seventies' — back again, flapping a hand — 'but I talked him round. If you're going to spend that sort of dosh you might as well put in ten grand extra and go for real quality, you know ...'

And Bonnie would get up and move around the kitchen because she couldn't stand to be that close to him, to be stuck there as he jabbered and gesticulated and the twins hung on every word and Pete ate his breakfast as if behind some invisible barrier, untouchable, removed. *Who the fuck are you to tell someone which expensive car to buy?* she might shout in

140

her head. Or just, *Shut up, shut up, shut up!*

And Pete would go out to the workshop, and Doug would hang around, performing for the twins who always provided such an infuriatingly willing audience, and she would peck around them like some sort of ineffectual chicken, trying to get the kids away, move them on to something else. Making comments such as, 'Come on, guys. Let's leave Doug alone now — he's got work to do with Dad.' And with what seemed at times to be simple blithe intractability, or at others a sort of indulgent tolerance — as if she really was a bird and if he wanted to he could just raise an arm and shoo her away — Doug would go on with his banter, his show.

Or he might not come, and they'd sit at breakfast with the spectre of his figure at the door. And at these times it was Bonnie who foisted on the others conversations they didn't appear to have much interest in. 'Looking forward to kinder today, Lou?' she might say, and receive absolute silence in response. Or, 'Be cold out there this morning' to Pete, who'd maybe offer a 'Hmm'. And she would feel her face get tense, hating the insistent blather of her own voice yet unable to stop it. In the pauses she'd sip her tea, and back her eyes would slide to the door, the waiting pane of glass.

A CD arrived in the mail, rough mixes of the Mickey recordings. Bonnie stood in the living room with an armload of folded towels. From the sagging old speakers the sounds opened themselves out, filling the room. She shut her eyes. The bass and drums and strum of acoustic guitar slid together and merged, a layered, solid slab, heaving and rolling. In dropped Mickey's voice, landing like a cat, soft-footed and sure, slipping from note to velvety note. And then, trembling in the distance, vast and silvery, a hovering mist of sound, Bonnie's guitar.

Shivers ran up her legs. She kept her eyes closed and

dropped her face into the pile of towels, mouth split in an unstoppable grin.

That night Doug stayed for dinner. Pete opened a bottle of red. Bonnie had a glass and felt her cheeks grow warm, her limbs relax.

'Remember at McKean Street?' said Doug. 'That backyard with the brick path and to get to the toilet you had to balance on the row of bricks and on one side was all the rotten plums that fell off that bloody tree — about a hundred of them every day — and on the other was all the dog shit?'

Pete smiled. 'Yeah. That was really disgusting.'

Bonnie smiled as well. Somehow, on this night, for what seemed like the first time in ages, possibly ever, she was able to block Doug, diminish his blaring presence. She focused on Pete, watched his face, felt the same old twist she always did when she thought about his past, or saw old photos — the person he was before she knew him. That sort of hungry wish to somehow get inside the history, share it, so she could have all of him, every corner of him and his life. And the other side of it — the sadness, the hollow pang of knowing that such access was impossible, that no matter how open he was, how much he told her, how many stories, there was a whole slab of his life, the things that made him who he was, that she had missed out on. That didn't belong to her and never would.

Doug tipped up the bottle, emptied the last few drops into Pete's glass. 'We had some parties there.'

Pete made a noncommittal sound. He drained his glass. 'There's more wine somewhere.' He stood up.

Bonnie lifted her own glass, but it was finished. She put it down and glanced at the clock. 'Come on, kids. Bath time.'

Pete put his hands on her shoulders. 'Do you want me to do it?'

142

'No, no — it's fine, really. You guys keep talking.' She got up. 'You sure?'

She looked at him. His skin under the kitchen light appeared smooth, cheeks flushed slightly from the wine. As if Doug wasn't even there the vision came easily to her: Pete, his younger, straighter self, balancing step after step along a line of bricks in a bare, untended share-house yard. She could see the back of his neck, his lean shoulders. His slim hips. She smiled, reached up and kissed him. 'Yeah,' she said. 'I'm sure.'

She ran the bath and got the twins in it. Left them to play while she took Jess to change her nappy and clothes. She switched on the oil heater and felt its waves of warmth at the backs of her legs. The room filled with its comfortable smell and quiet ticking sounds. Jess on the change table gripped a toy with fat fingers, passing it from hand to hand with open-mouthed concentration.

'Where's the mumma duck?' Louie was saying in the bathroom. 'Oh, here she is. "Hello, baby duck. Would you like to come to my house for a visit?"'

Bonnie paused at the doorway. 'You guys happy here while I just go and feed Jess?'

'"Hello, mumma duck. I'm your baby,"' said Edie, head bent over the floating toys.

'Okay then. I'll be back in ten minutes. Dad's in the kitchen if you need anything.' Carrying Jess she went down the hallway to the bedroom, put on the bedside lamp, bolstered up the pillows, settled herself and latched the baby on. She closed her eyes.

'Now it's your go with the baby duck,' came Edie's voice.

'... and they turned up with a slab of beer and two bottles of whiskey ...' came Doug's.

Bonnie hummed the opening of one of Mickey's new songs.

In her head she saw her fingers climb through her part, test out a variation, bend the strings on the last note.

She tucked the blankets firmly in around Jess, clicked up the side of the cot, checked the setting of the heater dial and went out. Pulled the door quietly shut.

'... and Deano said "Never heard of him" ...' said Doug in the kitchen.

Bonnie went into the bathroom. 'How's it going in here?'

'Go-ood,' came the chorus.

She stood watching the two heads, the two slender bodies, the incredible clarity of their skins. How could she regret it, any of it, no matter how ruined her own body, how fractured her life? She perched on the low stool at the end of the bath and leaned back against the cold tiles. The chatter of her children bounced around the small room. Across the darkened hallway a wedge of lit kitchen was visible. She could see Doug in profile, tipped back on his chair, one hand reaching to the glass on the table. His voice wound on, broken now and then with scrapes of laughter, or a palm-slap on one knee. Bonnie glanced back at the children. She should get them out and into bed. It was getting late. But she still felt loose and warm, and weary from feeding Jess. She sat a while longer and returned to the song in her head. Experimented with a picking pattern instead of strumming in the verse before the singing came in.

Something, some word in the endless drag of Doug's voice brought her back, tuned her in. She sat up and listened.

'... that girl,' he was saying. 'What was her name?'

A pause but no answer from Pete, invisible on the other side of the table.

'Remember?' Doug went on. 'She came with Sarah and Vicky, those girls. Oh, she was an absolute knockout. And you — you were like a little puppy dog following her around.'

144

That titter, an undulation on the chair. 'She had a tab of acid and a bottle of wine and there you were just following her around with your tongue hanging out. Oh god' — he hooted — 'I can see it like it was yesterday.' Under the light he shifted, brought the front legs of the chair back down to the ground, raised the glass to his lips. 'Little lovestruck Peter Holmes.' That hoot again, and then he swivelled his head, turned it to the hallway, towards her sitting there in her own pool of light. Across the darkness his eyes met hers, held them. 'Ooh, yeah.' His lips split to show the broken teeth dark with wine. 'You lost your cool over that one, Pete.'

No sound from Pete. Doug kept looking at her, the stained grin lingering. She stared back. Cold stirred in her stomach. Doug moved his head, dipped it in a slight nod like a formal acknowledgement. Bonnie got to her feet, lunged at the door. It swung almost shut, sticking soundlessly at the towel hung over the top. There was a moment's more silence, and then she heard Doug's voice start up again, resume its drone.

'Okay, guys.' Bonnie reached for the plug. 'Time to get out.'

'Bon?' Pete was sitting on the edge of the bed.

'What?' She rolled over, squinted in the dazzle of his bedside lamp. 'I was asleep.'

'Sorry.'

She pulled the covers up over her eyes. 'What is it?'

'It's all right,' he whispered. 'I was just seeing if you were awake.'

'Well, I wasn't.' She lay for a moment and then pushed back the cover and sat up. 'But I am now so you might as well tell me.'

'No, it's all right. It's … nothing.' Pete got in beside her. He lifted the full glass of water from the bedside table and slowly drank the whole thing, his swallows loud and regular. He smelled of pot.

'Did you smoke a joint?'

'Yeah. Just a bit. Douggie had some.' He slid down under the covers. 'You don't mind, do you?'

'Course not.' She stayed sitting up. Underneath the cold, awful feeling that had been there since that moment in the bathroom — all through drying the kids and getting them in their pyjamas, reading to them, taking them out to the kitchen to say goodnight, enduring the sight of them flinging their arms around Doug to receive his kisses — there was still the vision of the young Pete balancing on those bricks, the soft, sad love that came with it, that remained somehow untainted by Doug and his words, his look. She met Pete's reddened eyes. *Don't be a bitch*, she thought. *It's not his fault.* But still, as if it was beyond her control, she couldn't help saying something, one small barb. 'Must be nice though, not to have to worry about waking up if one of the kids cries in the night. Or staying sober to feed the baby.'

Pete closed his eyes, drew in a breath and let it out slowly.

'So.' She tried to lighten her voice. 'Did you have fun? With Doug?'

'Oh god, I can't win, can I?' He lay right down and turned away from her.

'What do you mean?'

'Well, you're always saying I should be his friend, you know — offer support by being his friend, rather than giving him work, treating him like a charity case, and then when I do the right thing you —'

'Oh, sorry, Pete.' She put her hand on his shoulder. 'I didn't mean to hassle you. You're right. It was the right thing to do — I really think it was. It's the way it should be — you should invite him for dinner, have a few drinks, have a chat, all that stuff. It's just ...' His shoulder under her touch was unresponsive. She sighed. She felt too tired to go into it now, to try to explain.

And it would feel silly, embarrassing, to say it aloud, to admit to feeling jealous of some girl at a party so many years ago. And how to tell him about Doug's look without seeming paranoid? She stared at the back of Pete's head, the curve of his ear. She couldn't see if his eyes were open or closed. And anyway, he was stoned. She lifted her hand away.

She fed Jess at six and came back to bed. Curled into Pete's warm body. Shut her eyes and slipped down under the covers, pulled up his t-shirt, kissed his chest, tasted his skin. Drew close, pressed into him, her head under his chin, her tongue against the few coarse hairs that grew in the hollow at the base of his throat. He lifted himself on one elbow, dragged off his t-shirt without opening his eyes. Sank back down and turned onto his back. The air was cold on Bonnie's shoulders as she took off her own clothes and got on top of him. She pulled the covers up around herself, but he loosened them, reached up and ran his hands over her. Her nipples stood out, her breasts hanging full and heavy. For a moment she crossed her arms shyly, but gently he pulled them away.

'I love them,' he whispered. She looked down, and his eyes were open. 'You're so beautiful.'

She bent to kiss him. 'You are.' He was beautiful. In the early light his face was calm, full of peace. She put her hand on his chest over his heart and kept looking into his eyes.

Later she was almost asleep again when Pete whispered, 'Bon?'

'Mm?'

'I just want to ask you something, before the kids get up, while I've got a chance.'

'What is it?'

'You know that money.'

'What money?'

'That we've got put away. The four grand. You know, for the holiday.'

She opened her eyes. 'Yeah?'

'Okay.' He moved a bit away from her, pulled himself up to sitting. 'I want you to think about this. Don't just get mad straight away, all right? Just hear me out and think about it.'

She turned to him. 'What is it?'

He looked away from her, towards the window. 'Douggie's given me this tip.'

'What?'

Pete lifted his hand. 'Wait — please just listen.'

She waited.

'Okay.' He took a breath. 'I've got this tip. It's from Douggie, but really he's just passed it on from this friend of his, who works for the trainer, you know?' He glanced at her, then back to the window. 'Anyway, it's — look, he says it's a sure thing, and apparently this guy's ... well, he knows his stuff. And say what you like about Douggie, but I reckon he's onto something here.'

She stared at him.

'So ...' Pete made a grimace. 'What do you reckon?'

'About what?'

'Come on, Bon.'

She shook her head. 'I don't get it. I don't understand what you're asking me.'

He rubbed his hand over his face. 'The money. It's a risk, but we could turn it into ten times as much. Even more. I was thinking we could maybe keep some of it — maybe keep half. So if we put on, say, two, and the odds stay at ten-to-one —'

'What?' She gave a dull bark of a laugh. 'You're not serious.'

'Please, Bonnie. I asked you to keep an open mind on this.'

She let her jaw hang slack.

'I mean ... Think about it. We've put that money aside

148

anyway. It's not — we haven't counted on having it for the mortgage or anything.'

'I can't believe you're suggesting this. I —'

'Will you just think about it? Please?'

She rolled her eyes, blew out her lips with a derisive puff of air.

'Bon? Please? The race is tomorrow night. Just — you can tell me tomorrow. Okay? Just think about it, okay?'

She closed her eyes. He got up. Bonnie could hear him pulling on some clothes. Then there was quiet. She opened her eyes again.

He was standing there by the bed watching her. In his striped pyjama pants he looked like a little boy. 'Think about it?'

She pulled the covers over her head. 'Okay. But I doubt I'll change my mind.'

Pete came in for lunch. Doug as well. She heard them in the kitchen, heard Pete call — 'Hey, Bon, you here? Had lunch?' — but she didn't go out. There was the sound of the fridge opening and closing, cutlery rattling. Doug's voice winding on, lifting and falling.

She passed through on her way to the clothesline. They looked up at her, Pete quickly, anxiously, Doug with that head-back grin, still talking.

'... and they put him up for a fifteen-hundred after a spell, blinkers on, and he just ab-so-fucken-lute-ly *caned* 'em ...'

Bonnie went out into the cold. She felt watched, clumsy at the line, her movements strained as she reached and stepped. When she came through again with the empty basket in her arms Pete kept his eyes on the paper and Doug paused in his monologue. As if allowing for a minor interruption he reclined in his chair, arms folded, thin lips open, teeth and tongue on display. She felt the heat rise to her face, her steps get awkward, his eyes at her back. As she started down the hallway she heard him take it up again, the tireless thread of talk.

In the bedroom, with the door shut, she sat with her acoustic, picking quietly, marooned in the weird stillness of a kindergarten day — no sounds from Jess asleep in her room. Only the enduring drone from the kitchen.

Around the room she wandered, picking things up and putting them down again. The ornamental perfume bottles that had been her grandmother's. The photo of her and Pete holding the twins, one each, in the hospital. Edie's drawing of a tree, coloured with scented textas that still smelled, faintly, like lollies. She ran her fingers over the cluster of laminated music-festival passes that hung from their lanyards, looped on the door handle. Long-ago logos and coded text: *Access all areas*; *Performer main stage*; *Artist day 2*.

She lay on the bed. After a while she heard the back door open and close, the faint bells, and then there was silence, Doug's voice gone. She pulled the blanket over herself and closed her eyes. In the warm lapping place between resting and sleeping her mind softened, draped itself over the idea of being generous, understanding, of saying yes to Pete. Giving it to him as a gift — that thing he needed, whatever it was. A last hoorah, a flight of nostalgia. Of them listening to the race together, jumping up with open smiles of triumph when the horse won, arms around each other, heads flung back. Even more: of Doug there too, the three of them shouting and jumping together at their collective good fortune. Pete in the middle, arms around the two of them: Doug the old friend, and Bonnie the warm, kind partner. The woman you'd want to be with, who you'd love forever.

She fell asleep for maybe a minute. Dreamed of being backstage trying to tune her guitar and the tuning pegs coming off in her hand, one after the other. Then the whole guitar falling apart. The house music going down and the lights up. The crowd falling quiet. Stepping out onto the worn gaffer-scarred carpet completely empty-handed, the last fragments of varnished wood and metal dropping away from her, the strap over her shoulder slipping to the ground. Going out there into the hot lights and the terrible hush holding nothing.

The baby's crying jarred her awake. She'd dribbled on the pillow. Her head felt thick — it was worse than if she hadn't gone to sleep at all. She lay for a moment and stretched out her legs until they trembled. Wiped her cheek with the back of her hand. Then eased herself up and swung out of the bed.

When she got back from collecting the twins Doug's van was gone.

Her phone rang as she was walking up the path. She reached for it, dropping the kids' backpacks and the nappy bag in a pile on the porch and shifting Jess to the other arm.

It was Mickey.

'Hey, Bon?'

'Yeah?'

'Have you thought about the shows?'

Bonnie resettled Jess on her hip. 'Yeah. I mean no — not really.'

Mickey said something, but it was lost under an outburst of bickering between the twins, who were trying to climb the squat front-yard lemon tree.

'Hang on, sorry, Mickey.' She moved further away, down the other end of the porch. 'Sorry,' she said again, 'what was that?'

'Sounds like I've caught you at a bad time,' said Mickey. 'But quickly ...'

'Get OFF!' yelled Louie.

'Mu-UM!' yelled Edie.

'... getting a bit late,' said Mickey. 'So I kind of need to know.'

'Oh,' said Bonnie, jiggling Jess, who was starting to whinge.

'... but I do have this other show, in Sydney, this kind of arts festival thing ...'

'Na-na-na-na-na!' went Louie.

'That's my branch!' went Edie.

'... be a weird one — they're calling it a showcase — but lots of money,' came Mickey's voice, tiny and fractured.

'Shh, shh,' she said to Jess, tucking the phone in against her shoulder and trying to bend her head away from the noise.

'Na-na-na-na-na!'

'Get off, get off, get OFF!'

'... crazy money, if that makes any difference ...'

Jess's whingeing was getting louder.

'Sorry,' said Bonnie. 'Sorry, Mickey, I think I'm going to have to ...' Real crying now from Jess. She pressed the phone closer to her ear. 'Sorry, can I call you back?'

'Sure.' Mickey laughed. 'Talk soon.'

Bonnie shoved the phone in her pocket and swapped arms again with Jess. 'Come on, you two,' she called to the twins.

'But I want to climb this tree, and Louie won't —'

'Na-na-na-na —'

'That tree's got thorns.' Bonnie bent and with one hand gathered all the bags up. She turned to the door, tried to reach the keys in her pocket, sighed and dropped all the bags again. 'Bloody hell,' she muttered.

'Oww!' came Edie's cry.

She slid the key in the lock. 'Well, I told you that tree's got thorns.'

'Ow-ow-ow-ah!'

Bonnie opened the door and slung the bags in one at a time. Marched quickly to the living room with Jess and plonked her on her play mat. Marched back out to the porch and knelt with her arms open ready for Edie who came, red-faced, tears spurting.

'Come here,' she said, folding the girl into her arms, taking the scratched finger and kissing it. 'Poor possum.' She put her lips to Edie's forehead, felt the hot fury of her tears.

Pete came in at five. 'What should we do for dinner?' he called from the bathroom over the water running in the basin.

'Oh god, I don't know.' She looked in the fridge. 'I haven't thought about it, sorry. There's some chops here.'

'Want me to do it?'

'Sure. That'd be great.'

Bonnie watched him pass, the glance he threw her. Under his tired face, the sag of his shoulders as he bent to the vegetable crisper, she saw again the shadow of that younger self, walking along the bricks. Or running back from the TAB with the phone-bill money multiplied by ten stuffed into his pockets. The crack of the champagne cork in the dingy kitchen of some share house. Pete and Doug and all those other long-ago friends, young and full of easy pleasure, raising their glasses, yelping and smacking palms on the table. *Just let him do it*, she thought. *Give it to him. Why can't you just be kind?*

She went out into the dimming yard to get the clothes in off the line. She couldn't tell if they were still damp or just cold. She kept testing each thing with her fingers as she took it down, gripping the fabrics at different points — the pockets of Pete's jeans, the toes of Edie's tights. She piled them loosely in the basket, carried it back inside and dumped it down in front of the heater. Then she started pulling things off the clotheshorse and sorting them hurriedly, tossing them into piles on the couch.

Louie ran in and almost knocked over the framed print that had been leaning against the wall since the wire broke. He clambered up the back of the couch and somersaulted into one of the piles of washing.

'Louie! Get off!' Bonnie flapped one of Jess's romper suits at him. 'I'm trying to sort clothes here.'

'But I need to hide,' said Louie, trying to burrow between the couch cushions. 'I need to hide from Edie.' Clothes slid to the floor.

'Well, hide somewhere else.' She picked the clothes back up.

'But I need to hide here.' Louie wedged himself behind a cushion. 'Please, Mum, can you put more cushions on me?'

She sighed. 'Okay. But you have to keep really still, all right? Until I've finished sorting this stuff.'

'Okay,' came the muffled reply.

Bonnie stacked up the threadbare op-shop cushions and stood back looking at the couch, the heaps of clothes, the room crowded with old, cheap furniture — the computer desk, the mismatched bookshelves crammed full. The cracks in the walls, the spotted mirror over the mantel, the wobbly coffee table Pete always said he was going to build a replacement for, when he got a chance.

'Is she coming, Mum?' said Louie's squashed voice.

'Not yet.' She stood with one of Jess's tiny singlets in one hand. It had once been white, but she'd washed it with something red and now it was a blotchy brownish pink.

A memory came, from her own early share-house days, when she'd missed most of her lectures to sit in her room with her shitty first guitar and tinny little amp, playing along to Sonic Youth albums. Further west, and about eight years later than Pete and Doug and their trifecta and champagne. There had been a house on the same street as hers, red brick, with roses in the front garden. The black-painted front door sometimes stood open, and Bonnie would sneak glances in at the quiet gleam of floorboards, the little hall table always with a vase of flowers; further in a pale couch, a clear expansive living area, big paintings on the walls. There might be the sounds of classical music playing, or the smell of coffee. She never saw any actual people.

One day she was passing and out on the edge of the veranda pillows and a quilt had been hung to air in the sun. Something, some hunger had stirred in her at the sight of those plump white shapes, their dazzling cleanness, and the square of bedroom visible through the opened window behind — simple dark timber furniture, a picture in a frame. The loveliness of order, of cleanliness, the pride and industry of those invisible inhabitants — Bonnie tasted it as she walked by, this morsel so foreign and beautiful in her life of mess and dim pubs and beer and smoky band rooms, of a mattress on the floor, of clothes in a pile.

She always looked for it, that house, and even when she moved to a different suburb she thought about it sometimes. It wasn't that it was what she wanted then. She had smaller, more tangible aspirations — the skeletons of songs she laid down on her four-track recorder, hunched in her room with the door shut; the *guitarist wanted* ads she scanned in record shops, her face burning just at the thought of ringing the numbers; the sweet-faced boy with the Dinosaur Junior t-shirt in her twentieth-century literature tutorial — but that house, that beautiful house waited there somewhere in the back of her mind as something she might one day like to have. A tempered, peaceful, ordered life.

'Mum?' It was Edie. 'Where's —'

'Ta-da!' went Louie, bursting up and out from behind the cushion, and Bonnie only just managed to save the stack of Pete's clothes before it was scattered all over the floor.

'Oh god!' But the energy wasn't there to tell them off. 'Look. Just please don't mess up any more of these piles, okay, you two?'

They were gone anyway, chasing and shrieking. She held

the bundle of clothes to her chest and went with it to the bedroom. Dropped it onto the end of the bed on Pete's side. Glanced over at the table and saw the slip of paper alongside a handful of coins. Unfolded, curving up at the ends, showing crease marks in an elongated cross. She didn't have to go much closer to read it. Blockish writing, all in capitals. Doug's. Amazing how a person's handwriting could evoke them so completely. The familiar tingle of discomfort, of annoyance, set up in her fingers as she reached for the paper, turned it slightly on the table so it sat square. *FRI NITE TROTS. MOONEE VALLEY. RACE 4 HORSE 7 — BRAGGART.*

'God,' she said. 'It's not even the real races.' She gave the paper a flick with her finger, and it twirled on the spine of its crease. 'It's the bloody trots.' She flicked it again, and it skittered, hit the coins and stopped.

'So,' said Pete the next evening, once the kids were in bed. He stood behind her in the kitchen. 'Um.' As if they both didn't know what he was going to say, as if it hadn't been hanging over them for two whole days. 'That race is on soon.'

Bonnie stood at the bench, her hands on the folded newspaper. She dangled the pen over the crossword, over her single pathetic answer straggling down one side.

Pete stirred, cleared his throat. 'So ... have you thought about it?'

Leviathan, read her word, the letters floating in their little boxes.

'Bon.' She heard Pete pull out a chair and sit down. 'I had a good look at it. At the form. I reckon it's a good chance. I know' — he brought his voice up as if she had spoken, challenged him — 'I know there's no such thing as a dead cert. But sometimes, especially with the harness racing — well, I reckon these insiders sometimes know something we don't.

And I reckon — that money, we weren't counting on having it. Maybe it's worth, you know, having a bit of a gamble. We could put two grand on, and still have two left. If we lose, well ...' She could feel him watching her. 'We could still go to Queensland for a week. Something like that.'

She stared down at the newspaper.

'I don't know.' His voice was muffled — he was rubbing his eyes. 'I just — sometimes I feel like all I do is work, and help you with the kids and, you know, fall into bed exhausted and then get up and do it all over again. I feel like my life's ...'

Bonnie turned. *Look at him*, she told herself. *Go close. Look in his eyes. Touch him.* If she did, she thought she might catch it again, that ripple of the younger him. Whatever it was he wanted to go back to, to get near again, just for a little while. And that vision of the two of them together, his arms around her, him gazing into her face, her kind, generous face, and her sharing it with him, the victory, the thrill of the win. But she felt stiff and unwieldy, choked by it all — Doug's leer across the darkened hallway, the dip of his head, his clamouring presence in the house day after day. The way he sat at the table, the way he ate and drank, the way he slathered himself all over everything like he owned it. She closed her eyes and saw the smashed pot, the naked roots of the plant, the spray of dirt on the cobblestones, the ruined towel. Her fingers buzzed. She gripped one hand in the other. She opened her eyes again but she couldn't look at Pete.

'Bon?'

Doug's clunking handwriting on that slip of paper.

Pete sighed. 'Bon?'

She stared at the floor, at his boots, at a hardened bit of pasta missed by the broom. 'I'm sorry,' she said. 'I just don't think it's worth the risk.'

She knew he was listening to the race. She saw him fiddling with the stereo tuner in the living room, heard the bone-dry voices in their ceaseless tides listing names and weights, jockeys, trainers, odds. She went into the bathroom and shut the door. Flossed her teeth and brushed them, taking as long as she could. But when she'd finished she could still hear it, faintly, through the door, so she got in the shower. Washed her hair. Let the water and the foam fill her ears. Closed her eyes. Her heart was pounding, and she had the water too hot. When she got out she couldn't see for a moment, and had to hold on to the towel rail. By then the radio was off again.

She went straight to bed and turned off the lights.

She must have fallen asleep, but she woke up when Pete switched on his lamp. He sat facing away from her, feet on the floor, still dressed. She lay with her hands over her eyes.

'It won,' he said.

'I'm sorry,' she said, almost at the same time.

There was a silence. 'I'm sorry,' she said again, pulling herself up on one elbow, looking at his slumped back.

'Fuck it!' He straightened, picked up one of his boots and hurled it into the corner. It landed with a deadened sound on a pile of dirty clothes. 'Fuck it!' He whacked his fist into the mattress.

'Pete.' She reached out but didn't touch him. Her hand hovered. 'I'm really sorry. But — I mean, it might not've won. It's always easy with these things, you know, afterwards, to say —'

'Yeah, yeah, I know.' His back sagged again. He pulled off his jeans and lay down, facing the other direction. Bonnie's hand was bumped away.

'Pete.' This time she did touch him. She put her hand on his arm. 'I really am sorry. I feel like such a bitch.'

He was silent, lying still.

She felt his flesh under her fingers. She pressed harder.

'I'm sorry,' she whispered.

He didn't move. 'Yeah, okay,' he said.

After a few moments she took her hand away again, and Pete switched off the light and rolled onto his back.

They stayed like that, like corpses in a tomb, side by side, a decent space between them. The house settled into night. Bonnie thought she would never sleep. She lay rigid, listening to his wakeful breathing beside her in the darkness.

At six Jess cried, and Bonnie went and got her and fed her on the couch in front of the heater. The red glow burnished the glossy hip of her acoustic guitar resting on the armchair. She sat empty of thought, the warm weight of the baby against her. If she moved her head from side to side, just a tiny bit, hardly at all, the flaming stripe on the side of the guitar stretched and contracted like the neck of a wading bird. Jess reached up and pinched the skin of her throat, squeezed with strong fingers, and the nip of pain rang through Bonnie's unresisting body. She took the tiny hand, prised it open and kissed its padded palm. At the window the light was not yet even a gritty grey. She looked down at her daughter, her last baby, so surprising every day in her singularity.

After a while she leaned her head back and closed her eyes, but she was starting to wake up properly, and in it crept at last, turned a circle like a dog, tucked its tail around and settled itself — a miserable, flat helplessness that had been waiting, it felt now, for a long time. It was too late. It was done. She couldn't change anything, or make up for it.

A first bird made a cautious chitter outside. Bonnie kept her eyes closed. It would get light soon. She could almost feel them, the others, Pete and the twins in the bedrooms at either end of the hallway, the gradual ebbing of their sleep, the coming-to of their thoughts.

She tried again anyway, when he was in the shower. Went into the bathroom and shut the door behind her. Stood watching his shape, the waterlogged mass of his hair, the blurred brightness of his warmed-up skin through the shower curtain.

'Pete?' Her voice came out rusty, and she had to clear her throat and say it again. 'Pete?'

'Yeah?'

'I really am sorry.'

He didn't answer. The water beat down, sluiced against the curtain.

'Pete?'

'I heard you.' He cupped his hands and sloshed at his face, then did it again.

She waited.

'I just' — he kept his hands to his face so his words were muffled — 'need a bit of time to get over this, okay?'

Bonnie stood a while longer with her back to the door, breathing the close, steamy air, the smell of soap. The helplessness spread through her, thin like watered-down milk.

'Where's Douggie?' said Edie at dinner on Tuesday.

Bonnie glanced at Pete, who was standing at the bench cutting bread.

'Where's Douggie?' Louie joined in.

Bonnie put a forkful of pasta in her mouth, eyes on her bowl.

'Where's Douggie?' Edie said again.

'I don't know,' snapped Pete.

Bonnie chewed and swallowed and shovelled in more, the food sitting heavy in her stomach. The weight of the tension crowded the room, the bank of accumulated unease between the two adults pressing at them all. *How long can this go on for?* she thought, eyes on Pete's back.

Pete sighed, and there was the click of him laying the knife down carefully. 'I don't know where Douggie is,' he said in a gentle voice. 'He ... he won some money. Lots of money. I think he might've gone on a holiday.'

'Can we go on a holiday?' Edie bounced in her chair.

Silence. Pete stood without moving.

'Why can't we go on a holiday?'

Bonnie put down her fork, reached across and took Edie's hand. 'One day we will,' she said, feeling Pete listening, her voice taut with self-consciousness. 'Just not right now.'

Bonnie filled the kettle and switched it on. She went down the hall to the living room, automatically checking the children sleeping in their rooms. Pete was at the computer. He didn't turn around or say anything when she came in.

'Cup of tea?' Her voice grated out stiffly.

No reply.

'Pete?'

He didn't look around. 'No, thanks.' He moved the mouse, clicked it, muttered 'Shit' under his breath.

'Sure?'

'Yeah. I've got to get back out to the workshop.'

'What?' She went closer, stood behind him. 'Why? It's nearly ten o'clock.'

He turned in his chair. His eyes looked blurred, tired. 'I have to get this Grant job done. Doug's — well, I don't think he's coming back, and there's just so much work.'

Something spurted in Bonnie, a flood of guilt and love together in an awful gush. 'Oh, Pete, I'm so sorry,' she said quickly. 'I didn't think ...' She stepped towards him, but he put his head down, rested his elbows on his knees, and she halted at the last moment, stood over him uncertainly.

'Yeah, whatever,' he said, rubbing his eyes, his voice thick.

'It's done now, and everything's fucked.' He glanced up for a moment. 'I've got payments to make, Bon. Suppliers. I thought ...' He shook his head. 'That money, it was really going to make a difference.'

The feeling cooled in her. She frowned. 'But to rely on a bet for paying suppliers? I mean, how could you even ...'

He didn't answer.

'How much do you owe?' The words felt foreign in her mouth. It was as if she was speaking a part, as if she'd somehow dropped into some other, different life. 'Pete?'

What was going on? Who were they now — a couple with money troubles, real ones?

'Pete? Why didn't you tell me?'

He made a movement with one hand. 'It'll be all right.'

'Well, will it?'

He moved his hand again, palm down, an erasing gesture. 'Don't worry about it.'

She sat on the arm of the couch, fighting to keep her voice under control. 'But what about Doug?' She ground her fingers into the couch fabric. 'Don't you know where he is? Haven't you heard from him?'

'No. I haven't.'

'So he's just gone?' She felt the familiar irritated buzz start up. 'He didn't say anything?'

Pete shrugged.

'Does he know you didn't put the bet on?'

He shook his head.

'He didn't call to find out?'

'Nope.'

She leaned forward. 'But wouldn't he want to, you know, celebrate together or whatever? If you'd won too?'

Pete sighed and sat up straight. 'Guess not,' he said. 'Every man for himself.'

'But that's so unfair!' She stared at him. 'He doesn't know if you put the bet on or not — he doesn't know whether or not you still need him in the workshop. He knows you've got this big job, that he'd be leaving you in the lurch.' She shook her head. 'I can't believe someone would do that — to anyone, let alone a friend.'

Pete stood. 'Whatever. It's done now.'

'But don't you want to ... I don't know, chase him up?'

Pete shrugged again.

'I would. I'd be tracking him down and bloody well letting him know how much deep shit he's left me in. You can't just walk off a job like that. Fucking hell!'

Pete moved past her. 'I'd better get out there,' he said. 'Try to get some work done.'

They lay in bed, the yawning space unbreached between them. Bonnie looked at the clock. One a.m. She blinked and her eyes were scratchy with tiredness.

Pete spoke quietly, almost formally, out into the darkness. 'I've got to get going early in the morning.'

'Oh.' She heard the stiffness in her own voice, its matching stilted tone. 'Okay then.'

'Yeah. I've got to take a load of timber over to Glenn.'

There was a pause. Bonnie swallowed. She hated all this between them, the caution she had to apply to everything, every word, the landslide of guilt tilting in her chest. She gathered up her voice, forced it out. 'Glenn?'

'Yeah.' Pete shifted in the bed, further away from her. 'You remember him.' As if her not remembering would be another example of her hopelessness, another failing.

She struggled to think, to remember, but nothing came. 'Um, sorry ...'

Pete took an impatient breath. 'Glenn. He worked on the

Juno job — you know, he's got a workshop in Footscray. Tall. Long hair. Does a lot of furniture from reclaimed wood.'

'Oh right. Yeah. Okay.'

She felt the pulse and bristle of the gap between them. At last he went on, his voice flat now, contained. 'Anyway, I'm subcontracting him. For the Grant job.'

'Oh.' Bonnie felt paralysed, pinned under a suffocating slab of guilt and fatigue. She closed her eyes. All she wanted was to fall asleep. 'Okay.'

'Yeah, well, it's not really okay.' His words kept their even measure, but the flatness Bonnie now recognised as held-in anger. 'I have to pay him three times what I was paying Doug. And even then he's not sure how much he can fit in — he's doing it as a favour to me.' He got up on one elbow and turned the pillow, thumped it back down. 'I had to beg him.' He dropped back onto the pillow and rolled to face away from her.

She lay still. The effort of speaking felt enormous, even if she'd known what to say.

'There's your holiday money,' said Pete. 'Gone.'

'And how's Pete?' said Suzanne at the swimming pool the next day.

'Good.'

'That feller still around?'

Bonnie didn't answer. She dug through the swimming bag for her goggles.

'You should do something about that, darling.' Jess started to whinge, and Suzanne reached to the pram, gave it a tentative rock. She clicked her tongue. 'You can't just stand back and hope these things will sort themselves out, you know.'

Jess's whingeing broke into a cry.

Bonnie folded her towel and put it on top of the bag.

'Darling?' said Suzanne. 'Don't you think?'

Bonnie turned and grabbed the handle of the pram, her hand beside Suzanne's. She jerked it, sideways, gave three big shoves. 'Hard,' she said. 'Like that.' Then she let go and walked to the water without looking back.

'Mickey?'

'Bonnie?' There was background noise — drums, someone clattering from tom-tom to snare and back.

'Hi.'

'Hi.' The drumming got louder, then receded. There was the sound of a door closing and then quiet. 'That's better,' said Mickey. 'Just at rehearsal. How you going?'

'Oh, sorry. Is it a bad time?'

'No, it's fine.'

'You sure? I can call back.'

'No, really, it's fine — we were just about to have lunch.'

Bonnie looked at the clock. It was half-past two. She turned away from the dishes piled in the sink. 'Hey, I'm sorry about the other day,' she said. 'I meant to call you back, but then I just, everything got ...'

'That's all right.'

'... and I know I've missed out on the tour ...'

'Yeah. Sorry, Bon. I couldn't wait any longer.'

Bonnie swallowed. 'But I was just thinking — you said something about that other show?'

Mickey laughed. 'Oh yeah, the' — she put on a posh voice — '*showcase*. You want to do that one?'

'What is it?' Bonnie perched on the edge of a stool. Outside, through the glass in the back door, Pete came around the corner and went towards the workshop.

'Well, it's this weird arts festival thing — they're putting on a series of shows, called *Nights Underground* or something. As far as I can tell it's pretty much just a normal show.'

Bonnie watched Pete walk, head down, slow in his heavy work boots. The wind caught his hair and ruffled it forwards and the back of his neck showed, exposed. She had a sudden, awful vision of him having to answer to one of the unpaid suppliers — him making excuses, shuffling, cowed.

Mickey went on. 'But it's really close to the tour, so I was going to say no, but then my booker said let's just ask for a ridiculous amount of money, what the hell, so we did, and they said yes. So looks like I'm doing it.'

'Um,' said Bonnie, and she sounded strange in her own ears, shrunken and distant. 'So, how much … how much could you pay me?'

There was a rustle and the click of a cigarette lighter, Mickey's intake of breath, then the exhale. 'Not sure. Let me suss it out.'

Pete went into the workshop and closed the door. She kept her eyes on the greyish timber, the rusted hasp dangling.

'All right?' said Mickey. 'Bon?'

She imagined the door opening again, Pete and Doug emerging, coming up the steps to the kitchen. Doug talking, waving his arms, filling up the kitchen. Pete taking a seat at the table, glancing up at her, his face soft and open, his smile ready.

'Bonnie? Hello?'

The faint noise of Pete's electric sander started up. 'Sorry,' said Bonnie slowly. 'That sounds' — she brought her gaze back inside the room, blinked, pushed the hair back from her face — 'that sounds good.'

'No probs.' The drums started up again in the background, and the rolling of a bass guitar. 'I'll get back to you.'

Bonnie slipped off the stool and stood over the empty table. Pete's sander droned on like a faraway insect.

On Thursday night there was an email from Mickey. *Festival show*, said the subject line. Bonnie opened it, scanned down the lines for a number. *$3,800*. She blinked, checked again. *Flights, hotel and taxis covered*, read Mickey's message. *And I'll buy you dinner*. She looked away from the screen, up at the faded curtain. She'd never been offered so much for one show. She sat, breathing slowly, waiting, but nothing came, no thrill. She went back to the screen, searched for a date. Next Friday.

Bonnie shut down her mail and closed the computer. The house was silent. She ignored the heap of unsorted laundry on the couch, went to the door and switched off the light. Walked slowly past the children's darkened bedrooms to the kitchen. Through the back-door glass lines of brightness showed around the workshop doors. Bonnie filled a big saucepan with water and put it on the stovetop. She knelt, opened a cupboard and started searching for the breast pump.

When Pete came in she was just putting the sealed bag of milk in the freezer.

He stopped inside the doorway. There was a pause. She went on with her movements, her back to him, taking the pump apart, awkwardly, self-consciously.

'Thought you'd be asleep,' he said at last.

'No.' Bonnie watched her own clumsy hands lift the pieces of the pump into the sink and turn on the tap. 'Had to do this.' Her face was hot. *What's your problem? Just tell him.*

Another pause. Then his voice, tired-sounding, mistrustful almost, as if expecting further trouble from her, further difficulty. 'What are you doing?'

Bonnie saw herself through his eyes, her tense frame at the sink. She swallowed down on the silly lump of embarrassment in her throat, willed her face to cool. *It's nothing to be ashamed of. You're helping — fixing things.* 'I was expressing milk.'

'Right.'

She turned and spoke in a rush. Water splashed up onto her cheek, and she tilted her face to wipe it on her shoulder, glad not to meet his eyes. 'I've got a show. With Mickey. It's next Friday, in Sydney, but it's really good money. Nearly four thousand dollars.'

Pete didn't answer.

Bonnie swallowed again. She glanced up, but couldn't hold his gaze. She turned back to the sink. 'I thought ...' She scrubbed at one of the plastic tubes. 'I thought it might help. You know — bring in a bit of extra money. To make up for ...'

No response from Pete.

She dunked the tube under the water, lifted it and scrubbed again. 'Nearly four thousand,' she repeated. 'All the other expenses are covered. The hotel and ... stuff.'

'So you're going to Sydney?'

'Well' — she faced him again — 'yeah. I mean, that's where the show —'

'For the night.' His expression was flat, unreadable.

Don't be mean. I'm trying to help. But then Bonnie felt her mouth go stiff. She knew what was coming; she hadn't thought things through. She stood lamely, wet hands dangling.

'For a night, and — what? — most of two days?'

'Yeah.' The word came out small and limp.

He sighed, as if preparing to explain something to a child. 'I have to work. Every possible moment. I have to get this job done for Grant.' He shook his head. 'I don't think you understand. I'm going to have to work weekends till it's done. Weekends, nights. It's ...' He spread his hands. 'Well, my reputation's at stake.'

She stared at the floor.

'Sorry, Bon.' His voice softened. 'Thanks for trying to help, but I can't take that time off to look after the kids. You know what these things are like: you'd have to leave by — what? — mid-morning Friday, and then you won't be back until —'

'Yeah, okay.' She felt tears come into her eyes. 'I get it.'

'I'm sorry,' he said again and yawned. 'I have to go to bed. I'm exhausted.'

'Okay,' she heard herself whisper. She turned back to the sink one last time and pulled out the plug.

'Mum?'

'Oh, hello, darling.'

Her stomach was clenched. She shifted the phone to her other ear, breathed in, tried to shake off the nerves. 'Can you talk?'

'Quickly, yes. I'm just on my way to bridge.'

'Oh. Okay.' *Come on.* Bonnie stood at the kitchen door, watching the twins out on the trampoline. She put her hand to the cold pane of glass. 'Well, I just ... I've got ...' She breathed and pushed the words out. 'I've got a favour to ask.'

'Yes?' Suzanne gave a short laugh, and Bonnie heard unwillingness, reluctance.

You're imagining it. She drove her voice out again. 'I've got some work — a show. In Sydney. Next Friday night, so I'll have to go Friday morning, and I won't be back till Saturday afternoon ...'

'That's great news,' came Suzanne's voice, slow and hesitating.

She's waiting for the catch. 'Yeah, it is.' Bonnie watched the children bounce round and round. 'But the thing is, Pete's ... Pete can't take any time off work. He's got this big job on and, well, Doug's disappeared, so he's on his own —'

'Disappeared?'

'Yeah.'

'What do you mean? He just left?'

'Yeah.' Bonnie closed her eyes and spoke rapidly. 'I guess so. Got a better offer maybe. Anyway, he's gone.'

Suzanne made a clicking sound. 'Told you that feller was a liability.'

There was a cry from the trampoline. Bonnie opened her eyes again. Edie was swinging Louie around by the back of his jumper. She glimpsed his furious crying face whisk by before she turned away. 'Yeah, I know.' She leaned over the kitchen counter, trying to ignore the screams. 'But, anyway, so the thing is, it would be really great for me to do this job — to bring in some extra money — but Pete can't afford to take any time off at all. He has to work weekends till ...'

'So you want me to babysit?' Suzanne's voice sounded small and cold through the phone.

Babysit. How detached the word was. As if Suzanne was someone who might be paid — someone with no connection or obligation. She willed herself to answer. 'Well ...'

There was a sigh.

Bonnie fought the shame that lay thick and choking in her chest. *She's your mother. You can ask her for help.* 'Sorry,' she heard herself say.

'It's not much notice, is it?' said Suzanne.

'I guess not.'

Another sigh. 'I'll have to cancel some things.'

The yelling outside was reaching a crescendo. Bonnie moved further into the house. She couldn't face the living room with its piles of laundry so she stood in the bathroom. 'Sorry,' she said again, hearing her voice echo.

Suzanne was speaking quickly now, brisk and clipped. 'So when is it again? Next Friday — from Friday morning till Saturday afternoon?'

'Yeah.'

'All right.' Another tongue-click. 'I'll get myself organised.'

Bonnie sat down on the edge of the bath. 'Thanks, Mum,' she said, hating her meek voice.

The kitchen door crashed open, and there was the sound of Louie calling. 'Mu-um!'

'Sounds like you're busy there,' said Suzanne.

'Mu-um!' Footsteps, running.

'Yeah. I'd better go.'

'All right then.'

'Bye.' Bonnie pressed the *end call* button and cradled the phone in her lap.

'Mu-um!' yelled Louie in the hallway. 'Edie hit me!'

Bonnie reached out with her foot and nudged the door gently so it swung shut.

'Let's jump on the couch.' Louie pushed away his plate and slid down off his chair.

'Yeah,' said Edie. 'And let's make a train with all the cushions.'

'Hang on,' said Bonnie, leaping up with a tea towel. 'Wipe your hands and faces first.'

The twins paused, taking it in turns to make brief scrubbing motions with the towel before running out of the kitchen.

'That's not …' She gave up and started to clear the table. 'Watch out for my guitar,' she called after them.

Jess leaned sideways in her high chair and let a rusk drop to the floor.

Pete picked it up and handed it back to the baby, who smiled, leaned over and dropped it a second time.

'Ah-ha,' said Pete gently, bending again. 'This old game.'

Bonnie stood on the other side of the table. She found herself averting her gaze, as if the moment between Pete and the baby was something she wasn't meant to see. She gathered up cutlery. 'So,' she said after a while. 'I've got my mum.'

'What?' said Pete.

'To look after the kids. Next weekend.' She added the leftovers from one twin's bowl to the other's.

'Really?'

'Yeah.' Bonnie's heart picked up. 'So I can do the Mickey show.'

He stared. 'Your mum?'

'Yeah.'

'And you reckon that'll be okay?'

She turned her eyes away from his face, its hard look. 'Yeah,' she said, hesitatingly.

Pete puffed out his lips. 'You sure?'

She stacked the two bowls and carried them and the fistful of dirty forks and spoons to the sink. Her throat hurt. Her body felt stiff with it all: guilt, worry, swelling anger. 'Yes.' Her voice ground out roughly. 'Why wouldn't that be okay?' She threw the cutlery into the sink.

'Well,' said Pete behind her, evenly. 'It's just — you know — she's kind of, hopeless, and I don't want her knocking on the door every three minutes asking me things.'

Bonnie clanged the saucepan down beside the stack of plates. 'I'm trying to *help*,' she said, her voice catching. 'I'm trying to help, to make up for everything — fuck it.' She leaned over the sink.

Pete stood, scraping back his chair. 'How much is it again? Four grand?'

She didn't answer.

Pete brought his plate over and added it to the pile. Then he went to the door. 'It's better than nothing,' he said. 'But — you realise, it'll just cover the difference between what I was paying Doug and what I have to pay Glenn.'

Bonnie closed her eyes.

'So' — Pete pulled open the door — 'we'll pretty much be

back where we started.'

She kept her eyes shut. The cold wind was rushing in.

'You'll be right with the kids, won't you?' he said, as he stepped out. 'I'd better get back to work.'

After she'd fed Jess in the early morning and put her back to bed, Bonnie used the breast pump. She huddled on the couch in the grey almost-dawn with the heater on and the rug around her, pressing the funnel to herself, squeezing the handle until one hand got sore and then changing to the other. When she touched the bottle she could feel the warmth still in the milk. It hissed against the plastic as it went in, its fine jets almost translucent. Outside various noises started up: a barking dog, a car engine, a few sparse bird calls. Bonnie pumped, both sides, until no more would come out.

She went to the kitchen and carefully poured the milk into a storage bag, labelled it with the date and quantity and put it with the others at the rear of the freezer. Then she returned to the living room, shut the door and got back under the rug on the couch. Picked up her acoustic and ran through her parts for Mickey's songs. She played them straight, one after the other. Then she mixed them up, spliced the verse bit of one with the bridge from another, went into the chorus from a third. The fingers of her left hand swung from note to note, the riffs ran and merged, took off in their own directions.

Bonnie forgot she was cold and the tired aches in her shoulders and throat. She swam into it, the bright-edged trails of notes, the hums of chords, the opening of the sounds as they lifted out of the belly of the guitar. Their shining ascent, their moment of life, their leaving.

She pumped every chance she got. The stash of bags grew at the back of the freezer. She went through the corner cupboard, the dusty collection of bottles, teats and white plastic accessories, sorted and washed them. Matched bottles, lids and teats and lined them up in ordered rows in a shallow cardboard box on the bench. She wrote a detailed schedule for Jess. Feed and sleep routine; times she was likely to need her nappy changed: *Usually does a poo mid-morning so don't forget to check her nappy before you put her down for a sleep.* She added general tips and rules, feeling stupid and obsessive but unable to stop. *Obvious of course but NEVER let go of her in the bath!! Always put her to sleep on her back.*

She stood at the kitchen bench with the pen in her hand. How much did Suzanne know or remember? Was any of this common knowledge? Was any of it the same as it was back then, when Suzanne was the mother, and she, Bonnie, was the baby? All she could think of was how when the twins were newborns, she'd begged for some advice, crazed with exhaustion, and Suzanne had only smiled vaguely and said she couldn't remember anything. *Sorry, darling. It all seems so long ago now.* Sitting there holding one of the blanket-wrapped babies as if it was a cake, or some extremely delicate or breakable thing, that she couldn't wait to give back.

Every now and then Bonnie would try to pack.

One show. One night. It should have been easy. The overnight bag stood in the middle of the floor waiting. But every time she actually went to the wardrobe, looked at the clothes, tried to make a decision, her mind slid away from it and her limbs felt weighted down with hopelessness.

She threw the last dress down on the end of the bed and put her hands to her face. 'Nothing,' she said. 'I've got nothing. What am I going to do?'

'What about this one, Mum?' Louie held up one of the unworn tops she'd bought not all that long ago, but that was still just a bit too tight, and anyway would require a proper bra. 'I like this one.'

'Yes, it's nice, isn't it. But it's just … It's not quite right.'

'I'll put it in your bag.' Louie went over and stuffed it in.

'Thanks, Lou.' Bonnie heaved a sigh and looked down at her thighs, her old underpants, faded black, with a hole at one of the side seams, her pale, ruined stomach. 'What am I going to do?' she said again. She took the small pile of clean underwear and her best pyjamas, went over, pulled out the top and pushed them to the bottom of the bag.

'The top, Mum.' Louie picked it up and tried to stuff it back in.

'Oh, no, I actually don't think I will take that one after all. Thanks anyway though, Louie.'

'But it's my favourite.' Louie shoved it right down into the bag, gazed up at her with satisfaction.

'No, really, Lou — I think I'll have a bit more of a look at what else I've got.' Bonnie bent to pull the top out again.

'No.' Louie kept his arm stuck in the bag, his hand pressing down on the top.

'Come on, Louie. I'm trying to get packed here.'

'Na-na-na-na-na! Na-na-na-na-na!' went Louie in a chatter of protest, resisting her efforts, bearing down with all his weight.

'Louie. Lou.' She gave up and sat on the edge of the bed. 'Can you please go and see what Edie's up to? I'd really like to do this by myself.'

'Na-na-na-na-na!'

'Oh god, Louie. Come on. Please?'

'Na-na-na-na-na!'

'Forget it.' She stood up and pulled her jeans back on. 'I'll do it another time.'

On Sunday she tried to go clothes shopping. Mel came over with Freddie, and Bonnie left all the kids with her and caught the tram into the city.

She was so early none of the shops were even open. She got a coffee in a laneway cafe and sat looking out at the passers-by — middle-aged or elderly, all of them — who seemed to share the same tentative, hesitant movements. Cautiously they crept, as if aware of their status as trespassers in this half-asleep city whose rightful owners — younger people — had only temporarily receded and would soon return. A grey-haired couple in sturdy khaki pants walked with backpacks. An elderly woman in an immaculate wool suit and a hat took on the cobblestones with her twiglike legs. As she passed she turned her head, and Bonnie saw the careful placement of colour on her face — the coral lips and dabs of blush.

Young people, Bonnie realised, would still be asleep, or only just waking for the day. She thought of the time, one early morning, when the twins, still babies, had been up screaming since five and in desperation she'd stuck them in that horrible double pram that never fitted through any doorways and taken them out for a walk. The muted, secret colours of a winter dawn. Everything brittle with cold. Waiting gardens and the sleeping windows behind them. She'd gone all the way to the 7-Eleven and bought the paper, and it had been on her way back that she'd passed the two girls walking arm in arm, inadequate jackets buttoned, gauzy scarfs floating, make-up and hair still holding some of the glossy promise of the night before. For a second she'd actually thought, *They're up early*, before the realisation hit and in the same moment she saw herself as she would appear to them: heavy-thighed and pale, hair tucked into her beanie, the pram before her like some kind of giant prosthesis, an extension of her body, of her, the person she was. The girls passed, heels clipping on the pavement, stepping around Bonnie and the pram heedlessly, as if around a tree or a rubbish bin. Bonnie found herself slowing, twisting to look round after them, full of a kind of irate sorrow. *Hey,* she wanted to call. *Stop — wait!* She came to a halt, stood and watched their backs, their easy passage past and away. Before she knew it they'd gone. *Wait!* The dew on the empty street shone. The words sat in her mouth like stones.

She finished her coffee and wandered until the shops began to open. Then she went into them, one after the other, riffling through the racks of clothes, taking things out and putting them back again, her heart beating harder, the time seeming to leap relentlessly further forward every time she looked. Only forty minutes till she'd need to start heading back. Then only half an hour. Twenty minutes.

She made the mistake of thinking about Jess, and her milk let down so she slunk in and out of the shops with her coat pulled close and her arms folded.

'Need some help?' a sales girl might ask, and Bonnie would smile apologetically and creep out again. Or, possibly worse, the girls, leaning on their counters, gazing at their phones, wouldn't even acknowledge her. One stood at a mirror, adjusting her own outfit with such intimate absorption that Bonnie felt embarrassed and left without even looking around.

At last she got back on the tram empty-handed and dropped into a seat with a mixture of panic and relief. Sat and watched the buildings flick by — shops, cars, people. The industrious, impersonal world full of girls that cut swathes, that negotiated with aplomb.

When she got home she sank onto the bed with Jess. Closed her eyes against the still-not-packed bag crouching on the floor. Tipped her head back against the wall, empty of everything except the even, hungry drag of Jess's sucking.

'You okay?' Pete turned towards her in the bed. 'You crying?'

For the first time since the night of the race his voice sounded normal again, unguarded, and it pulled Bonnie undone, sent her into real, proper sobbing.

'I'm sorry,' she said, pushing up to him, butting blindly against his chest with her face.

His arms went around her. She heard him sigh, felt it against her skin. 'It's okay.'

They lay still for a while.

She let herself cry, taking in big hungry sniffs of Pete's warm smell. But there was a tightness in her shoulders and across her temples that didn't go away. She lifted her head. 'I just feel so overwhelmed,' she said. 'I don't feel like I can manage all this, trying to get organised for this show, and … everything. I feel like I'm falling apart.'

'You don't have to do it.' He moved his hand up and down her back.

'But I want to.' Bonnie struggled to see his face in the dark. 'I want to help, you know, because …'

'Yeah, I know. And' — his hand stopped, he moved slightly, away from her, and his voice changed — 'I appreciate you doing that, Bon. It will help.'

'I really am sorry.' She was still crying.

He rolled onto his back, letting go of her. 'Let's not talk about that.'

The pillow was cold and wet under her cheek. She let out a breath, long and tired and trembling. 'It just … it just seems so ridiculous that I can't even, you know, get my bag packed, or think about what to wear, or — I don't know — print out the set list and stuff.'

Pete reached for her hand. 'I know,' he said. 'It's hard to get anything done with the kids around. You just have to accept it — factor it in; plan for things to take four times as long.'

178

'But it's not just the kids. It's like … it's almost like I get paralysed. I can't do anything. It's like I don't know how to do things any more — anything in the outside world. It's like I've lost the knack. I mean, remember when I did those really long tours? Before the kids? For months I wouldn't even come back to Melbourne. I just lived out of a suitcase. And now it's like the opposite. I feel like I'm — I don't know — submerged or something. Like I'm in quicksand.'

'It gets easier. Everyone says. When the kids are older. You get your life back.'

'I'll be too old by then. To go on tour.'

'You could do other stuff. Recording. Soundtracks.'

She slid lower under the covers. The tight feeling around her head was getting worse. 'Oh god,' she said. 'Can you just stop being so reasonable for a minute?'

Pete laughed. 'Sorry.' He moved down as well, put his arms around her. 'I'm trying to be nice.'

She rolled over to face the other way. *He is — he's trying. Just be nice back. Be grateful.* 'Yeah, I know. I'm sorry I'm being such a bitch. It must be hormones.'

'That's okay.' He reached into her top and put his hand on her breast.

Before she could help herself Bonnie clamped her arm down.

He pulled his hand away. 'God,' he said in an injured voice. 'Sorry.'

'Oh, Pete, I'm sorry.' She faced him again. 'I just — I can't stand one more thing touching my boobs at the moment. Between Jess and the pump I seriously feel like a cow. They really don't feel …' She sighed. 'I've never felt less sexy.'

'Yeah, okay.' He switched on his bedside lamp and picked up his book. Now he turned away.

You've ruined it now. Idiot. She tried to curl into him, reached her arm around his waist. 'I'm sorry,' she whispered. 'I'm sorry. I actually do have a headache. Can't we just, you know, have a cuddle?'

Pete flipped a page, adjusted his pillow. 'Whatever.'

'This is ridiculous,' said Suzanne on Wednesday, at the swimming pool. 'You need to buy a new outfit. Something that makes you feel good.'

She looked at her mother's crisp white slacks, the cashmere jumper and soft leather shoes with little heels, like a child's dance shoes. Her fingernails painted a mild pink. Her blow-dried hair. 'It doesn't matter really,' said Bonnie. 'I've got clothes. I'll dig something out.'

'No,' said Suzanne. 'You can't go off to Sydney feeling second-rate. This is important. And I'm not going to make all the bloody effort to …' She grimaced, broke off, then worked her face into a smile. 'You know,' she leaned towards Bonnie and dropped her voice, 'when you were three weeks old —'

'I know,' said Bonnie in a flat tone, rolling her eyes. 'You left me with Granny and went and got a Vidal Sassoon haircut.'

'Yes.' Suzanne sat back, looked out over the pool. She put one hand to her hair and smoothed it. 'And it did me a world of good. I think women these days feel too much at the mercy of their children. You're not doing them any favours being a drudge, you know. You need to have some life of your own.'

Bonnie breathed the muggy air and tried to will away the familiar stab of annoyance. *I don't see you putting your hand up to babysit while I get my hair cut.* 'Well, I do have a life of my own,' she said aloud. 'I just — I'm having trouble getting everything else organised around it.'

Suzanne reached to the pram, pushed a dangling toy back within reach of Jess's hands. 'Tell you what,' she said. 'Why don't you go this afternoon, just for a couple of hours. I'll come back and take care of the children.' She glanced at the narrow gold watch on her wrist. 'I'll need to get going by half-past two at the latest.'

'Are you sure?' Bonnie watched Jess clutch at the toy.

'Yes, of course.'

'Well, thanks, Mum. If you're sure. That would be really great.'

Suzanne crossed her legs and brushed at the fabric of her pants. 'I think it's important you make the most of this opportunity.'

Bonnie watched her. Into her head came Suzanne's words from nearly six years earlier. *Oh well, you might as well do it now, I suppose. I really enjoyed getting properly back into my career in my forties.* She remembered putting the phone down, going to the mirror. A hotel room in Brisbane. The savage sun through the slatted blinds. The glitter of the river behind, the faint rush of cars on the bridge. Her guitar case and gear bag at the foot of the bed with her jacket dropped over them. The thin scatter of her travelling possessions, ready to be scraped together and taken, leaving no trace. The white stick of the test lying on the bedcovers with its two pink lines. And in the foreground herself, her body, just the same, not yet betraying any secret. She'd run her hands over her breasts, her flat belly, her hips and her thighs. Leaned in to study her face. *This belongs to you,* she'd said to that face. *You and Pete.* It hadn't mattered then what anybody else thought.

In a boutique she tried on a long top, a kind of tunic. Black floaty silk with a textured pattern. It hung, it drifted, it skimmed. She checked the price tag. It was on sale; her heart surged. She turned in front of the mirror in relief and a flurry of hope.

'Got the day off?' The sales girl folded the top and nestled it in tissue paper.

'Not really.' Bonnie stood at a rack of belts. 'Just a couple of hours. My mum's looking after the kids.'

'That's nice.' The girl pulled out a stiff paper bag. 'How many kids have you got?'

'Three.' Bonnie glanced at her and waited.

'Three! Wow.' There was a pause, and Bonnie felt her heart wilt. But then the girl passed the bag across and smiled. 'You don't look old enough to have three kids.'

She strode out into the watery sunshine. She bought a takeaway coffee and walked with it back to the car, the shopping bag hooked over one arm. In the plate-glass windows of the shops her reflection, narrow and light, leaped up to flash alongside her, again and again.

On Thursday night she checked again the lists of instructions for Suzanne, the rows of bottles and teats. She opened the fridge and felt the bags of milk that sat there, defrosting, ready for the morning. Closed the fridge. Stood in the house full of sleeping children, listening to the lonely grind of a power tool from the workshop.

In the bedroom she refolded the floaty tunic, placed it gently on the top of the overnight bag. Checked again her toiletry bag with its cache of make-up untouched in years, toothpaste and toothbrush, bobby pins and hair elastics. Hotel soaps with their pleated paper wrappings. Mini bottles of shampoo and conditioner. All still there in their little slots, the make-up jumbled in its separate case. More than she could possibly need for one night. She pulled the zip around the whole thing and tucked it in the side pocket of the bag.

She took out the guitar and wound the strings slack, ready for the flight. Laid it back down. Let the lid of the case fall with its whoosh of cool smoky-pub air. Clicked the latches. Opened the gear bag and checked leads and pedals, spare strings, batteries.

When she finally went to bed she couldn't sleep. Pete's words from the other night kept sounding in her ears. *Pretty much back where we started.* The shapes of her packed baggage hulked behind the door. She had an urge to get up and kick them, send them slamming into the far wall. Tear open the zips of the two bags and fling their contents out all over the floor. Jump on the guitar case until it caved in. She turned onto her other side so she couldn't see them.

In the early morning, after she'd fed Jess and come back to bed, she lay watching Pete's sleeping face in the thin grey light. The helplessness ran through her again. Her limbs felt stretched by it, the joints weakened. It was as if she could sense, heaped in the space between their two bodies, all the small horrible moments of the past two weeks — the banal string of tensions laid in a coil, the ignoring, the resentments. And, beneath them, the greater, lurking weights of blame and anger.

It suddenly felt very important to do something now, before she went, to get Pete to look at her softly again, with love. To reach through the air between them, stir it up, send everything flying, so they could be with each other properly again, openly.

But there were dark circles under his closed eyes, and she couldn't bear to wake him.

And then she heard Edie crying and calling out — a nightmare — and by the time Bonnie had gone in and settled her, lain with her in her narrow bed for a while, it was too late, and Pete was up and busy.

He came to the door while she was in the shower.

'Your mum called,' he said, and her stomach shrank at his tone.

'Yeah?' She tried to see his face through the shower curtain, but it was a blur.

'She's running late.'

'Shit.' She turned the taps off, pulled back the curtain, reached for a towel. 'Why?'

'Da-ad!' came a voice from the kitchen. 'I need some more toast.'

'I don't know.' He stood with the phone in his hand, his thumb on the *call* button, pressing it on and off in regular stabs. Bonnie could hear the tiny bursts of dial tone.

'Da-AD!'

'Coming.' Pete pushed himself up off the doorframe.

Bonnie caught sight of her own drawn face in the mirror, and looked away. 'Well, what did she say?'

'I don't know, some excuse. Traffic.' He was turning back to the kitchen. His work shirt had a rip at the elbow. 'I knew this would happen,' he said quietly.

'I'm sorry,' she said, to his back.

He didn't answer.

'Fuck,' whispered Bonnie. She picked up the moisturiser and the bottom of the plastic jar fell from the unsecured lid, plopping upside down onto the tiles. 'Fuck!' she said out loud. She straightened, stuck her face out towards the empty hallway. Rage throbbed in her, hot up her spine. 'I'm SORRY!' she yelled.

Bonnie held the spoon to Jess's lips. 'Did she say how long she'd be?'

Pete said nothing.

She watched him leaning over the bench, his back to her, stubborn and unfriendly. 'I'm sure she won't be too long.'

Pete unfolded an old newspaper.

'Come on,' she murmured to Jess. She had that tired, scratchy feeling she always got before catching a plane: the bad night's sleep, waking up worrying that she'd forgotten to pack something or — an outdated fear from her life before children — that she'd somehow sleep in and miss the flight.

'Are you going on a plane, Mum?' Louie spooned up some porridge and slurped the milk from around it.

'Yes. I'm going to Sydney.' She took the spoon back out of Jess's mouth and used the edge of it to scrape rice cereal from the baby's chin. 'But only for one night. I'll be back tomorrow.'

'What're we doing?'

'Grandma's coming.' Bonnie flicked a glance at Pete. 'Dad'll be here though. Out in the workshop. And he'll put you to bed and everything.'

'What're we doing, Dad?'

'Mm?'

'What're we doing today, with Grandma, while Mum's on the plane?'

Pete kept reading.

Bonnie scooped up more rice cereal. 'Try again, Lou,' she said. 'Use a big, loud voice and say, "Excuse me, Dad."'

'Excuse me, Dad!'

Pete looked up from the paper.

Louie put down his spoon.

'Yes, Louie?' Pete refolded the paper and put it aside.

'What're we doing today, while Mum's on the plane?'

'Well, that'll be up to Grandma, I guess. If she ever gets here.'

Bonnie noticed the way he was narrowing his gaze to only see Louie, blinkering himself against her sitting there. There was a thin dryness in the back of her nose and throat, like that dizzy, ill feeling cigarettes always gave her.

Jess flailed an arm and caught the spoon. Rice cereal flicked over Bonnie's sleeve. 'Shit.' The ill feeling swamped her, surged in a panic, tinged with hateful self-pity. She felt her lips shake.

She reached for Jess, for the spoon trapped in the fat fingers, dribbling white mess, but then she stopped, dropped her hand and stood up. Jess raised the spoon and wiped it over the side of her head. Beads of runny cereal clung to the fine baby hairs. 'Sorry,' Bonnie heard herself say. 'I can't ...' She turned and left the room.

In the hallway Edie sat with socks and one shoe on but no pants, laboriously fitting the strap of the other shoe into the buckle.

'Oh, Edie,' she said automatically. 'You'll need ...'

'What?' said Edie without looking up.

'Never mind.' Bonnie went into the bathroom.

'But, Mum,' called Louie, 'Jess is getting that stuff all over her head.'

Bonnie caught her own frown in the mirror, her ugly resentful face. The surge of self-pity went careening into anger. The mouth opened. 'Dad's in charge,' it yelled.

The taxi honked its horn, and the twins went running to the front porch. Pete followed with Jess, and they all stood watching as she lugged her things out to the car. The driver, a tall, impossibly thin African man, helped her put everything in the boot, and then she went back to say goodbye.

'Bye, Mum!'

'Bye, Edie. Bye, Lou. Love you. See you tomorrow, okay?' Bonnie bent to them, felt their fast kisses glance off her face, both of them. She made do with pressing her lips to the tops of their heads, breathing their sweet, musty smells. It was cold. She pulled a tissue from her sleeve and wiped her nose. To kiss Jess she had to go right up to Pete. There was a strange, unbalanced moment as they, without speaking or looking at each other, juggled the baby between them. Then Bonnie took her, kissed her face, the round cheek, the springy flesh. One of Jess's hands connected with her chin, the fingers closing and opening again in a brief uncontrolled pulse.

For a second Bonnie saw them all from a distance, as if on a movie screen: a scene where a woman leaves her husband and bewildered children, gets into a car and is driven away. The brave, uncertain smiles and waves of the boy and girl; the innocent baby; the grim-faced husband. The woman ducking into the seat, her hair hanging like a curtain.

'You'd better go.' Pete nodded at the taxi. She kissed Jess one more time and passed her back. Her hand and Pete's overlapped on the small, warm body and slipped apart again with the politeness of strangers.

'See you tomorrow.' Her gaze was stuck at Jess's jumper, the faint stain on its front. With an effort she went higher, up Pete's chest, his neck, his stubbled chin, to his eyes.

They looked at each other. Pete's face had absolutely no expression, like someone sitting on a tram, thoughts secured, turned inwards, or elsewhere.

Do you hate me? Bonnie wanted to say. *Don't hate me.*

'See you tomorrow,' he said.

'Mum.' Louie pulled at her sleeve. 'The taxi.'

Bonnie went down the path and out to the taxi. She climbed in the back, shut the door and turned to see them: the twins jumping and waving, Pete still with that no-one-home expression, Jess in her little halo of immediate focus, bent to a button on Pete's shirt. The car began to move.

'Sorry about that,' she said. 'Just to the airport, please.'

She lifted her eyes to the street ahead, and there was Suzanne's little hatchback, her smile flashing, a wiggle-fingered wave. Bonnie raised her own hand as the two cars passed, dragged her lips back in an answering smile, but in her held-tight body there was no happiness, no softening relief. She pulled her tissue out again and started to cry into it. Hard, dry sobs like vomiting. The muscles in her brow and jaw aching. She hunched in the seat, swaying as the driver took a corner. Mercifully, out of courtesy or embarrassment, he didn't speak to her or look around.

'HELLO?' SHE PUT THE KEY CARD DOWN ON THE NARROW HIGH bench of the little kitchen alcove and set her bags and case on the carpet. They made no sound. She went past them, further into the room with its familiar neutral comfortless calm — white paint, framed abstract prints, the couch in a beige faux-suede fabric, glass-topped coffee table, the floor-length sheer curtains and beyond them the bare boxy balcony. There was an empty can of Coke on the small table, and what looked like the plastic wrapping from a pack of cigarettes. The couch cushions were in disarray, and the TV remote lay on the floor.

'Hello?' Bonnie moved down the short hallway. The door to the first bedroom was open. A big soft bag lay on the bed, unzipped, clothes spilling out, jeans, t-shirts, a single not-too-clean sock. The bedcovers were rumpled. At the foot of the bed stood a long, metal flight case, bass-guitar size. It was covered in band stickers and *Fragile* and *Handle with care* labels, neon orange and yellow with black checks. A bristle of severed elastic ties sprouted from the handle. She kept going. There were two more doors. Another bathroom — in darkness, the faint gleam of tiles through the half-open door — and the second bedroom, empty of either people or baggage. A queen-sized bed and a single, covers smooth and impersonal. One whole wall taken up by a built-in wardrobe with mirrored sliding doors.

She sat on the nearer bed. Her reflection faced her — eyes, knees, feet. The mirror looked plasticky, like it would give if she pressed a finger to it. The dark circles under her eyes showed,

189

and her cheeks looked hollow. She turned away. Pulled her legs up and lay back on the pillows. There was a smell of cleaning products, deodorisers. The air tasted recycled. She glanced over at the window. It opened, she could see. *In a minute I'll get up and open it*, she thought, but she felt exhausted, wrung out. She shut her eyes.

At one point the thought of the show that night came drifting in, and she woke with a start and an eddy of nerves, but when she really faced it, tried to grip it properly with her mind, it seemed somehow like a job another person would be doing, something that wasn't her concern, and the nerves drained away again. She still had her coat on and her boots, but she didn't take them off or climb under the covers. She turned on her side and went back to sleep.

A door slammed. A voice called. 'Bon?'

She opened her eyes.

'Bonnie?'

She sat up and looked blurrily around. 'Yeah?'

'So she is here.' There was a movement in the hallway, and then Mickey came in. 'Oh, sorry. Were you sleeping?'

'I guess I was.' Bonnie ran her hands over her face, tried to straighten her hair.

Mickey sat on the end of the bed. She patted Bonnie's ankle. 'I've been trying to call you.'

'Oh, sorry, yeah. My phone's in my bag. I guess I didn't hear it.'

'Doesn't matter. I was just wondering if you made it okay.'

'Yeah, fine.'

'Have you met Beth yet?'

'No, I just —'

'She's great. Come and meet her.' Mickey bounced off the bed again and grabbed Bonnie's arm.

As they went out the door Bonnie caught sight of herself in the hostile mirror: her sleep-swollen face, her crumpled clothes, her messed-up hair. She followed along behind Mickey out to the main room where a woman wearing tight black jeans and a leather jacket was smoking a cigarette in the doorway to the balcony.

'Bonnie, this is Beth,' said Mickey, and stood back happily.

'Hi,' said Bonnie.

'Nice to meet you,' said Beth. She had an English accent.

A phone sounded, and Mickey pulled it out, answered it and started pacing up and down the hall as she talked.

'Tired?' said Beth without smiling.

'Yeah, I guess so.' Bonnie could feel how puffy her eyes were. She ran her hands over her clothes, trying to smooth them. Her stomach felt hollow and her mouth dry. She went over to the kitchenette and took down a glass from the cupboard, filled it with water.

'Don't drink the tap water,' said Beth behind her. 'It's really disgusting. There's bottles in the fridge.'

'Oh.' She stood with the glass in her hand. 'It's just,' she said, 'you know, the minibar — I hate paying so much just for water. I usually buy some bottles myself from the supermarket ...' She trailed off.

Beth had swivelled to blow smoke outside. 'Fair enough,' came her turned-away voice.

Bonnie watched her. The sharp flick of her haircut, the dark polish on her fingernails, the soft-looking leather of her jacket. Without pleasure she drank down the sulphurous water and felt dislike welling, ready.

But then Beth stepped onto the balcony and stubbed out her butt in an ashtray, leaned on the wall and said, 'Oh, it's just beautiful out here. Come and see.'

Bonnie went and stood next to her, and there it was, the

harbour of course, and the unmistakable curve of dark metal, but there was also all that lay in between. The unprepared, back views of buildings. Flat rooftops like mountain steppes. Rows of windows. Offices, apartments, low lines of shops along streets. So full of colour and scrambling life — cars, buses, people, birds. Trees that even from this distance seemed glossy-leaved and verdant. Almost directly below was some sort of halfway house. Narrow concrete steps up to a second-storey walkway and a series of brown-painted doors and barred windows. A group of men in tracksuits stood in the car park talking to a plump man in a uniform. One of them laughed and clapped the uniformed man on the shoulder.

'You'd think it'd get depressing, wouldn't you?' said Beth. 'Watching cities from hotel-room balconies. But I love it. I never get sick of it. I don't know — it makes me happy. Watching people just — doing whatever they do.' She spoke softly and unashamedly.

There was a silence. *I like her*, Bonnie thought with a throb of surprise. She watched the uniformed man below get into a car and the mob of tracksuit men slope out into the street on foot. Two birds came shooting up from a cluster of umbrella palms. She followed them with her eyes, and when they were gone she looked back down and watched people on the footpath. The tracksuit men had already moved off, but here came a group of high-school girls in green uniforms, and there the other way went a man in a suit with the jacket hung over his shoulder. An Asian man on a bike. A grey-haired woman holding the hand of a child, gripping it at the wrist in her thickened brown fingers.

Bonnie leaned on the bricks and watched their passing, the tops of their heads, their strange, foreshortened bodies, their varying airs of urgency or ease. She watched and somehow it all cushioned her, held her, loosened her.

192

'Sound check.' Mickey stood behind them. She clapped her hands. 'Let's go.'

Through the weary, dark room they moved, pushing amps in wheeled metal cases, lugging bags, instruments, boxes of t-shirts and CDs. The dusty chandeliers hung unlit, the floor sprawled emptily. The domed ceiling, swathed in shadows and deprived of an audience, failed to soar. A missed plastic beer glass lay on its side at the base of the stage. There was that smell, musty, closeted, of spilled drinks and, somehow, still hanging there in the curtains and carpet, old cigarette smoke. It smelled like the end of a night.

Every sound rang: the roll and clunk of the amp-case casters, the thud of cables as the mixer laid them out on the thin stage carpeting, the coarse wrench and rip of gaffer tape coming off the roll.

'A-one, and a-one and a-two,' went the mixer behind the desk, popping and honking through the PA.

'Chips?' Mickey held out a bag, and Bonnie dived her hand in gratefully, licked at the salt at the corners of her lips.

'So have you met everybody?' Mickey held a chip between thumb and forefinger and put her tongue to the underside of it.

'Um ...'

'Everyone, this is Bonnie.' Mickey put an arm around Bonnie and turned with her. She pointed with the chip to the drummer, a small man with thick straight dark hair that hung low over his forehead. 'Henry.'

Henry and Bonnie exchanged nods and smiles.

'Lloyd.' Mickey aimed the chip at a guy with messy blond hair and a checked shirt who was setting up a keyboard.

'Hi,' said Lloyd.

'Hi.'

'And Beth you know,' said Mickey. 'And Tom of course you know.'

'Yeah, of course.' She waved to the mixer who waved back.

'All right.' Mickey pulled her closer. 'I'm so glad you could do this show. It's going to be great.'

'Well, I hope so.' She looked down at her feet, the toes of her boots. 'It's been so long. I hope I can ...'

'You'll be fine.' Mickey squeezed her again and then let go. She put the chip properly in her mouth at last and picked up her guitar, plugged it into a tuner and started twanging strings.

Bonnie took her own guitar across the stage. As if from some sunken internal hidey-hole she watched as her hands opened the case, took out the instrument, tightened the strings, tuned them, slung the guitar around her body, plugged it in, flicked switches and twisted knobs, moved over the fretboard. Sounds rose from the amp, full and certain.

'Okay, and snare,' came Tom's voice from the fold-back wedge, filtering through the fractured, busy garble that was everyone getting sounds. 'Okay, thanks, and now some more kick drum ... Okay, keys?'

One at a time they turned to him, straightening, looking out at his face above the desk, way off there in the gloom, down the back near the bar. One after the other cycling through their sounds, loud, soft, effects on or off. Waiting for the nod, the 'Okay, thanks' through the speaker before sliding once more into the tangle of noise.

'Shall we do a song?' Mickey went out to the mic at the front of the stage. She strummed a few chords, and Henry started up a shuffling beat. Lloyd pressed some buttons and began to send long, wavering organ drones floating out into the people-less room. Alongside Bonnie Beth swung her hips and rolled out a bass line that swaggered and swayed, climbed up the drums, jumped off, flew back down and began to climb again. And from

Bonnie's own telecaster, from her fingers that seemed not to belong to her, in and then out of the amp and through her own numbed body came spangles of notes, notes that hovered like points of light, that trembled and merged, that ran into riffs that rippled and sang. And even though it didn't seem to be her that was doing it, even though it swelled through her like she hardly existed, at the same time it was like listening to the throb of her own blood.

It was only six o'clock when they finished, but Mickey wanted to eat so they all went to a Greek place. They drank beer and ate small whole fish, fried, and dolmades and salty lamb and olives and cucumber. The ceiling was low, and the paint peeling and dark. A framed tourism poster hung behind Mickey's head — square white buildings, harsh light and blue sea, boats lined up on a rocky shore. Outside there was sun still, low and late.

The beer lifted Bonnie, and she ate and drank and watched the others, their hands, their fingers, their lips shiny with oil, their mouths biting and chewing and talking. The coming show hovered. Everything seemed intensified, sharp-edged with nerves.

'Good we've got this show,' someone said. 'Good warm-up for the tour.'

Lloyd smiled at Bonnie. 'I love your guitar playing. You were in Need Police, weren't you?'

'That was a long time ago.' Bonnie felt a shaft of embarrassment. She lowered her eyes to her plate. 'It was a pretty dumb band.'

'No, it wasn't — you guys were great. You were one of my favourite bands when I first moved to Melbourne.' Lloyd sipped his beer. 'I moved from Adelaide and I just couldn't believe how many great bands were playing all the time — like every night. It blew my mind. I used to go and see Need Police all the time.

Such a great band. You and that other guitarist — I'd never heard anyone play like that.'

She drank, tried to make a humble shrug.

'Who wrote the songs?' said Lloyd.

'Richie, mostly, the singer. I wrote some.'

'So did you ever have your own band?'

'No.' Bonnie looked at the tide-line of foam on her glass. *Better not drink too much.* Inside her head, blurred and dim, she saw her battered old box of four-track tapes squatting on the workshop shelf, furred with sawdust. Those long-ago sketches of songs, guitar and makeshift drum kit, borrowed bits and pieces, her unadorned voice. Lyrics that were still catalogued somewhere deep in her mind. Lonely, shy bedroom songs that she'd cringed to listen back to, even at the time. But still she'd written them, still she'd laid them down. And kept them. She drained the beer. Reached for an olive and bit into the salty flesh.

Back at the hotel Beth flopped onto the couch and switched on the TV. Bonnie sat at the glass-topped table, on one of the hard white plastic chairs. For the first time that day she checked her phone. Only the two missed calls from Mickey. It was eight o'clock. The kids would be asleep by now anyway. She let the phone drop back into her bag.

Under the shower she expressed milk by hand. Creamy runnels washed across the tiles, swirled with the water down the drain. She kept going until her hands were sore and her breasts felt eased and softer. Then she shaved her legs, using the little plastic bottle of shower gel. It smelled like coconut and something else, some tropical flower. She stood in the shining room drying herself. In the spotless mirror she turned her head to one side and then to the other. Wrapped the towel tighter. Stood up straight. *You're only thirty-four.*

She shared a cab to the venue with Mickey and Beth.

Bonnie sat behind the driver, fingers spread on her knees, nail polish not quite dry. She could smell it, as well as the deodoriser thing that dangled from the rear-view mirror — harsh, synthetic smells — and there was also, softer and more intimate, the perfume one of the others was wearing, or maybe hair product. Her own make-up, the shower gel.

Her nerves were running now. The others' too. They spoke but didn't listen, flung out chatter to fill the space. Legs jiggled, sighs heaved.

Down the long, crowded street the car moved, slow in the stop-start traffic. Bonnie looked out the window. A small queue outside a nightclub — girls in short skirts and bare legs, arms wrapped around ribcages, shoulders hunched. Lights, signs. Rubbish on the ground. Bouncers at the entrance to a strip place. She put her window down a bit. The air blew cold on her face, put tears in her eyes.

Someone had hung some placards with *Nights Underground* on either side of the stage and over the merch table, but other than that it seemed just like a normal show. The crowd a bit older maybe. Bonnie had forgotten how dark it always was, how people stood in bunches, making the place feel cramped even when it wasn't. The way you always seemed to be squeezing past.

She stood beside the mixing desk. The support band was loud. They looked so small, so far away on the stage. Little figures, bright-lit, grinding away at their instruments, yelling into microphones. Their faces just blurs.

'I don't know — they're just a bit *blah*,' a woman shouted into her friend's ear.

'They're trying too hard,' the friend shouted back.

'Let's go to the front bar.' They turned and pushed past.

Bonnie drank, felt the dry beer fizz at the back of her throat.

She shook back her hair and looked up at the chandeliers now glowing softly, the ceiling's vault filled at last with the right kind of mystery. She straightened her shoulders, felt the strap of her bag, the sweep of her new clothes, the lift in the heels of her good boots. The mask of make-up on her face. Slid her thumbnail under the edge of the label on her beer bottle, worrying at the wet gluey paper.

The backstage room was a white-painted box with fluorescent lighting. Dirty blue carpet. Plastic chairs with cracks in the bottoms. On the wall next to the mirror, above the tubs full of bottles and icy water, someone had written *Check you'r rider — tightarse alert.* Bonnie reached over and took another beer, twisted off the top.

'Fuck, I wish we could smoke.' Beth sat low in one of the chairs, unplugged bass guitar cradled in her lap, strings buzzing and clacking under her fingers.

Mickey stood at the mirror, putting on lipstick. 'How long have we got?'

'About fifteen,' said Henry. 'These guys should finish any moment.'

Bonnie found her guitar case and opened it. She took a seat beside Beth and began her own warm-up. The tinny, depthless twanging hardly sounded over the booming of the band up on the stage. She leaned her beer-thick head against the wall and watched the busy clamber of her fingers, up and down.

On the stage it was hot. Only the first couple of rows of faces showed in the spill of the lights, all the rest like a dark blanket spreading further than she let herself look. She turned back to her amp, fiddled with her levels just for something to do.

'Hello,' said Mickey into the mic, and a wave of cheering rolled up off the crowd. Two spotlights, bright almost-white glares of yellow and pink, lapped across the stage to meet in the middle, locking in together over Mickey and her guitar. Bonnie watched her there in the dazzle, face lifted, one arm raised, open to the invisible sea of people. Her cheek in profile curved with her smile. There was no way she could see any more than Bonnie, but still she looked out there, smiled, kept her eyes raised as she dropped her arm, dipped her shoulder and hit the opening chords of the first song.

Bonnie thought of something she'd read in a review once. *Meyers' performance is so generous it's hard not to feel like every song is being sung just for you.* She saw the lit-up front rows, the heads all turned to Mickey, tilting like a field of sunflowers.

Further over, Lloyd, Henry and Beth were ranged level with Bonnie along the back of the stage. Bathed in their own softer lights they appeared, on the outside anyway, to be incredibly calm. Composed, focused. She breathed, and felt her own wash of nerves take a useful shape. She glanced down at her guitar, checked the volume and tone knobs, then back up at Henry. They were here to work. Out the front Mickey started to sing the first verse. Henry nodded, adjusted his grip on the drumsticks, and they gathered themselves. Reined in all their slow-built heaving energy, smoothed it, held it down with an even pressure. Went into the song.

Afterwards they stood around the band room. The white light showed the sweat on their faces, the slip and blur of Mickey's lipstick, the dark stains under the arms of Henry's shirt.

People edged in the door. Mickey hugged and kissed and laughed and made introductions that were lost in the whirl of talk. More drinks were passed around. Someone opened a bottle of champagne. It was crowded and noisy and the lights seemed even harsher than before, but Bonnie stood with a beer in one hand and a plastic cup of champagne in the other, half listening to Henry and Lloyd saying things like 'I had too much of myself in the fold-back at the start' and 'I reckon *Catching Birds* works better when we play it slow like that', and felt it still surging in her, the high of the show. The feeling she'd known she'd missed but forgotten how much, the glorious soaring that was so much better than any drug she'd ever taken.

'Excuse me.' A woman slipped around Henry and stood next to her. 'I just wanted to say I love your playing.'

'Oh.' Bonnie stared down at her two drinks. She felt stunned and slow. 'Thanks.'

'It's really beautiful. The sounds and the … the … what you make …' The woman laughed. 'Well, anyway, it's just beautiful.'

'Thanks.' Bonnie drank from the beer.

The woman lifted her plastic cup. 'Cheers.'

'Cheers.' She bumped it with her beer bottle, and then her own plastic cup, and they both laughed a cut-short laugh, then drank and looked away from one another.

'Anyway …' said the woman, and moved off again.

'Here you go.' Henry held out a poster and a pen.

'Oh, I don't need to.' Bonnie held out her drinks. 'I mean, I'm not really in the band, I just —'

'No — he wants you to sign it too.' Henry tipped his head towards a young guy standing in the doorway, who put his hands together in a prayer shape and gave a little nod, shoulders curved in with self-consciousness.

'Okay, then.'

Henry took the beer and gave her the pen. He spread the poster against the wall and held it there for her, and Bonnie added her own scribble to the others in the white space under the photo of Mickey.

'Haven't seen you in a while.' It was a tall guy with glasses. Long, badly cut hair tucked behind his ears. He held a bundle of

200

CDs and wore an old Mickey t-shirt, from a tour years before, worn and faded.

'Um. Sorry, I don't think we've …?'

'Yeah, yeah, I know. So many nights, so many faces.' He rolled his eyes. Behind his glasses they were small and flat.

'Sorry.' She glanced around. Henry and Lloyd had moved off. *Bugger*, she thought.

'Bret,' said the man. 'I met you last time you played with Mickey. Here, actually.'

'Oh.' She tried not to keep looking around so obviously. 'Sorry. I've got a terrible memory.'

'I'm not very memorable.' The man shrugged.

'No, it's not that. It's just, you know …'

'Yeah, yeah.' He stood square and close, unmoving.

'I'm Bonnie,' she heard herself say weakly.

'I know.'

They stood in a bubble of silence within the frenzy of chatter.

Oh god, just leave me alone. I can't be bothered with weirdos tonight. She drew in a breath and gestured vaguely towards the door. 'Well, I guess I'd better …'

But he was turning anyway, his head swivelling, beacon-like. 'Yeah, sure.' He swung his long body around, and Bonnie caught a whiff of laundry detergent. His arms gangling out of the t-shirt sleeves looked white and soft. She followed his gaze and saw Mickey alone in a little clear spot, momentarily abandoned. *Whoops*, thought Bonnie, but relief bubbled up too, and she wended her way to the door and out.

She passed the stage scattered with half-packed equipment and crossed the room that yawned its emptiness, so total, as if none of it had ever happened. The carpet was littered with plastic glasses, and she clipped one with her toe.

In the toilets the door echoed and clanged. She sat in

the cubicle and heard the loudness of her own breathing, her pee in a full drunken stream. When she washed her hands she didn't look up at the mirror.

The group — band, friends, hangers-on — had moved from the back room to the area in front of the stage. A security guy had appeared and was circling heavily, making shooing movements and saying, 'All right, people. Time to move on.'

What was everyone doing now? Was anyone going out? There was a party. There were two parties. People hovered, made suggestions, lifted shoulders and tilted heads, spread palms in an offer.

'I live around the corner. We could swing by the bottle-o, pick up some beers ...'

'There's an indie night at Spectrum. Could be okay ...'

'You know Max, from Higher Mountains? There's a party at his place in Stanmore ...'

Bonnie parked herself beside Mickey. The voices darted, and she tried to follow, dragged her gaze from face to face. Under the dimmed chandeliers nobody looked old or sweaty or pale or tired. She gave up on following the talk and settled into admiration. The sweet, round contours of Beth's face with its sharp frame of hair. Henry's lashes showing in thick dark curves when he looked down. Mickey's full mouth with its smudged lipstick. How alive they all were — how quick and young and clever. She was with them. She didn't want to think about anything else.

A decision was made. Coats were dragged on, bags shouldered. Away they went in a jumble, over the carpet, past the bar, leaving the bouncer dangling his meaty hands.

Outside the road was wet and car tyres loud. Specks of rain drifted, sparkled on hair and clothes. Under orange streetlights, against darkened shopfronts they dived into three taxis that pulled over like magic. Bonnie scooted in beside Mickey. The seat cover was ripped and her hand sank into foam only half covered by a web of tape.

'Oh no!' Mickey stabbed a finger at a looming figure on the footpath. Hunched in the cold, head lowered to peer in at the car window, glasses reflecting twin slashes of light. The bundle of CDs clutched to his chest like a tourist's map. 'Quick! Get down!' Mickey grabbed her, and they bent flat over their knees, giggling. She felt the blood beat in her face. Her ears sang with it. The car slid out into the traffic and away.

A room with a long curved orange couch, worn vinyl, missing buttons. Old carpet, pale in the dimness. A tall lamp with a green shade. Music, loud. People. Standing, talking, drinking, smoking, dancing.

Bonnie felt it all swell and heave around her. Amazing, to think she used to do things like this all the time — play shows, stay in hotels, go to parties full of strangers. Feelings moved through her like streams of air from passing cars. Bravado, a nostalgic kind of swagger. Fear, anxiety, rising to clog her chest and throat. A thin tide of the helpless guilt from home. Someone gave her a beer, and she swigged at it.

'Cheers!' Henry materialised and raised his stubby.

'Great show!' A woman nodded and smiled, then slipped back into the fold.

'Hi, Bonnie. How's it going?'

Faces appeared. Men and women from other bands, or who'd worked behind bars or for booking agencies. People Bonnie had met years before and not thought of since. Names drifted in and out of her head, and scenes, little snatches from long-ago nights, flickering way off in the distance. A lock-in at a pub in Surry Hills — sitting at a table by the stage still full of equipment, the bartender lining up shots of something.

Palace Brothers playing on the PA — the first time she heard them. A bar in Kings Cross, some party full of film people — impossibly beautiful women, men with their shirts halfway unbuttoned, the smell of frangipani, the flowers fallen from someone's hair, their creamy petals crushed on the floor of the second-storey deck. A fight on the street outside — a man face down on the footpath, a cop kneeling on his back. Blood under the flashing lights.

'So how many have you got?' said a woman.

Bonnie tried to focus on her face. 'Um … sorry?'

'How many? Kids?'

'Oh.' She looked down at her hand around the bottle of beer, her fingers with their unfamiliar bright polish. 'Three.'

'Wow.' The woman wrapped her arms around herself and did a little wiggle. 'That's amazing.'

'Well, it's …'

'You must be so happy.' Her lipstick gleamed, a hot pinkish-red, and her teeth were small and white like a child's.

There was an acrid taste at the back of Bonnie's throat. 'Yeah, of course I am,' she said. 'But it's, well, it can be really hard work, and …'

'Oh, I'm sure it's hard. I don't know how you do it. My sister's only got one kid and she's changed *so* much. She doesn't even go out any more. Ever. She doesn't even *try*.' The woman rolled her eyes. 'But look at *you*.'

'Well. I don't really … I mean, this is just a one-off. Normally I pretty much just …'

'But you wouldn't have it any other way, would you? Like my sister — she complains, but then I say, "Well, what do you want? Would you change it all back again?" and she's like, "No way."' The woman threw back her head and did that body-wiggle again. 'Oh, I love this song.'

Bonnie drank. She didn't know the song. She swallowed down on the bad taste and the new feeling that was rolling in, that she couldn't quite recognise, that was somehow panic and sadness and a restless kind of lust all running together. It was the feeling she used to get as a teenager, pacing the kitchen floor on hot weekend nights, stealing white wine from her mother's cask, listening to the radio and looking out at the whispering dark that seemed full of everybody else's happiness, of parties, love and sex. *Unknown Pleasures*, like it said on the Joy Division poster in her bedroom. Her aloneness a pool that barely lapped as she floated at its centre in a kind of miserable glory.

'I hated it.' Another woman, with dark hair cut in a thick fringe. 'The most boring film ever.'

'Oh,' said Bonnie, trying not to sway.

'It was all right,' said a man. 'I liked that other film he did — what was that film?'

'They all suck.' The fringe woman lit a cigarette. 'All his films. He just sucks.'

'So, Bonnie,' said another man, and she swung her head to look at him.

Did she know him? Had they met, been introduced, some other time? Or perhaps she'd introduced herself just now, earlier, in the whirling blankness of this night. She tried to haul out a memory, short- or long-term, but nothing came: her mind sank into murk.

The man smiled. He had crooked teeth, the canine more prominent on one side. 'It's nice to see you again.'

'Yeah, it is. It's ...' She tried to shape her face into a casual smile. So they had met before. Maybe he played in a band. She couldn't remember. In her stomach and at the back of her throat there was a rising queasiness. She swallowed. 'I might just ...' She dragged her eyes round the room but there was no sign of anyone familiar. 'Is there a …?' She caught sight of a glass door, of black sky and the leaves of a plant. 'Are people outside?'

'I'll take you.' The tall guy opened out his arm. His shirt sleeve was rolled up, and as Bonnie moved forward and the arm settled across her shoulders she felt its hairs brush against her cheek. She could smell him, his warm body, strongly unfamiliar.

Outside in the cold air the sick feeling dissolved. She tipped her head back to the clean, open sky. 'Look at the stars.' Her voice went gliding out as if of its own accord.

A raggedy patch of lawn, fences shaggy with vines, a shed. An aeroplane passed low over the horizon, tiny lights blinking staidly. People stood in clusters on the oblong of brick paving. Pot smoke drifted, sharp, grassy.

'Let's go over here.' The man guided her across the bricks.

Bonnie let herself be led. She didn't look at who was standing by the door, who might be watching. Everything felt blurred, fractured. Sounds crashed in on her and receded — the throb of the music inside, a shard of talk, her own breathing. Out over the grass they went, and to Bonnie it was as if the darkness had weight, as if there were slabs of it that pressed at her, that shifted to let her through, and closed again behind.

'I've always wondered about you, Bonnie.' The man kept his arm around her. They stood side-by-side, backs to the fence, like spectators at some event. 'I always thought you were' — he spoke down into the cold air — 'different. Special.'

She couldn't help the sound, half snort, half giggle, that welled up in her throat. 'Really?'

'Yeah.' He sounded injured. 'Don't you believe me?' His fingers closed slightly further round her arm. He was leaning in, bringing his face level with hers.

'Not really.' A memory flared, tiny, distant — this man at other parties, at nightclubs, backstage after shows. Tall, long-limbed, a shock of hair. Always bent over some girl, slipping off with his arm around her. People smirking after him, raising eyebrows. He was a player. A cruising shark. *He says this to everyone*, came a small, very faraway warning in her head, but at the same time something fluttered awake, a response, flattered and heedless.

'Come on.' His fingers were touching her, lifting her chin. 'I've been watching you. Working that guitar. Doing your thing. Don't you know how beautiful you are?'

Bonnie didn't answer. She looked at him, his angular features, the dark of his eyes. *What are you doing?* sounded the warning voice.

'Bonnie.' His hands were either side of her face, on her hair, cupping her ears. Everything went muffled and close. She kept her eyes open as he kissed her, as he took her lower lip between his teeth and gently bit it, pushed his tongue into her mouth, but still — with her ears blocked and his face right there filling everything, and his body looming over her and moving even closer — still it didn't really feel like it was happening to her. Their teeth clashed. She wobbled, and the guy took her shoulders, steadied her.

She stared over at the shed, its one unlit window like an eye. 'I can't ...'

'Let's get out of here.' He ran his hand down her arm, took her hand. 'Where are you staying? Have you got a hotel room?'

She slid her eyes around the garden, the inky ruffles of the vine-draped fences, the spread of grass, the yellow windows of the house, the black shapes of people standing with arms folded, drinks catching the light. 'Okay,' she heard herself whisper.

And so together they were walking back into the house, through the rooms, the noise, the faces and figures and smoke in the air. Out again, the front this time. Down the narrow street, his arm around her, their steps moving in and out of time. To the main road, and before she knew it another taxi, another door opening. There was no thinking, no control, it was happening and she had nothing to do with it.

His hands on her. Their two bodies in the back seat. His mouth, his tongue, the air cool on her wet lips and chin when he pulled away. His fingers at the crotch of her jeans, working at the zip. His fingers inside her, the sting of her not-ready flesh catching, embarrassment dim and faint at how dry she was, at the legacy of three births — could he tell? — a distant voice, his, hers, or maybe it was both, whispering, 'Sorry.'

His breath tickling her ear. His murmur, 'Oh, Bonnie, Bonnie,' warm and close. The awful urge to laugh. He was putting it on. He was a bad actor. She didn't even find him sexy. *What are you doing?*

Him trying to kiss her again.

Then blankness, nothing.

'Bonnie?'

Or an echo of blankness because it was gone again, finished, she was coming straight back out of it. And down she came, rushing, sliding, hurtling dizzily, and — slam — like leaping awake to an alarm there she was back in her body.

'You okay? Bonnie?'

Lights through the car window, haloing his head. His arm across the seat back, across her shoulders.

'Bonnie?'

'Yeah. I'm okay.'

The feeling of his arm behind her neck, her hair pushed up at the back. Her jeans open, the scraped feeling in her vagina. The night flying by outside, whipping past, faster and faster. She gripped the door handle and tried to fix her eyes on the seat in front, to hold something still, to hold herself steady.

'Have you got a card?'

'What?'

'I think we need a card to make it work.'

The bank of buttons hung lifeless. A finger jabbed at one of them, kept jabbing. Bonnie watched it. The nail had purplish polish with a big jagged chip out of it. She closed her eyes and opened them again. The wall, the rows of buttons bulged towards her, wavered, and then smoothed out. She watched the finger and its hand drop and looked down at herself, her boots, her jeans, her top. Heard her own voice, thick and slow. 'Oh. It's me.'

Beside her the guy laughed. She turned to him. There was a mirror behind him, smoky glass. The lift. They were in the lift.

He laughed again, but then his face went serious. He bent towards her and frowned. 'Are you sure you're all right?' he said. 'I didn't realise you were so ...' He dropped his eyes. 'I think maybe I should just help you up to your room and then go.'

In the mirror Bonnie saw him reflected, his long back, the worn strip of his leather belt, his shirt half tucked in. And, peering out from around him, her own bleared empty face. She closed her eyes, shook her head, tipped forwards on her toes and pressed herself to his chest. She felt his arms go around her. *Fuck it*, she thought. *Fuck it, fuck it, fuck it.*

'Bonnie?'

She straightened up, let her bag slide down her arm and started digging through it. 'Got a card here somewhere.'

He kept a hand on her elbow as if she was an old woman. 'I'll just come up with you and then I'll leave,' he said. Even through the blur she could hear the edge of embarrassment in his voice.

Fuck it. 'No — stay.' She caught hold of the card, drew it out and fumbled with it at the slot. 'One more drink.'

'Bonnie?'

She opened her eyes. Tiles. Her elbows on her knees. Her head heavy in her hands.

'Bonnie?' A tapping at the door.

'Hang on.' She lurched to her feet and pulled up her jeans. Flushed the toilet and ran the tap in the basin. Liquid ripples of black hung at the edges of her vision. She felt huge, loud, her body crowding the tiny room. Her boots crashing on the floor. She tried to look in the mirror but she couldn't see her whole self, only bits at a time — her chin, her mouth with its traces of lipstick. Her hair, an earring. She leaned in, got a fix on one eye, right up close so it floated, enormous, the threads of red veins like a web dragging to the centre, the glaring pupil. *I hate you.* Her forehead touched against the cool surface.

'Bonnie?'

She scrabbled at the lock, wrestled the door open.

He stood uncertainly in the small dark hallway. 'I think I'm going to go.'

'Oh no — don't.' She saw her hand reach out, for his sleeve, clutch at it. 'Come on.' The weight of his flesh as her hands tried to turn him, manoeuvre him in the direction of the kitchenette. 'We're doing this now. Let's just have one more drink. We can sit out on the balcony.'

He stood still, resisting. 'No, look, I really think I should go.'

'Come on.' She left him, went past and opened the bar fridge. 'Let's see.' She watched her hand touch the bottles. 'We've got Crown Lager or very nasty white wine. Or UDLs that cost a frightening amount of money.'

He moved forward, near to the main door. 'This was a nice idea, Bonnie, but I think I should go.'

'Why?' She straightened up with a beer in each hand.

'I just — I think you're way drunker than me. I don't want to take advantage of you.'

210

'Oh, come on.' She went towards him, held out one of the bottles.

He kept his hands by his sides. 'No, really.'

'I promise it's okay.' She could hear her voice, slurring, brash, the words bouncing around the small room. *Shut up*, she thought, but there was something there, making her do this, pushing the words out, some flattened need that came from somewhere, she knew, that had some reason but she'd forgotten it, lost it in the fog.

'Thanks, anyway.' He went to the door. 'See you next time.' He went out and the heavy door swung and sighed shut behind him.

'Fuck,' she said. One of the beers slipped from her fingers and smashed on the floor. 'Fuck.' She shuffled away from the mess. Put the other bottle down on the bench. Found a tea towel — pristine, folded in a perfect rectangle — and knelt. The overhead light sparkled on the pool of beer, the glitters of glass, the lace of foam, the whole mess of it. She tried to pick up some of the glass and felt a piece push into her finger. A delayed intake of breath and a childish sob sounded, faintly, as if coming from elsewhere. She put her finger to her mouth, tasted the blood, warm and sweet.

She woke up sometime around dawn. The curtains were open, and the sky showed pale and pinkish. Birds were calling, rough, loud and exotic-sounding. A call she'd never heard before. Bonnie thought of claws gripping, solid bodies hung upside down from branches, big, curved beaks.

Her breasts ached, pushed against her bra. She could feel her pulse in them, and in her splitting head, her throat, her throbbing finger. She looked down at herself under the covers. All her clothes still on. Without sitting up she undid her jeans and wiggled out of them. Kicked them off the end of the mattress. She groped at the bedside table but there was no bottle or glass of water. She closed her eyes again, tried to ignore the dry of her mouth and the insistent fullness of her breasts. Breathed shallowly, drifted in and out of a hot, queasy doze. Started awake, turned to the other side, drifted again.

'Bonnie?'

She opened her eyes. There was someone at the door — a shadow with dark hair. Just for a second she thought it was the guy again, come back somehow. Hadn't he gone? Didn't those doors lock themselves when they shut? She covered her face with her arm, felt her throat fill with sick embarrassment.

'You awake?' It was Beth.

'Mm.' She kept her arm over her face. 'Kind of,' she said, and the words rasped out brokenly.

Beth's soft English voice was apologetic. 'It's almost eleven. The housekeepers are here. They want us to get out.'

'Okay.' Bonnie lay still.

Beth moved away, pulling the door shut behind her.

She lay a moment longer in the tick of her thick pulse and the grip of her nausea and slashing headache. She didn't want to think about anything, but her mind was beginning to creep towards it anyway, to send out tendrils. Back to last night, poking at that nerve-end of exquisite shame, the details that lay waiting in their drunk, fogged shrouds. And forward — and she threw back the covers and hauled herself up, hunched over the threatening heave of her stomach, reached with shaking hands for her jeans, her boots, her bag — forward to the flight she was about to miss, to the new flight she'd then have to pay for, to the heavy hopeless guilt of home, and Pete.

She hobbled from the lift, pushing her sunglasses onto her face. Half dragged, half carried her luggage to the desk. Leaned at the high marble counter. Caught sight of herself in the mirrored door to the office — a drained death-mask of a face, scarecrow hair, the black lenses of the glasses with their promise of hidden damage. There was a moment of fascinated shock that registered in the receptionist's eyes before she was able to recover her air of professional composure, and it almost brought a laugh swimming up through the churn of Bonnie's pain.

Her voice wavered out in a croak. 'Can you get me a cab, please? I'm running late.'

'Certainly,' said the receptionist, picking up a phone. 'Where are you going?'

'To the airport.' Bonnie sagged at the counter. She looked down at her pale wrists sticking out of the cuffs of her jacket, the bulging blue veins on the backs of her hands. She put the left hand over the right, to hide the brownish streaks of dried blood.

In the taxi she tried to clean her hand with spit and a tissue. The cut was small and pink, swollen at the edges. Bonnie dabbed at it, and it oozed new, thin blood. She wrapped the tattered tissue around her finger, clenched it back into her fist. She kept having to stop and lean forward, hold herself taut against surges of nausea. Every movement seemed a mammoth task. Slowly and laboriously she prepared for the airport: checked the printout with the flight details, readied her driver's licence, checked her mobile phone — no messages — and switched it off.

'I'm running really late,' she said to the driver, for possibly the third time.

'Doing my best, love.' He made no change to his driving. His left arm lay slack, the hand resting on the gearstick. Bonnie tried looking out the window, away from his infuriating calm. But the grey concrete barriers that lined the road — tall, like walls, like battlements, with their rows of rectangular holes from which the occasional plant sprouted, wildly, clawing skywards — made her feel worse, and she turned her eyes back to the safer immediate view of the seat in front, and the driver's unsympathetic arm.

She ran, past smokers and trolleys, through automatic doors, over the buffed floor. A thickset teenager carrying some enormous piece of sporting equipment in a soft case moved with impossible slowness in front of her, and she skittered from side to side, arms wrenching at the handles of her own baggage, elbow joints aflame, head pounding. 'Excuse me,' she hissed. 'Sorry. Excuse me.'

Past him and past one of the check-in lines, darting in while the man at the desk was still clicking something on his computer, and two wheelie suitcases blundered along the conveyor belt.

'Hey — there's a queue!' came a voice as she hefted her gear bag and guitar case onto the belt and slapped her licence on the counter.

'I'm sorry,' she panted. 'Melbourne. Can I still make it?'

The man gazed at her, then back at his screen. Then back at her. 'It's about to board,' he said. He looked about twenty. His eyebrows appeared to have been waxed.

'You can't just push in!' came the voice from behind.

Bonnie tried to swallow. Her mouth was so dry her tongue stuck to her teeth. 'Please?'

He picked up her licence, turned briskly to the screen. 'You'll really have to run.'

Through security, past the juice bars and coffee places, the doughnut shop, the displays of scarves and cosmetics. Dodging people, her overnight bag thumping on her shoulder, her full-to-bursting breasts shooting pain, the boarding docket gripped sweatily. The breath rattling in her chest.

'Just made it!' The woman in her neat uniform took her slip of paper and scanned it, smiling cautiously. 'You're the last one,' she said, and made a stiff, open-palmed gesture towards the empty low mouth of the boarding bridge.

Bonnie couldn't answer. Mutely she took back the docket and willed her legs to keep going, slower now but still an impossible effort, into the tunnel and along its airless length. Through the concertinaed entryway and into the whooshing hum of the plane. Down the aisle, wading through the false calm and the piped music, keeping her face upturned to the numbers, not looking at the rows of seated people, so close, giant blurred blobs. Reaching for the headrests as she went, hands shaking. Sweat prickling cold under the air conditioning. Her seat at last, almost at the back. She edged past someone's knees — a man, pants those light tan colour golfers wore — and sank down. Dropped her bag and pushed it under the seat in front with her foot. Clicked on her seatbelt. Leaned her head against the window. Jammed her trembling hands between her knees.

She could smell herself: stale and boozy with an acrid, panicky edge of sweat. Behind her sunglasses she snatched a look at the passenger next to her. Older, grey-haired, big and solid. A checked shirt, a newspaper. He appeared comfortably uninterested. *Calm down.* She closed her eyes. A recorded voice sounded, modulated politely, outlining safety and emergency procedures. She could hear the flight attendants going through their measured, purposeful demonstrations — the clink of seatbelt buckles, the rustle of lifejackets. The engines notched up their roaring. The plane began to move. She tried to steady her breathing, slow her heart, but the panic didn't recede. Instead a new terror rose, as if it had been waiting all along for her to stop, to sit still, to pay attention. Her heart knocked, the cold prickles broke afresh. *One hour and it'll be over. Just hold it together for one hour.* But up it shot, a vicious queasy dread. She couldn't sit still. Feverishly she shifted her legs and feet, crossed and uncrossed her arms. Twice she reached for the seatbelt, made to undo it, to get up, to barge out into the aisle and — do what? Scream? Vomit? Fall to the floor? She pictured the flight attendants rushing to her, calls for medical help or security, being led or carried back off into the airport. The rows of watchful faces, craning necks, papers and magazines lowered, whispers rippling.

The plane turned a corner, pulled out of its wobbling crawl. The sound of the engines built to open-throated gunning. She licked her lips, swallowed, took long, slow breaths. They were powering along the ground, swaying and jolting, and then with a surge they were up, climbing, the angle steep and sudden.

PETE OPENED THE DOOR. 'HI,' HE SAID, HIS VOICE CAREFUL, neutral — not normal and not unfriendly — and he smiled, a small smile. Then he registered her pallor, the mess of her slept-in make-up, and his expression faltered.

She reached out and gripped the doorframe. Time narrowed, and way off in the darkness she saw the tiny, lit-up circle of yesterday, shrinking even as she watched — yesterday, when the only thing between them was the whole business with the bet. Her legs trembled, and saliva ran into her mouth. She tightened her fingers. *He's ready to forgive you.*

'You okay?'

But she was pushing past him, running to the toilet. A flash of Edie's surprised face in the hallway, and then Bonnie was flinging the door shut behind her, lurching to her knees on the tiles, gripping the cold seat with both hands, vomiting.

She slumped on the couch with the baby at her breast, the twins either side, jumping on the cushions and yammering at her.

'Just go to bed,' said Pete, from the doorway.

'But hasn't my mum left?'

'Yeah, she's gone.'

'But don't you have to ...?' She couldn't look at him. She kept her eyes on Jess.

'It's all right.' No anger in his tone, but something — or was she imagining it? — some strangeness, some hesitation. 'Just go to bed.'

And so she did — dragged off her dirty clothes and sank into sleep.

When she woke up she could hear them in the kitchen. There was the smell of sausages. Bonnie lay staring at the wall, heavy and restless with guilt. She threw back the covers and sat up, but then lay down again. How could she face Pete? Look at him, talk to him? *Nothing actually happened*, she tried to tell herself. *Nothing serious.* But she could feel it still, as if her mouth was swollen, and her flesh tender where he'd touched. She bit her lips. *Act normal.* She cupped her hand between her legs and pressed. *Nothing happened.*

She showered, washed her hair. Put a bandaid on the cut on her finger.

Pete was sitting with his back to her when she entered the room.

'I'm sorry,' she said, softly, as she passed him.

'So you had a big night?' His voice sounded friendly, jovial — intentionally so — and she was unprepared for the flood of fresh guilt it brought, awful, coarse, as unbearable as physical pain.

She bent to put her arm around Edie, hid her face in the girl's hair. 'Yeah,' she mumbled.

'How was the show?'

'Good.' She fetched herself a plate and cutlery. Her face was hot, her damp hair and scalp itchy. She glanced at Pete this time, as she sat down, but he was busy cutting up Louie's sausage.

She put a sausage on her own plate, and a mound of mashed potato, carrots, peas. 'Thanks for cooking,' she said, eyes on the food.

Louie's voice rang out, like an actor speaking a part. 'What happened to your finger, Mum?'

Edie sat forward. 'What finger?'

Bonnie looked up. Their clear faces, waiting. She held up the finger, the fresh bandaid glaring under the light. The twins leaned in. 'I cut it,' she said, her voice thick and stupid in her ears.

'How?' said Edie.

'On a guitar string.' She kept her eyes on the finger, Pete a shape at the edge of her vision.

'But how?'

Silence from Pete, but she felt frozen under his gaze. 'Well' — and even this little lie seemed to advertise itself in the way the words came out, misshapen, ugly — 'you know how the strings of a guitar are wound onto the tuning pegs at the top?'

No answer from anyone.

Bonnie sat with her stupid finger upheld, her voice clanking on and on. 'Well, the strings are wound onto the pegs, and then you cut them off, and the ends are really spiky and sharp.' Was anyone even listening? She couldn't raise her eyes to check. 'And sometimes they can sort of stab into your finger. If …' She lowered her hand at last. 'If you forget to be careful.' She stared down at her plate. *This is impossible. You can't keep this up.*

There was a pause, and then Louie said, 'More tomato sauce, please.'

They ate. Bonnie couldn't stop. She bolted the food, gobbled it, everything on her plate and then a whole second helping of everything, and then the twins' leftovers. She ate until her stomach hurt, cramming in the mouthfuls, watching only her own hands slicing with the knife and loading the fork.

And somehow, with the busy screen of her eating, and the demands and noise of the children, the meal passed with no further talk between her and Pete.

Then there were the dishes, and the bath, and pyjamas and reading books and bedtime, and Bonnie lumbered through it all with her head down, riding the sawing waves of guilt, feeling like her every movement, her every interaction with Pete — 'Did you brush Edie's teeth?' 'Do you know where Louie's pyjamas are?' — groaned and strained with the same falseness as the bandaid conversation, and the heavy certainty that Pete must know something had happened, he must be able to tell, there was no way he couldn't. She could feel it hanging anyway, waiting — the moment when they would be alone together, and he would look at her properly, when she could no longer hide from him.

'Did you see my new lucky charm?' said Louie, as she sat on the edge of his bed to kiss him goodnight.

'Lucky charm?'

'Yeah.' Louie sat up and reached into the shelf beside the bed. 'See?' He held out a small dark object. Bonnie took it. A wooden carving, some kind of warrior with popping eyes and bared teeth, jagged hair, arms akimbo. Between the sturdy legs a little penis and testicles.

'Wow,' she said, handing it back. 'Where'd you get that?'

'Doug.'

A coldness stirred in her chest. 'Doug?'

'Yeah.' Louie reached into the shelf again and set the carving carefully down, as far from the bed as possible. 'Edie's got one too. It's meant to be good luck, but I'm a bit scared of it.'

'Look at mine, Mum,' said Edie, sliding down from her bed and coming over. 'It's a woman one.'

Bonnie held the carving in her palm. It had the same staring eyes. Round breasts this time, wide hips and a triangle between the solid thighs. An etched grin that seemed lascivious, knowing.

'I'm a bit scared of mine too,' whispered Edie, leaning over Bonnie's legs.

'They are a bit scary,' said Bonnie slowly. She closed her fingers over the carved woman's face. 'So ... did Doug ... come over?'

'Yeah.' Edie climbed up onto her lap. 'While you were in Sydney.'

'Yesterday? During the day?'

'It was night-time. We were in bed, but Dad let us get up.'

'Oh.' She pulled Edie close, kissed her hair. 'So he's back from his holiday.'

'He gave Dad a bottle of wine or something,' said Edie. 'Booze. But he didn't have a present for Grandma.'

'Guess what he did?' Louie bounced on his knees on the mattress. 'On his holiday?'

'What?'

Louie put his face close to hers, eyes wide. 'Rode on an elephant!'

'Did he? Wow.' She stood up, sliding Edie from her lap. 'Okay, into bed and lie down now, you two. It's late.'

She still had the carved woman in her hand when she left the room and went out to the kitchen. She stood on tiptoe and tossed it onto the top of the fridge, right at the back behind all the other junk.

She waited while Pete said goodnight to the children. She stood in the middle of the room, not knowing what to do with her hands, and then at the last moment when she heard him coming she scuttled to the bench and started wiping the dishes and putting them away.

He came up behind her, and when he reached around her in a hug she jumped.

'Oh.' Her voice was high and breathless. 'You gave me a fright.'

'Sorry.' Pete loosened his grip and rubbed her arm. 'You okay?'

She gripped a plate inside the tea towel. Her fingers felt weak. 'Yeah. I just — I'm really tired.'

Pete kept touching her, his hand moving slowly up and down her arm. He leaned into her. 'I'm sorry about yesterday,' he said. 'I was just so pissed off that your mum was going to be late.'

Bonnie lowered the plate carefully to the bench. 'Did she … was everything okay?'

'Yeah, it was fine.' Pete kissed her on the neck. 'She was quite good actually. She cooked a nice dinner. And she did Jess's bottle at six this morning, and made breakfast and everything.'

'That's great.'

There was a pause. Pete's breath tickled her neck. 'Doug came round.' His voice sounded easy, normal.

'Oh.'

'Yeah — he's back. He's looking for a flat I think, so he can finally get out of that shed or whatever it is. He's going to try and get a business going, fixing up vintage furniture.'

She felt a stirring of the old irritation. 'So he's not coming back here? To help finish off the Grant job?'

'No.' He kissed her again. 'But we'll be all right. We'll get through it. I had another look at the books last night and it's not as bad as I thought. The debts … it's not impossible, it'll just mean a few lean months. I just … you know I don't like owing money.'

She tried to pick up the frying pan to dry it, but Pete's weight over her shoulders made it awkward. She stopped and just stood, holding the tea towel, her head down. 'I'm …' She put her hands up and over his. 'I'm sorry about today,' she said. 'Sorry you had to give up your afternoon to look after the kids.'

'It's all right.' He pulled her closer. 'So what happened?

You were a mess. Did Mickey take you out on the town?'

Bonnie felt her throat go thick. 'Yeah.'

'Where'd you go?'

She closed her eyes. 'Just to a bar.'

'Oh yeah. Was it fun?'

'Not really.' Her heart thrummed. How could he be so unsuspecting? Couldn't he feel her strangeness, her nerves? She bent her knees, tried to ease herself out from his hold. 'I mean, it was okay … I don't know how I got so drunk. I guess I'm just out of practice.' She moved forward, away from him. 'I'm so tired.' She picked up the frying pan. 'I'm just going to finish these and then I have to go to bed.'

'Really?' He moved in again, arms around her waist this time.

She wiped the tea towel over the pan. The thought of sex with Pete, of being close, their two bodies, their faces, kissing, set her jangling with fear. He would know then, for sure — see it in her. She could picture him, drawing back, his gentle, questioning frown. 'I'm sorry,' she said. 'I'm just exhausted.'

'Fair enough.' He yawned. 'Wish I could go to bed.' He kissed her quickly one last time, reaching round to her cheek. 'I'll be in later. Sweet dreams.'

His footsteps over to the door, the chime of the bells, the rush of cold air, the door closing, and he was gone.

She stood twisting the tea towel, wringing it in her hands. *This is crazy.*

She finished the dishes. She checked the children and brushed her teeth. She moved slowly — her body numb and clumsy, like a car with bad steering and worn brakes. All she wanted was to sleep, to get to bed and to sleep, to shut herself down.

In the bedroom her clothes still lay on the floor — her best jeans and the tunic top. The zipper of the jeans caught the light from the hallway, open in a grin. She stepped over them and then turned and kicked, her foot hooking under the denim. They flew out of sight, behind the door.

She woke in the night, woke herself up talking aloud, speaking out from some black dream.

Quiet. Pete's even breathing beside her. The hallway light through the gap in the almost-closed door. Their house, its smell, everything the same, but inside her this insistent balloon of guilt straining, bringing her out of sleep. She put the heels of her hands to her eyes and pressed. Circles of silver and blue burst and faded, and from them an image swam up: Pete, all those years ago, sitting at a share-house kitchen table on their first morning together. The happy jolt she'd felt when he spoke those words like a child. *I wish you could stay.* As if he was presenting her with an offering — the gift of his honesty — and the coming-home feeling, the recognition she'd felt in accepting it.

She turned to him sleeping beside her. She could see the rise of his cheek, the line of his brow. She could smell him, sweet wood, sawdust, and his own warm smell, his skin.

Under the covers her thumb sought out the sore finger, picked at the bandaid, pushed it down. With her thumbnail she dug at the cut, brought pain flaring bright in the darkness. There was no hiding. Even if he never noticed, if her guilt never showed enough to alert him — and he wouldn't be looking for it anyway — she couldn't keep carrying it around like this. She curled on her side with her knees up, tucked her hands in together against her chest. *You'll have to tell him something.* She trawled for words. *I was so drunk ... there was this guy, and ...* She mashed her lips between her teeth. *I just, I was so drunk. But, Pete, Pete — nothing actually happened.*

Jess didn't cry for her early feed the next morning. Bonnie woke to Louie crawling in under the covers on her side of the bed. She wriggled over, and Pete's arm went round her automatically. She lay sandwiched between them, and there was a delicious long moment before she remembered — before it came lunging at her again, snapped her completely awake.

Then Jess did start to cry.

'What time is it?' said Pete.

She lifted her head to see the clock. 'Quarter to seven.' When she lay back again she could feel him behind her, their bodies touching all the way down, the easy way his arm resettled around her, and her flesh shrank in shame.

Pete yawned. He gave her a squeeze and sat up. 'I'll get her.'

She stayed where she was, Louie tucked in at her front. The guilt gave a fresh surge. *Oh god, Pete*, she thought. *Don't be extra nice — don't make this even harder.* She put her nose to the soft nape of Louie's neck. 'You sure?'

'Yeah. I'm up now.' Pete, in his t-shirt and boxer shorts, was groping around on the floor. 'Are these my jeans or yours?'

There was a crash from the other end of the house, a pause, and then Edie's cry. 'Mum!'

Bonnie sat up. 'What was that?'

Pete didn't answer.

'Watch out, Lou.' She pulled back the covers and climbed over him. 'Did you hear that?' she said to Pete.

Pete was standing near the doorway, his back to her.

'Mum!' came Edie's call. 'I accidentally dropped the milk!'

Jess wailed.

'Bloody hell,' muttered Bonnie. She grabbed her dressing-gown. 'I'll get Jess then, if you can deal with Edie?'

'She's dropped the milk,' said Louie helpfully, from the bed.

'Pete?' Bonnie looked up from tying the belt.

No answer.

'In the kitchen,' said Louie.

Jess was screaming now.

'I'll get Jess,' she said again, and went out to the hallway. As she passed Pete he shuffled around, keeping his back to her, his shoulders forward, as if protecting something. She was hit by a displaced, uncomfortable feeling of having intruded on some private act, like masturbating, or an intimate hygiene ritual. *Strange*, she thought, rushing towards Jess. *What's he doing?*

She heard him while she was in Jess's room, his heavy tread in the hallway. Then, back in bed, as she lay feeding the baby she could hear from the kitchen the reedy voices of the twins, crisscrossing, and the occasional deep bass note of Pete's. She closed her eyes, felt Jess's dense body against hers, listened. There was the sound of the shower starting up, Edie yelling from the living room, 'Louie! Come and play train tracks!'

Bonnie kept her eyes closed, anchored in the warm dark by the pull of Jess's sucking. She let herself drift into hope. If she could just find the right way to tell Pete, the right thing to say, then maybe it was possible, after all, for everything to continue. The five of them, their family, spinning on, moving in the paths of their beautiful, sensible constellation. What happened in Sydney absolved, erased, dropped into the black.

She put Jess in her baby chair on the bathroom floor and showered. The smell of Pete's shaving cream was in the face washer when she used it, and the grain of guilt rose again, insistent, caught and snagged.

Jess kicked in her chair.

Bonnie pushed aside the curtain and reached for a towel.

Jess frowned and made a wet, protesting sound.

'It's okay, Jess.' She dried herself, wrapped herself in the towel, lifted the baby. She kissed her hungrily, held her close, but it didn't work. In the cold air of the bathroom the hope was evaporating.

When she went into the kitchen Pete got up from the table, brushing past her without speaking or making eye contact.

Bonnie stood frozen. *He knows.* The certainty came dropping down inside her, quick and final, like a coin falling into a slot.

After a moment she followed. He'd gone into the bedroom and shut the door.

'Mum,' said Edie from the living-room doorway. 'Will Douggie work in the workshop again now?'

'I don't know,' she said, faintly.

'Can I have more toast?' said Edie.

'Please?' said Bonnie, automatically.

'Please?'

Bonnie went back into the kitchen, strapped Jess in her high chair. Her heart thumped. She moved into the hallway again, towards the bedroom door. *How could he know?* She crept closer.

The door opened. Pete stepped forward, doing up the zip of his jacket. He saw her and stopped. His face was closed, stony.

She spoke before she could think. 'I need to talk to you.'

He didn't answer. He dropped his eyes and moved past.

Bonnie turned and went after him. 'I need to talk to you,' she said again, hearing her voice, its desperate upwards slide.

Pete walked down the hallway, through the kitchen and out the door.

She faltered by the table. 'Maybe later?'

But the door was shut. He was gone.

She took the children to the park.

She sat with Jess on her lap while the twins ran and climbed and swung and slid.

How could he know?

'Look at me! Mum!'

All of a sudden, like that?

'Mum! Mum!'

Could someone have told him? A phone call, this morning? An email?

'Mum!'

Someone who was at the party?

'Mum!'

Who saw the kiss?

'Mu-UM!'

She let her mind dip into the awful shame-filled black of her recent memory — the night, the party, the man. *Who was there? Who saw you leave with him? Who would know Pete, be able to contact him? Mickey? Would she do that?*

'Mu-UM!'

Who cares? He knows something happened, that's what matters. And he probably thinks it was worse than it actually was.

'Look at me! Watch this!'

He knows, and he thinks you were never going to tell him.

'Mu-UM!'

'Great!' called Bonnie, weakly. She held Jess closer against the cold wind and stared out at the street, the passing traffic. A van went by, yellow, shabby, rust-spotted. Her scalp prickled. She pictured Doug sitting on the end of Louie's bed, holding out the little carvings, the warrior and the sly-smiling woman. Her two children in their pyjamas, arms reaching, receiving. Doug's own sly grin, his cigarette stink and dirty clothes, his presence reaching into every corner of the room. Her children's bedroom. Rage and fear tore at her. She stood, clutching Jess.

The wind blew her hair into her eyes and mouth. Why was she so hopeless? She should have done something ages ago, stood up to Doug, forced him out. A sound broke from her, a wild, despairing sob. She sank back down on the bench. She was hopeless, hopeless; she'd fucked it all up.

When she returned to the house there was a note on the kitchen table. Pete's writing, but unsigned. *Back later,* was all it said.

She marched into the living room and put on the television, found a kids' show.

'TV?' said Edie.

'TV!' said Louie.

Like zombies they stood before the screen, arms dangling.

'Sit on the couch,' she said, and slowly, stares fixed, they reversed up to it, climbed on.

She went to the bedroom, lay on her side in the bed, feeding Jess. The baby looked up at her, one hand gripping the edge of the covers. She watched her daughter fill up, her sucking slow, her long and searching look waver, her eyelids drop, once, twice, slowly, reluctantly, and then a final time, into sleep.

She waited a bit and then pulled away gently. Jess's mouth made a languorous empty sucking motion, and then she sighed and slept on. Bonnie rolled over and faced the other way. She lay gazing at Pete's pillow. What was she going to say, to tell him, when the time came? *Think, think,* she told herself, but a great, desolate blankness settled in her. She tried to let go, to feel, but nothing came — she didn't even want to cry. After a while she closed her eyes and slept too.

'Mum?'

It was Edie, standing by the bed. Bonnie gasped, half sat up.

'I'm hungry.'

Jess was stirring, frowning and stretching out her arms, eyes still shut.

'Shh.' Bonnie put her finger to her lips.

'I'm hungry,' Edie whispered.

Jess's eyes opened.

'She's awake,' whispered Edie.

Bonnie sighed. 'I know.' She drew back the covers and picked up the baby, glanced at the clock. 'Oh my god,' she said. 'It's two-thirty.'

Edie flopped onto the bed and kicked her legs up. 'We watched *so* much TV,' she said in a satisfied voice.

Bonnie groaned and stood up.

She went out into the hallway. No sign of Pete. In the kitchen she checked her phone, and the home phone. No messages, no missed calls. She walked around the room with the baby in her arms.

'I'm hungry,' said Edie.

'Okay, okay,' she said, pacing. 'I'll get you something to eat. Hang on.' She went to the fridge and opened it, stared into it, closed it again.

'Mum!'

'What?' She tried to focus on Edie's face, but her head felt too fuzzy. Jess wriggled and she switched her to the other hip.

'I'm hungry!'

'Okay, okay.' Bonnie opened the fridge again and took out a block of cheese. She set it on the bench and picked up a knife, struggling to pull back the wrapping from the cheese with Jess in one arm. The knife fell to the floor. 'Oh god.' Her voice sounded like someone else's, a feeble whine. 'What am I doing?'

She went around the table and tried to put Jess in her baby chair, but the child clung to her arms, grizzling.

'Mum?' It was Louie now, coming in from the living room. 'I'm hungry.'

'I know!' She knelt, still holding the baby. 'I know!' Tears rose at last, hot in her eyes. 'I can't …' She put her head back, looked up at the ceiling and away from the watching faces of her children. 'I just can't deal with this!'

Pete didn't come back. Neither phone rang, and there were no text messages. She stumbled through the afternoon and into the evening, making cheese on toast, cutting up fruit, leaving the mess on the table, wiping noses, doing up shoes, reading stories in automatic mode, staring sightlessly at the pages. She paced, unable to keep still, wandering from room to room, driven by some mindless, restless energy, the thinking part of her brain switched off. It was like being in labour. What she might actually say to Pete, how to explain herself — coming up with any kind of plan — was unreachable, beyond her.

She heated baked beans for dinner, bathed the children, put them to bed.

'Where's Dad?' said Edie at one point.

'I don't know.'

But Edie was waiting, and Bonnie saw that more was expected of her.

'Out somewhere,' she said, trying to sound normal. 'He'll be back later.'

It seemed to be enough.

She stood with the phone in her hand. She selected the *recent calls* icon and *Pete mobile* came up, top of the list. She hovered her thumb over the *call* button.

But then she saw his note on the bench, the two stark words. *And don't call me*, it might as well have said — and she took her thumb away, put the phone back down.

She woke, and it was dark. The house quiet. The bed empty beside her. She fumbled for the bedside lamp. Outside the pool of light the edges of the room retreated. A terrible thought came to her: what if Pete had returned, taken the children and gone? What if she was alone in the house? Fear wrenched at her.

She got up. The floorboards were cold. She pulled on her ugg boots, tugged the old blue dressing-gown off the edge of the chair and put it around herself. Crept out into the hallway. Silence. The tangle of kids' clothing where she'd left it outside the bathroom door. Shoes kicked off.

She went to Jess's room. Turned the knob in practised silence and opened the door. There she was. Sleeping. Arms up either side of her head. Blankets tucked in. The side of the cot up. The heater on, ticking comfortably. She closed the door again. Went to the twins' room. Checked them, a head on each pillow, their slow sleepers' breaths.

In the hallway again she stood and listened. Silence and darkness in the living room. She went to the kitchen. Light on but empty. The dishes as she'd left them, half done. Crumbs on the table. But a bottle of wine on the bench, open. And a pack of tobacco and papers.

She stood at the back door, peered out through the glass. Pete was sitting on the porch steps. She saw the glow of the tip of a cigarette, then the flurry of sparks as he stubbed it out on the concrete and got up.

She stepped back.

He came right in before he saw her. 'What're you doing?' he said, as if talking to one of the children. 'I thought you were asleep.'

Bonnie drew the dressing-gown closer around herself. She felt self-conscious, ridiculous in her layers of clothing, vulnerable next to Pete in his day clothes and jacket, shoes still on.

'You should go back to bed.' He went to the bin and threw in the cigarette butt, poured more wine.

She swallowed. *Don't cry. It'll just annoy him.* 'Can we talk?' she said. 'About what's going on?'

He sighed and picked up his glass. 'Okay.' Annoyance did seem to show on his face, as if she really was a child making untimely demands, someone he had to both indulge and be responsible for. He didn't offer her a drink.

Bonnie followed him down the hallway and sat while he lit the heater and perched at the far end of the couch, away from her.

'So,' he said, staring down at his glass. 'What're you going to tell me?'

'Pete.' Bonnie's voice blared in her own ears. She had no idea what she was going to say. In the light from the heater he looked so young. Younger than her. He could be twenty. *How were you — how were they, the two of them — supposed to manage something like this?* Her shoulders ached, and her back.

He didn't move or look at her.

'I've never lied to you,' went her blaring voice. 'You know that.'

He didn't answer.

'In Sydney. I did something.'

'Go on.' He was rubbing one thumb over the knuckle of the other. She could hear the rasp of his rough, dry skin.

'I just — after what happened with the bet and everything — I just felt so horrible. I hated myself so much.' Her voice was coming back down now, sounded closer, more real. 'After the show there was a party. I was so drunk. And this guy, some guy, I don't even know his name ...' She leaned towards him. 'I didn't even *like* him, Pete, you have to believe me.'

'But you still fucked him.' He kept his eyes down. Bonnie

had never heard his voice so thick and mean. He made it sound like the ugliest word in the world.

'No — no!' Her hands were clenched in her lap. 'I didn't. I ... I was so drunk. He just helped me back to the hotel. And he left.'

The heater hummed and zipped, liquid orange now. One side of Bonnie's face felt scorched. She put her hand to her cheek.

'Are you sure?'

She dropped her eyes. 'What do you mean? Of course I'm sure. Nothing happened. We just ... we left the party together and ...' She crossed her legs, squeezed all the muscles in her thighs and between her legs, feeling those fingers again, the rawness of her too-dry flesh. *Oh, Pete. How can I make you understand? It wasn't sex. Or lust or fun or anything. It was the opposite.*

'So what about the condom?' Pete's thumb kept up its rasping.

'What condom?' But even as she said it the memory came bouncing up, as if a lid had been lifted, a button pressed. The hotel, the bathroom. Her hateful reflection in the mirror. Swivelling, her boots echoing in the tiny room. Swivelling back, swaying, leaning over the counter. Beth's make-up bag. The spill of tubes and pencils, toothbrush and paste, the strip of little squares with their perforated seams. Their padded feel under her fingers, their anonymous neat shapes.

'The condom that fell out of your jeans pocket when I picked them up this morning.' He turned back to the heater, lifted his glass.

She could see the anger in the movement of his arm, the jerk of his head as he drank. She squeezed her muscles tighter. *Shit.* The memory floated before her, luminous. Her crumpled, drunken face, her voice slurring, begging him to stay. *Nothing happened. Nothing happened. You wouldn't have gone through with it.*

'Pete.'

'What?' There was an edge to his voice now.

'I didn't mean to …'

'What, you didn't mean to stop the taxi and go into a shop and buy condoms? Or, I don't know, get one from one of those vending machines at a pub or something? How can you not mean to get a condom, Bonnie, to put it in your pocket?'

There was a catch in her throat, a hopeless ache. 'I was at the hotel. I went to the toilet, to the bathroom — I was sharing with the bass player — and her stuff was in there. Her make-up and stuff. In this bag, on the bench, and it was open.' Tears were in her eyes and through them her hands turned into fat, pink blurs in her lap. 'And I just — I just took one, without thinking, you know. I was so drunk.'

'So the guy had already left and you were just so drunk you took a condom and put it in your pocket for no reason.'

'No.' She blinked and the tears fell onto her laced fingers. 'No, he was still there.'

'I thought you said he just took you back to the hotel.'

'No. He came up to the room.'

'Bonnie.' Pete shifted abruptly on the couch, licked his lips. He spoke slowly, as if having to let each word out with restraint in order to prevent an avalanche of anger. 'Can you just please tell me the fucking truth because I can't — I really can't sit here much longer trying to piece it together, okay?'

'Okay.' She was crying properly now but she didn't try to stop it. Her face felt raw and strained. 'Okay. We went to the hotel, just to have a drink. And he was about to go and I went to the toilet and I saw the condoms and I took one because I — I don't know why.' A sound burst from her, a kind of choked flat laugh. 'I didn't like him. I wasn't attracted to him. He didn't turn me on. When he said stuff to me it made me want to laugh. When he touched me it was embarrassing.'

235

Pete sat with his head down.

'I was so drunk, Pete. I didn't know what I was doing.'

He didn't move.

Bonnie's words were blurred with her sobbing. 'Nothing happened, Pete. Nothing actually happened.'

He stood up. He didn't look at her.

She put her hands over her face. 'I know you probably don't want to hear this right now and I don't know if it'll make any difference, but I love you. I love you so much, and the kids, and everything, our life together. I don't want to lose any of it.'

She pressed her fingers to her eyes. She heard him move. He was going to the door.

'I can't listen to any more of this,' he said in a low voice.

Bonnie lay in the dark. She took one hand in the other and squeezed it, pushed at the scabbed-over cut. A jab of soreness, but not enough. She dug with her nail, dug till pain came shooting and fresh tears popped into her eyes. *Fuck*, she thought. *Fuck, fuck, fuck.*

She woke to the sound of Jess crying. She pulled back the covers and sat up, but there was movement in the hallway and the crying stopped.

Pete came in carrying the baby. He was still in his clothes.

'What time is it?' She reached for the clock. 'Jesus, Pete, it's five-thirty. Have you been up all night? What've you …?'

Pete passed Jess down. 'I'm going.'

'What?' she said, thickly. 'Where?'

'I don't know. To stay with friends.' He wasn't looking at her. 'For a while.'

Bonnie sagged back into the pillow with Jess grabbing at her, rubbing her face on her top, making hungry sounds.

Pete went back across the room.

'Wait!' She sat up. 'How long for?'

'I don't know.' He pulled his overnight bag from under the chest of drawers and stuffed clothes into it.

Jess started to cry.

'But where are you going? Which friends?'

He didn't answer. He zipped the bag and went out.

'He's what?'

Bonnie held the phone further away from her ear. 'It's probably just for a little while,' she heard herself say. 'It's not —'

'What happened?'

'Nothing!' She glanced down the hallway. 'Nothing actually *happened*, but …' She went into the bedroom and half shut the door. 'Mum.' She stood in the middle of the room, head down, spare arm clamped across her body. She tried to speak quietly. 'In Sydney. The other night. I — Pete and I, we'd been fighting, and I just …'

Don't tell her.

Bonnie gulped, struggled, but the words were coming out. 'I just hated myself so much.'

Suzanne's tongue-click sounded through the phone.

Don't tell her.

But she was sliding towards confession now, the collapsing relief of it. 'I got really drunk, and there was this guy, at a party.' She spoke in a rush. 'And I took him back to the hotel …'

The click again.

'And, I mean, nothing really happened, in the end. I mean, we didn't, you know, have sex.'

'Bonnie!'

'But I still — I betrayed Pete.' She tried to control the crying, to keep it quiet — she could hear one of the children running past — but it was getting away from her.

'Bonnie.' Suzanne's tone was firm. 'Calm down. I'm sure

this isn't as bad as you think.' There was a moment's pause, and Bonnie pictured her mother glancing at her watch. 'Look.' A brief sigh. 'I'll come over, okay? I'll be there soon.'

'Mu-um!' It was Edie, out in the hallway.

'Okay?' said Suzanne. 'Darling?'

Bonnie's whisper wobbled and scraped. 'Okay.'

'Mu-UM!'

Bonnie hung up the phone and crouched by the bed, trying to breathe evenly, to rein herself in.

'MUM!' yelled Edie. 'Where are you?'

She flattened herself to the floor and pressed her face into the crook of her arm.

'What did you *tell* him for?' Suzanne pulled out a chair and brushed her hand over the seat before sitting down.

'Well, he kind of … It's complicated, but he would've found out anyway.' Bonnie stood at the back door.

'But I thought you said nothing actually happened.'

She put her face closer to the glass. 'Yeah, but …' The twins digging in the dirt were two blockish shapes, bright red and blue in their jumpers, the garden around them layers of watery grey and green, the black workshop hulking behind. Bonnie let her gaze float past them all, up into the cold white sky. 'I still … It was a betrayal.' Her voice was high and caught at the back of her throat. 'I've fucked everything up. I mean, I didn't even *like* the guy.'

'But, Bonnie … Look.' Suzanne shifted in her chair. 'These things happen. You'd be surprised how often they happen. And you'd be surprised who does them.'

'But —'

'What I'm saying is, it's not the end of the world.'

'But how can he … how can … I mean, if Pete did something like that to me I don't know if I could ever …'

'Don't start thinking about that. None of that matters. You have a life together. You have children. There's a lot at stake.'

'Yeah, but, Mum —'

'So what's going to happen now?'

Bonnie put her hands over her face. 'I don't know.'

Suzanne drew a breath in through her nose. 'Well, the two of you would be fools to throw it all away — everything you've got.'

'I realise that.'

'It's not easy on your own, with kids.'

'Jesus, Mum, I know.' Bonnie could feel her face getting hot.

'Remember Jan? I mean her life was bloody miserable — cooped up in that council flat all on her own. Those kids just constantly —'

'I know! I know how hard it is, Mum. I don't want to break up with Pete.'

'Bonnie. Listen. These things happen. You need to get Pete back, you need to both just forget about all this, and you need to just … get on with it.'

She lay on the bed. She could hear Suzanne and the twins in the living room.

'No — Edie. You stay here with me, please. Mummy's just having a lie-down. She needs a bit of a rest. Now. Who can do this puzzle?'

Bonnie closed her eyes. *Think*, she told herself. But nothing came. None of it seemed real.

Sleep then. Rest. But every time she closed her eyes they opened again. She stretched out her neck, made her arms and legs soften into the mattress. Then felt them all draw back into tightness again, as she stared at the ceiling.

'Where's he gone anyway?' said Suzanne later, as they hung clothes on the line.

Bonnie looked up into the grey sky. 'I don't know.'

'Well, where did he say he was going?'

'To stay with friends.'

'But he didn't say which friends?'

Bonnie sighed. Her throat hurt. 'No,' she said in a low voice.

Suzanne clicked her tongue. 'Well, did you ask?'

'Yes, I did.' She picked up more clothes from the basket. 'But he didn't tell me.'

Suzanne clipped pegs on briskly. There was the sound of the twins shrieking in the house.

She thinks you're hopeless. She felt her ears go hot. 'He just said he was staying with friends,' she repeated.

'Not what's-his-name,' said Suzanne.

'Who?' Bonnie could feel the heat creeping into her face, and at the same time a shrinking feeling in her stomach, the tender trembling of her own suspicions. Pete's words, the other night. *Doug came round. He's looking for a flat.*

'You know — the lame duck, what's-his-name? The one who was helping in the workshop, making a pest of himself.'

She swallowed. 'Doug.' Her voice shook.

Suzanne made a sharp, frustrated sound. She turned to Bonnie, a towel in her hands. 'Why didn't you do something about that, that … situation?'

Bonnie kept her eyes on the line, on her own hands spreading a pillow case. 'I don't know.'

'Why didn't you bloody well get rid of that feller? Pete was never going to — you knew that.'

In her head Bonnie saw Pete and Doug, the two of them, together in a flat with no furniture. Drinking and staying up late. Watching the races on some crappy little TV. A record player set up maybe, a crate of old records from their punk days. Eating toast and takeaway, getting the newspaper from the local milk bar. Like old times. Two men with nothing to worry about but their own immediate needs. Going on with their unfathomable, unexamined friendship as if more than ten years hadn't passed. As if she and the kids, Pete's business — none of it — had ever happened.

Suzanne bent to the basket. 'Someone has to take charge, with these things. You can't just drift along and trust everything will be okay.'

Bonnie stood staring at nothing.

Suzanne clipped up the last towel and turned. 'Can you? Darling?' She came closer, reached out and touched Bonnie's arm. 'Never mind,' she said. 'It'll be all right. Come on. I'll make you a cup of tea. God knows, I need one myself.'

Jess had a fever. She whinged all afternoon, protested during her usual naptime. Her eyes and nose ran, she rubbed at her ears.

'Can't you just dose her up with something?' said Suzanne impatiently as they stood at the kitchen bench, Bonnie jiggling the baby on her hip. 'Panadol? Or what's that other one — that makes them sleep?'

'Phenergan?' Bonnie allowed herself a dry laugh. 'I think they've changed the rules on that one. I don't think it's actually very good for kids.'

'Well, you had it.' Suzanne lined up a handful of green beans on the chopping board and sliced off their tops. 'You turned out all right.'

Bonnie took a careful breath. 'I'll give her Panadol if she can't sleep tonight,' she said. 'But they say it's best not to, if they're not suffering too much — it's best to let the fever do its work, fighting the bug or whatever.'

Suzanne sniffed.

Jess put the backs of her little fists to her face and began to cry.

'You're not feeling too good, are you, possum?' Bonnie sat down and put the baby to her breast.

'Didn't you just feed her?' Suzanne brought the knife down on another bundle of beans.

She didn't look up. Her neck ached. *Just ignore it*, she told herself. She smoothed the moist hairs back from Jess's forehead.

'I'm sure you just fed her only half an hour ago. Won't she have some dinner? Doesn't she have solids now?'

Ignore it. Bonnie tried to sit straighter in the chair, to ease her neck and shoulders.

Suzanne lifted the chopping board and swept the beans into the top of the steamer. 'Surely you don't need to be wearing yourself out breastfeeding all the time. Shall I pop her in the pram and take her for a quick walk? Would that settle her?'

Bonnie touched the backs of her fingers to Jess's burning cheek. *If it was up to you*, a voice inside her shouted, *you'd shove her in a room and shut the door and leave her to cry, like you probably did with me.* She breathed slowly. 'Thanks, Mum, but I think I'll just feed her and try to put her to bed.'

There was quiet for a while — the muted burble of the twins' talking book from down the hall.

Suzanne pulled open a drawer. 'Well, you're not helping anyone being a martyr. Least of all yourself.'

Bonnie adjusted her grip on the baby and, with her still attached, stood up and left the room.

They fed the children and got them to bed, side by side, cool and careful, not looking at each other. *This is ridiculous*, thought Bonnie. *Someone else to feel weird around.* But the prospect of a confrontation exhausted her. It was easier just to press on like this, to retreat into wounded distance. To let her tiredness push aside the frustration, the guilt, the whole tricky mess of feelings.

'Where's Dad?' said Louie as he lay in bed.

Bonnie looked down into his waiting face. 'He's — just gone away for a little while.'

'To get more wood?'

'No.' She smoothed the covers, tucked them in around his compact little shoulders.

'No,' said Edie from the other bed. 'Of course not. He's got so much wood. He doesn't need any more.'

'Dad just ...' Bonnie sat up straight and spoke into the middle of the room, the space between the two beds. 'He just needs a bit of time to himself.'

Silence from the children.

'Okay?' Her voice trembled, but she recovered. 'Okay?'

'He might've gone to get more wood, Edie,' said Louie. He got up on his elbows. 'You don't know everything.'

'He's got heaps of wood!' Edie's voice rang against the ceiling.

'Shh.' Bonnie pushed Louie gently back down. 'Okay, quiet now. Time to go to sleep.'

'He just needs some time to himself!' said Edie.

'Shh.' Bonnie crossed to Edie's bed and bent to tuck her in. 'Night-night. Sweet dreams.'

'Louie's stupid.' Edie kicked up her covers and thumped her heels on the mattress.

Bonnie rearranged the bedding. 'Edie — come on. Lie down properly and be quiet, please.'

'Well, he is.'

'Shh. No, he's not.'

'I'm not!'

'Yes, you are. Stupid. Stupid. Stupid.'

'Na-na-na-na-na!'

'Enough!' Bonnie stood up. Her hands were shaking. 'Lie down both of you and go to sleep! Or I'll have to turn off the hallway light and shut the door!'

The phone rang later that evening — the landline. A man. 'Is Pete there, please?'

'Um, no — sorry.' Bonnie's heart started to race. She didn't recognise his voice. *What to say?* 'He's … not here just now.' She felt she was speaking ridiculously slowly, the words oozing out. 'Did you try — have you got his mobile?'

'Yeah, I tried it. It went straight to voicemail.' He had a faint accent.

'Who … who is this?'

'Sorry.' He laughed. 'It's Glenn. I've got some joinery for him. He was in a hurry for it, kept calling me all last week, but now it's ready I can't get a hold of him.'

'Oh, Glenn, right.'

'It's Bonnie, isn't it?'

'Yeah. Sorry, yeah — Bonnie.'

A pause. He cleared his throat. 'Well … when will he be back, do you know?'

'Um.' She swallowed, pushed the words out. 'Soon. He's — he's just out for the evening, so I'll let him know you called and he'll …' She glanced towards the hallway, the living room where Suzanne was watching television, lowered her voice. 'He'll probably call you back tomorrow.'

She hung up. Pete's work, abandoned. His pride. His reputation. Pete just leaving, going off to live with Doug, of all people. She went into the hallway, stood in the dark, a sliding, tilting panic gripping her. *How has this happened?* She reached out and touched the walls on either side. Their house: draughty, cold, full of piles of things she never seemed to get around to putting away. All just as it was, but changed somehow. Everything — the rooms, their furniture and belongings — seemed flat, insubstantial. Like a stage, a set. As if she could reach her arms out and knock it all down, break it apart and see, as the pieces fell, the light of real life come flooding through. Real life, the way it was before.

It just wasn't possible that everything had changed so quickly.

She took the phone into the bedroom and shut the door.

Pete's mobile rang and rang until the voicemail kicked in. Her heart leaped at the sound of his recorded voice. When the beep sounded she laboured for a moment in the waiting silence, trying to muster words.

'Hi,' she said at last. 'It's me. Um. Glenn rang. The joiner.' Her voice jumping out in staccato spurts. She heaved in a breath. 'But that's not really why I'm calling.' She sat down on the end of the bed. 'I need to talk to you, Pete. Please — please call me.'

She let the hand holding the phone fall onto the mattress beside her. Then she flopped her whole body down. Lay looking at the phone, its blank screen. She tried to imagine what Pete might be doing — sitting in an op-shop armchair drinking beer, the stubble on his face dark with anger — but what came to mind were the old photos, of his youth, his real share-house days. Eighties hair and thin faces: Pete and Greg and Deano and various others, and Doug, always Doug, a bit older, a bit more weathered, hovering in the background, grinning narrowly, eyebrows cocked.

She washed her face and brushed her teeth. Checked the children. Jess was sleeping peacefully, the heat gone from her body.

She went towards the bedroom but then stopped, sighed. Dragged herself back to the living room. Stood just inside the door for a moment, cleared her throat.

'Goodnight, Mum.'

Suzanne looked up from the screen. 'Goodnight.'

Her face was in shadow. She had the crochet rug around her shoulders and her knees pulled up. In the flickering light she looked small, almost childlike, and Bonnie had a sudden vision of her alone like that, every night, across town in her little apartment.

She folded her arms over the unexpected spurt of pity and went closer. 'What're you watching?'

'Oh, I don't know, one of these panel discussion things. It's pretty boring.'

'Will you be okay sleeping here, on the couch?' she said. 'Are you sure you don't want to take the bedroom?'

'No, no — I'll be fine. I slept here the other night, remember?' Suzanne reached over and patted her hand. 'It's quite comfortable actually.' She kept her hand on Bonnie's. 'You go and get some rest. Go on — you need it.'

'Thanks, Mum.' Bonnie felt her voice go watery with tears. 'Thanks for coming over.'

Suzanne patted her hand again. 'That's all right, darling. And don't worry — you'll sort something out, you and Pete. I'm sure you will.'

She lay on her side with her knees pulled up. She slid her hand against the sheet, still feeling Suzanne's touch. The image wouldn't go away, of her mother, small and lonely on that couch, the rest of her mother's life stretching out, strung with night after night of aloneness. Bonnie took one of her own hands in the other and gripped it. She could feel it there, ready to open up and swallow her — the kind of stiff and desolate loneliness she'd only ever tasted, fleetingly, on school camps, or in the last week of a too-long tour.

She reached over and grabbed Pete's pillow, shoved her face into it and breathed.

She wore her sunglasses the next morning, dropping the twins at kinder, imagining strange looks from the staff and other parents, thinking it must be written all over her: *damage, crisis.* Kissing the children a hasty goodbye and slinking out again.

She was sitting in the car, keys in her lap, staring at nothing when Mel tapped on the window.

'Hi,' Mel mouthed, and the sight of her, her work clothes and her everyday, unknowing smile, brought tears out of Bonnie like something shaken loose.

They sat together in the car, and Bonnie cried and talked, lips numb and shaking, reaching up to swipe at the tears rolling down from under her sunglasses.

'So you were going to tell Pete?' said Mel. 'Anyway?'

'I guess so. I didn't really get a chance to think about it. I mean, he was acting so weird I just — well, I thought he'd found out somehow, that someone had told him; maybe someone saw me leave the party with the guy and, I don't know … Anyway, I didn't know he'd found the condom.' She shook her head. 'I can't believe I forgot all about it.'

Mel gave a dry laugh. 'You must've been so drunk.'

Bonnie's teeth were clenched. That night, the party, the taxi, the hotel — it all loomed there, vast and dark and shameful, nudging at her as she tried to keep her back turned.

'So.' Mel lined her handbag up across her knees. 'If he hadn't found the condom — if he wasn't acting weird — do you think you might not have told him?'

'I don't know.' She thought about the day between her getting back and it all coming out, being with Pete in the house, the doubt and guilt dragging at her. 'No,' she said slowly. 'I would have told him. For sure. I don't think I could've lived with the strain of not telling him.'

Mel frowned. 'It's a tough one though because — well, nothing really happened, did it?'

'Yeah, but it was only because he left that nothing happened. The guy, I mean. Something *could* have happened.' She put her hands up and gripped the steering wheel. 'I let it get as far as it did. And isn't that just as bad?'

Mel looked down at her bag. 'I guess so,' she said after a while. 'But there's still a big difference between nearly doing something and actually doing it. I don't think you could ever really say what might've happened if things went any further. You might've — when it really came down to it — you might've, well, changed your mind.'

Bonnie took off her glasses, touched the skin around her eyes. It felt swollen from all the crying. She breathed in deeply, trying to dislodge the weight in her chest. 'I just feel like the worst person in the world.'

'People do these things, Bonnie. You wouldn't believe the stories I hear through my work. And from friends too.'

'But …'

'God knows I've been tempted.' Mel lowered her voice, glanced at the window.

'Really?'

'Yeah, of course. Haven't you?' Mel leaned back in her seat. 'You know — life gets boring, you feel a bit neglected by your partner, you meet someone at work or at a party or whatever; they pay you attention and it feels good.'

'Yeah, I guess I've had … crushes.' She thought of the lanky blond man at the cafe she used to go to, near the old house — that extreme self-consciousness that came over her whenever she saw him, the way he'd drift into her thoughts sometimes afterwards, unexpectedly, and she'd feel guilty even about that.

'But of course I always just think, Well, what could I do? I could leave Josh for this guy, and break up a household and a family, and start all over again only to end up in the same place after a few years. Except with an ex-husband and having to share custody of a child.' She looked at Bonnie. 'I mean, usually I'm attracted to them because they kind of remind me of Josh. Or at least what Josh was like when I first met him.' She grinned. 'So might as well stick with the original model, I guess.'

'Yeah.' Bonnie bit her lip. 'I know what you mean, and I guess I've thought similar things. But this thing, with the Sydney guy — I wasn't even attracted to him. It was weird. What you were saying about someone paying you attention, someone noticing you — I guess that was part of it. But …'

'I could understand you feeling a bit neglected by Pete,' said Mel. 'You've sacrificed a lot — your music, your career — you're very supportive of him.'

'But he's supportive of me too. He always encourages me to do music stuff.' Tears pricked her eyes again. 'He's pretty amazing actually. He does just about an equal share of the housework. He's always bailing me out, you know, making dinner and going off to the supermarket late at night because I couldn't get my shit together …'

'Of course.' Mel shifted in the seat. 'I didn't mean he wasn't pulling his weight. I just wonder how much you acknowledge what you've lost — or put on hold. And I'm not saying he made you do that, but, well, you did it, didn't you? I mean, his work comes first.'

'Yeah.' Bonnie touched the skin on her face again, rubbed her eyes. She felt suddenly weighed down with tiredness, hardly able even to speak. 'I'd better get going,' she said. 'My mum's probably freaking out because Jess needs a nappy change or something.'

Mel gave her a sideways hug. 'Give Pete some time.' She rubbed Bonnie's arm. 'Where is he, anyway? Where's he gone?'

'I don't … know.' Bonnie put her sunglasses back on. 'He just said he was going to stay with friends.'

'Not Doug, I hope.' Mel made a face and got out of the car.

Bonnie's stomach contracted.

'Or has he vanished again?'

'No, he's — he's still around.' Bonnie fumbled with her keys, leaned forward to reach the ignition. 'I've got a bad feeling it is Doug,' she said, the words blundering out as if of their own accord.

Mel bent to look in at her. 'But isn't he — I mean, I thought he was living in someone's back shed or something?'

'No. He's rented a flat apparently.' She tried to rein in her voice, make it light. 'He won lots of money, remember, on the horse?' A forced eye-roll. 'The one I wouldn't let Pete have a bet on.'

'Oh right. That.' Mel gave a pinched smile. 'Oh well. Hopefully he'll drive Pete mad quickly — give him an extra reason to come straight home to you.'

Bonnie tried to return the smile.

Mel sighed. 'It'll be okay, Bon. Pete loves you. You love each other. He'll come back.'

'I don't know, Mel.'

'Give him some time,' said Mel again. 'He can't stay angry forever.'

'How do you know where anything is?' said Suzanne, on hands and knees on the kitchen floor. She reached into a cupboard. 'All these cans back here' — she pulled some out — 'I take it there's no system?'

Bonnie wiped Jess's face and took her bib off. 'Not really.'

'Okay then.' Suzanne leaned into the cupboard again.

'Just leave it, Mum.'

'It won't take long.' Her voice was muffled. 'Might as well sort it out, while I'm here.'

'No, really — it's fine. I've been meaning to —'

'Won't take long.'

She noticed Suzanne had a tea towel spread under her knees.

'And someone needs to do some shopping.'

'Yeah, I know.' The bib fell from Bonnie's hand, and she bent awkwardly with Jess on her hip to pick it up again. 'I'll …'

'Now what have we got here?' Suzanne took her head out of the cupboard. 'Chickpeas. Lentils. More chickpeas. Beans.'

'I'm going to put Jess to bed.'

'Okay then.'

'And then I might lie down myself, for a bit.'

'Yes, you should.' Suzanne didn't look up.

Bonnie settled Jess and went to her own room to lie awake and tense, staring up at nothing. From the kitchen came the faint clack and burr of a can falling to the floor and rolling. She tried to shut her eyes, to push away the image of Suzanne's industrious back; the cupboard full of cans in new, neat rows. *She's trying to help.* But she couldn't stop herself from seeing the flimsiness of the new order, how quickly it would all come undone again.

'I'll do the shopping tonight, if that's okay with you,' she said to Suzanne over dinner. 'Later, I mean. Once everyone's asleep.'

Suzanne nodded and went back to her plate. 'Good idea.'

Jess whacked her spoon on the highchair tray.

'When's Dad coming back?' said Louie.

'Soon.' Bonnie reached across and pushed his sleeve up. 'You're getting pumpkin all over your jumper.'

She moved out into the car park with the full trolley, swinging in a wide stiff turn, arms braced, fighting a dodgy wheel. The wind blew her hair into her eyes, and she had her usual out-without-kids weird feeling. It was dark, the lights orange against the overcast sky. She paused to hitch her bag higher on her shoulder.

She thought about Suzanne, back at the house, sitting alone in front of the television, and it rose again, the tender confusion of feelings, swamping, paralysing. Could there be any way around it, the hugeness of habit, the worn rut of their relationship?

Bonnie shook her hair out of her face and pushed on, to the car. She loaded in the bags and returned the trolley. Then she got in and sat, hands on the wheel, watching people walk in and out of the car park, and up and down the street.

Was there any answer? She tried to imagine some parallel life, Suzanne living with them, in a granny flat perhaps, or a house nearby. Suzanne there every day, in their house, Suzanne bringing her own rules and expectations. Suzanne clicking her tongue and sniffing.

And Suzanne's own needs, her own sadnesses, whatever it was she carried around with her, stitched in behind the wall of activities — work, bridge, book club — that only occasionally came leaking out. What about all that? Could Bonnie open herself up to that? After all her other responsibilities — the children; Pete, if he was to be a part of the equation; herself; her music — did she have anything left over to give?

She watched a woman waiting to cross the road to the pub opposite. She thought about Pete, about a summer weekend afternoon, them together in the house, one of those easy days when the children played and didn't fight, when they listened to music, lay outside on the grass, when they might cook a meal together and it wouldn't seem a joyless task but the opposite — full of joy, full of pleasure.

When it worked, the two of them, with the kids — when they were rested and together — it really worked. It did. But of course it couldn't always be like that. The two of them weren't enough. So what was the solution? Suzanne? Could you open the closed circuit? Could you, after so much time, draw together people who didn't know how to be together, graft them onto one another like bits of a tree?

Who knows, anyway? she thought. *All this might be the least of your problems.* She tried to imagine Pete not coming back, to really feel the possibility, but she couldn't do it, couldn't make it seem real.

She backed out of the parking spot. Shifted gears, checked her rear-view mirror. Braked. Two small figures framed by the rectangle of black plastic, going along the street opposite. She stiffened her legs, raised herself in her seat, turned and craned her neck to see through the back window. There they were, bigger, real. One man walking head down, hands in pockets. The other in front, striding with purpose, chest thrust out.

Bonnie's whole body tensed. There was a car behind her, waiting, headlights in her eyes, but she squinted past. 'Shit!' she heard herself say.

The car bipped its horn. Bonnie stayed in her twisted position, squinting. 'Shit!'

Towards the pub door the two figures moved. Pete, round-shouldered, heavy-stepping. And, lunging into the building as if launching an attack, Doug.

'So what's happening?' said Suzanne over breakfast the next morning. She folded her hands under her chin. 'What's the plan?'

Bonnie lowered her head, mumbled into her muesli. 'I don't know.'

'Well, have you' — Suzanne glanced at the twins and put on a whisper that seemed somehow louder than a normal speaking voice — '*heard anything?*'

Bonnie shook her head.

Suzanne's lips formed a line.

'Why can't we have porridge?' said Edie.

'Where's Dad?' said Louie. 'Why is Grandma here all the time?'

Bonnie didn't have the energy to answer, or to look up at Suzanne's told-you-so face. She swallowed the last mouthful of muesli, stood, and began to gather up the plates.

'More Vegemite toast, please,' sang Louie.

'I'll get it.' Suzanne followed Bonnie to the bench. 'You'll need to tell them *something*,' she went on in her stage whisper.

'Tell them what?' said Edie from the table.

Bonnie stacked the dishes and wiped her hands on the tea towel.

'Tell them what? said Edie again.

Bonnie went to the high chair and lifted Jess out of it. 'Come on,' she said, not looking at anyone. 'Let's get ready for swimming.'

She stood in her bathers and towel, Jess on her hip, watching the twins splashing laboriously up and down with all the other children, belly-up, kickboards clutched to their chests.

'Shall I take her?' said Suzanne.

'Thanks.' She passed the baby over.

Suzanne took her but didn't move. She sighed. 'I'm going to need to get back to work, Bonnie. By Monday, at the latest, but if possible —'

'Okay.'

'I'm sorry, darling, but I can't take any more leave. I used it all up on that Tasmania trip last year with Gail. And anyway, we've been short on staff since Brenda left and —'

'It's *okay*, Mum.' She looked down at her toes, feeling the sweat pop on her face. 'Don't worry about it.'

'Well' — Suzanne glanced around, lowered her voice — 'I *am* worried about it.' She brought her voice down even further. 'What are you going to do, Bonnie?'

'I'll work something out,' she said. 'I'd better get swimming.'

'Are you calling him?' whispered Suzanne. 'Pete? Have you spoken to him?'

She felt like a teenager, wooden with unhelpfulness, dumb with it. 'Don't worry about it, Mum.'

'Bonnie!' Suzanne put her hand on Bonnie's arm. 'This is ridiculous! You need to —'

'Don't *worry* about it!' Bonnie's voice ripped like an arrow into the moist cushions of air, shot through and up to bounce off the giant metal beams that ran overhead. People turned to look.

Bonnie pulled her arm from her mother's grip and marched past her, over to the deep end where she entered the pool in a clumsy unpractised dive, too shallow, so the water smacked her thighs.

She swam churning laps, breathing raggedly. Through her goggles she stared down at the tiled bottom, the black lines falling away at the deep end, but what she saw, couldn't stop herself from seeing, was Pete trailing Doug into the pub, Pete the shadow to Doug's forceful figure, Pete following blindly like a dog.

She tried his mobile that afternoon, and it went to voicemail again. She hung up without leaving a message.

'Who was that?' Suzanne was there behind her, a basket of

folded clothes in her arms.

'No one.' Bonnie put the phone down. 'You don't have to do that. Just leave it — I'll do it.'

'I might as well keep myself busy. You'll have to put them away though. I don't know where anything goes.'

'Thanks, Mum.' She stepped forward and reached for the basket.

Suzanne kept her grip on it. 'Was that Pete?' She raised her eyebrows.

'Sorry?' Bonnie felt the block-of-wood teenage feeling descend again.

'Pete. Was that him? Have you got onto him yet?'

'I've tried,' she said, dully. 'He's — he's not answering.'

'Well, have you left a message?'

Bonnie felt the basket between them, her mother's insistent hold on it. She tightened her own fingers and pulled. 'I'll put these away now,' she said in a mumble, trying to move off.

Suzanne held on. 'You need to leave messages,' she said, taking a step closer. 'I mean, it's all right for him to go off in a huff for a day or so, but he's got responsibilities.' Her voice rose. 'The children. It's just not fair.'

The plastic basket was cutting into Bonnie's fingers. *Fuck this*, she thought, and anger flew open like a parachute. 'Unfair?' she said, and heard herself laugh, high and gasping. 'Unfair on who?'

Suzanne gaped. 'Well —'

'Jesus, Mum!' Bonnie let go of the basket, and it tipped. Clothes fell to the floor. 'You don't mean me, do you? Me, that it's unfair on?' She laughed again, low this time, and shook her head. 'I don't think you mean me. *Actually*.' The cut of the word. Suzanne blinking. 'I think you're talking about yourself. That's who you're worried about, isn't it?'

Suzanne tried to steady the clothes tipping from the basket

as it swung against her legs. 'Help me,' she said, head down. 'Help me here.'

Bonnie stood back, arms folded. 'You don't care about me and Pete,' she said. 'Whether or not we love each other. Whether or not we're happy.' She watched Suzanne's bent head. The grey roots of her hair caught the light, and a thread of pity rose, but Bonnie ignored it, stayed with the anger, the wide-open feeling of it, its power. 'You're terrified Pete and I'll break up, aren't you?'

No answer. Suzanne stayed bent over the basket, holding it with both hands now, steady at knee level, the pile of spilled clothes at her feet.

'You're terrified,' she went on, 'that you might have to help me. Regularly. That you might have to spend time with your grandchildren. More than one hour a week. One hour! Fuck!' She ran her hands through her hair. 'Do you know what other people do? Other grandparents? I have friends, Mum, whose parents take their kids for *whole weekends*. Whose parents take their kids for *weeks* while they go overseas. Whose parents look after their kids *regularly*, for *whole days*, every week. Jesus! I mean' — she laughed drily — 'even if you're not interested in your grandchildren, which you're obviously not, I can't believe you're not prepared to help out for my sake, to help *me*. Your daughter.'

Suzanne dropped the basket. She folded at the knees and bumped down to the floor beside it. At first Bonnie thought she was going to pick up the clothes, but she didn't touch them. She lowered her face into her hands. Her shoulders shook.

Bonnie waited, the anger leaving her like the black twist of smoke from a blown-out candle.

'I put,' said Suzanne at last, 'the best years of my life into you.' She spoke into her hands. 'You and Luke, and it was bloody *miserable*.'

Bonnie's legs felt weak. She let them bend, slid down to sit on the floor opposite Suzanne.

Suzanne dropped her hands. Her face was red, the powdery foundation gone from her nose, mascara veined in the lines under her eyes. 'I don't know what makes us do this,' she said, as if to herself. 'This, this ... urge, this drive, to have babies.' She straightened. 'I remember it, still. Clear as day.' She smiled then, looking somewhere down near Bonnie's feet. 'My mother warned me, you know.'

Bonnie waited.

'Oh yes. "Don't do it," she said. "It's a death sentence. Get your tubes tied before anything happens."' Suzanne pulled a tissue from her sleeve and blew her nose. 'And that was in the sixties. No one said anything like that back then. You were supposed to *want* to be a mother.'

A hurt-child feeling uncurled in Bonnie. 'But ...' She heard the shyness in her own voice, felt an urgent, embarrassed smile flit across her face. 'But surely — surely it wasn't all bad?'

Suzanne glanced at her, as if only just realising who she was. 'Of course not,' she said. 'You were delightful, both of you. I told myself that every day. You're wasting it, I told myself. Why can't you enjoy this, this precious time?' She refolded the tissue, wiped under her eyes with it. 'You were delightful,' she said again. 'That made it even worse — it was like a, a *pressure*. Knowing that I was getting it wrong somehow.'

She watched her mother's hands holding the tissue in her lap. 'Mum,' she said, feeling enormous all of a sudden, swollen with pity. 'You probably had post-natal depression.'

'Oh, I'm sure I did.' Suzanne flashed one of her regular, bright smiles. 'But no one talked about that back then. I'm not sure if it even existed.'

'But that's terrible.' Bonnie leaned forward, voice loud in her own ears. 'I mean, to struggle all on your own like that.'

Suzanne made a rueful face. 'Oh well. That's just the way it was.'

'But didn't ... didn't Dad ...?'

'Him?' Suzanne laughed. 'He was always at work. He did nothing — *nothing* — to help with you children. Oh' — she flapped a hand — 'he read your stories, at bedtime, when he got home from work. Once I'd fed you and bathed you and got you all ready.'

There was a pause. No sound from Jess, sleeping in her room. Bonnie stared down at the scuffed toes of her boots. The warmth of her father's giant body, the smell of his clothes — like newspapers, and pencil shavings — the rumble of his voice, the vibration of it as she rested against him. She felt her mouth twist, the swim of angry tears. She couldn't look up at Suzanne. How unfair, that this vision of her father was so readily available, so alive and full and easy, when if she tried to summon the mother of her childhood all she got was impressions: a blurred figure always moving; a weary voice pleading *Hurry up*; impatient hands busy and full; a turned back.

'You're much luckier,' said Suzanne after a while. 'You've got Pete.'

'Now,' said Suzanne, the next morning, when Bonnie got back from dropping the twins at kinder. 'I've got bridge tonight ...'

'That's fine, Mum.' She spooned mashed banana into Jess's mouth.

'And I was thinking, it's at Marg's, all the way over in Hampton, and afterwards — I mean, you won't need me anyway, because the kids'll be in bed.'

Bonnie looked across at her. Nothing showed of yesterday's cracked, raw face. Suzanne's make-up was in place again, her expression contained.

'So,' Suzanne went on, 'I thought perhaps it would make

more sense if I just went home.'

The thin winter light in the room, the two of them there, trapped together in this, whatever it was, this unwilling union, this stasis. *Neither of us wants this*, thought Bonnie.

'It's fine, Mum.' She scraped creamy dribble from Jess's chin. 'That sounds fine. And I think you should go back to work tomorrow. I'll be okay.'

Suzanne sipped her tea. She leaned forward in her chair, opened her mouth. Sat back, closed it. Came forward again. 'But Bonnie, what —'

'It's up to me, Mum.' Bonnie was surprised at how firm her own voice was. 'It's my problem.'

That night she walked around the hushed house. Stood in the bedroom doorways, listening to the breathing of the children.

The couch cushions smelled of Suzanne — floral perfume and expensive hand cream. Bonnie turned the television on and sat down. Then she turned it off and stood up again.

She paced emptily. What could she do? What could she say to Pete, to convince him? How long should she leave it for, let him be like this, silent, cut-off? How long before it was up to her to force something, some confrontation? She stood in their bedroom looking at his row of shoes against the wall, a jumper hung over the back of the chair. How could she do it anyway? If he didn't call her or answer his phone how could she find out where he was? She tried to picture herself staking out the pub across the road from the supermarket, following them back to Doug's flat or wherever it was they were staying. Banging on the door, the demanding woman, the shrew. Their two faces, side-by-side, safe in their calm allegiance.

She was brushing her teeth when someone knocked on the front door. A long, hard hammering, and then what sounded like a voice. She jumped. Went into the hallway. *Pete?* She started towards the door, but the knock came again, a shuffling and a bump.

'Anybody ho-ome?' came the voice, quiet, almost sing-song.

She froze. It wasn't Pete.

Another knock, insistent at first, and then slowing, petering out. 'Mis-sus Bon-nie,' came the sing-song voice.

Bonnie stood a few paces from the door, body tense with fear. She put her hands over her mouth and waited. *Go away.*

'Hul-lo-o?' The knocking again, another shuffle. 'Come on, Missus Bonnie, let us in.' A long inhalation of breath, audible through the door. 'I need to talk to you.' A clink, like glass against wood, and the voice lowered for a moment, guttural, slurred. 'It's about Pete.'

He's drunk, she thought. The fright swelled. What about Pete? A series of ugly scenarios flipped through her mind. Pete had left town. Pete was moving in with Doug permanently and he'd sent Doug to get more of his things. Pete wanted to see the kids, and he'd sent Doug to mediate.

'Mis-sus Bon-nie!'

She shrank at the volume of his voice. What time was it? Ten-thirty? Eleven o'clock? What was he doing, turning up like this, making such a racket?

'Yoo-hoo!' More hammering.

She moved closer to the door, cringing. *He's going to wake the kids.*

'Yoo-hoo!'

Fuck!

'Mis-sus Bon-nie!'

She took two quick steps, wrenched open the door. Doug fell in, stumbling past her. His shoulder grazed her face, and she felt the cold outside air on his jacket, breathed smoke and booze and his dank smell.

He stayed on his feet, lurched round to face her. He was holding two stubbies of beer — Coronas — and he raised one. 'For you.'

She didn't answer. She couldn't even open her mouth. Her rage roared so strongly she couldn't keep still. She trembled on the spot, speechless with it, opening and closing her hands.

Doug waved the bottle at her, head back. 'Peace offering,' he said, but his eyes were wandering upwards, as if inspecting the ceiling for cracks. He took a couple of staggering steps backwards.

She drew in breath, struggled for words. 'What …?'

But his head snapped back down into position. 'Now when is this going to stop?' He eyed her sternly. 'Eh?'

Bonnie stared.

'This — this' — Doug brandished the bottle — 'rubbish you two're going on with.' His eyes had lost their focus again.

She tried not to look at his mouth as it hung open, waiting for the words.

The words obviously didn't come. 'I need a drink,' he said at last, swinging round. 'Where's your bottle opener?'

He headed off towards the kitchen, and it took a moment for Bonnie to gather herself and follow. *What's wrong with you?* She felt slow and bulky, dragging her anger. *Just kick him out, for fuck's sake.*

When she came into the room he was around the other side of the bench, going through the cutlery drawer.

Bonnie stood in the doorway. 'What're you …?' She couldn't seem to raise her voice above a weak bleat.

'Ah-ha!' Doug ignored her, came over to the table with the bottle opener held aloft. Bent and levered the top off one of the beers, then the other, sending the bottle tops flipping and bouncing across the table. Pushed one bottle towards her and seized the other. 'That's the way.' He pulled out a chair and dropped into it, took a moment to balance one ankle on the other knee and raised the bottle. 'Cheers,' he said, and drank.

Bonnie looked down at the floor. The rage was like a black hole in her vision, quivering, liquid. Who did he think he was, coming here like this, in the middle of the night, making so much noise? Stomping through the house as if he owned it, rummaging through the drawers? She tried to breathe evenly, to calm herself enough to think, to decide what to do.

'He won't listen to me,' said Doug, looking at his beer. He might have been at his own table, musing to himself. 'I've tried.' He shook his head. 'He's wallowing — that's what he's doing. Starting to get a bit sick of it actually.'

Slowly Bonnie opened her mouth, slowly she raised her head, fighting the dumb weight of the anger.

'Boring,' said Doug. 'That's what it is.' He sipped meditatively, tipped his chair back on two legs. 'Getting a bit boring now.'

She gaped. She blinked at him. She felt her head shake, heard herself give a broken laugh. *He's sitting here, in our house, in the middle of the night, complaining that Pete's boring, that our break-up is boring — that this thing, the worst, most terrible thing that's ever happened to us, that's ripped our lives apart, is boring, is a drag for him, getting in his way.*

Doug seemed to notice her then. He slid his lips back in a smile. 'I know you don't like me, Missus Bonnie. But the thing is —'

The numbness went. The anger ruptured, blew open. Bonnie shot across the room, seized the back of his seat and tipped it forward. '*Get out,*' she hissed. 'Get up out of my fucking chair and get the fuck out of my house.'

Doug stumbled but recovered himself, swayed upright, knees bent, arms raised, the bottle still in his hand. Beer flicked up the wall. 'Easy,' he said loudly.

'*Shut up,*' she hissed. She felt huge with rage. '*Get out!*'

'Easy, easy,' went Doug, hands still raised as if in protest. But he was moving, unsteadily, in bursts, like a dodgem car. Over the floor, through the doorway, out into the hall.

Past the darkened rooms of the sleeping children they went, Bonnie behind him, fists at the ready.

He wavered for a moment, and her throat stung with the force of her whisper. '*Move.*' She had an urge to lift her foot and kick him.

'I'm going,' said Doug. 'All right — I'm going, settle down.'

Teeth clenched, she followed him to the front door.

He stopped there again, slouched against the wall, grinning at her as if it was all a joke.

'You're all right, Missus Bonnie.' He sucked at the foam that was erupting from the shaken beer and wiped his mouth with the back of his hand. 'You're my favourite tough lady.'

Bonnie opened the door. 'Get out.'

'All right, all right.' He pushed himself up off the wall, groaning like someone getting up out of a comfortable chair. 'Not the first time I've been kicked out of a party.' Out on the porch at last he faced her and lifted the bottle again. 'Well, cheers, Missus Bonnie. To you. And to Pete, the stupid cunt who doesn't know his own luck.' He drank, swaying as his head went back.

Bonnie shut the door. She stood listening. She could hear him breathing, the shift of his weight as he turned towards the street. She heard him laugh softly, and then sigh. His feet across the porch to the steps, then a sudden scraping sound and a thud. The muffled scrunch of breaking glass.

Shit. She stood with her hand on the lock.

Silence.

Shit. Bonnie opened the door again. She could see the shape of him at the bottom of the steps, dark against the concrete path. She saw his head come up, and his shoulders, and then he was kneeling, his back to her.

'Doug?' She stayed in the doorway. 'You all right?'

He didn't answer.

'Doug?'

He mumbled something, tried to get up, but fell back into a squat. She heard the crunch and skitter of the broken beer bottle on the concrete.

'Doug?' She reached back inside the door and switched on the porch light, and he came properly into view, in colour, his hair, his jacket, worn at the elbows, the backs of his ears. 'Doug? You okay?' She went across the porch and started down the steps.

'Uh-oh,' he said suddenly, and gave a pale version of one of his titters.

She came down behind him. She could see the broken glass on the concrete, and bubble-edged splashes of beer, and — rich and dark — blood. A little trickle of it moving downhill, making for the edge of the path. Her heart started to hammer. Doug's knees sticking out sharp in front, his shoulders hunched, him swaying and bobbing like some giant injured bird. She edged round him.

'Aw, me new shoes,' croaked Doug.

She stared at the shoes. She hadn't noticed them before. They were awful, both cheap-looking and ostentatious, long and shiny, pale grey. There was blood on one of the toes. *Funny,* she thought, distantly, behind the pounding of her heart. *Why would you buy only those crazy shoes, and still keep on wearing the same crap old clothes?*

Doug made a noise, a kind of half-laugh, half-whimper, and she yanked her gaze away at last from the mess and the shoes and saw the hand he was holding out between his knees, palm up. It was bright and wet with blood, covered, slick, and Bonnie could see small pieces of glass sticking out of it. But the blood was coming from further up, from the wrist, where a cut — not big, but deep, like a miniature toothless mouth — was spewing in regular pulses. She drew in breath hard between her teeth. Too much blood. She could hear the busy drip of it on the path, see the puddle spreading between his ugly shoes.

Doug raised his face then, his skin drained and waxy under the light. 'Shit, sorry, Missus Bonnie,' he said, and moved his lips in an awful faint smile. 'I've done meself a bit of a ...'

Oh god, the fucking idiot. Bonnie reared back, clenched her arms around her own torso, turned her face away. *Oh god.* She scanned the empty street. *Help. Someone.* But there was no one, and there was no time anyway. She straightened, dropped her arms. She was going to have to deal with this herself.

'Stay there.' She darted back past him, into the house. Ran to the kitchen and grabbed a bundle of tea towels. Ran back. Heard her own voice rapping out — 'Sit down properly' — and then she was behind him, touching him, pulling him to the bottom step, moving him away from the broken glass. She smelled his dirty hair, his unwashed clothes, the stale smoke of his cigarettes. She felt his ribs under his shirt. His blood ran down warm over the back of her hand. It was shocking how warm he was, how solid his body.

He let her move him. He didn't say anything. She could hear his breathing, jerky and fearful.

Kneeling, she folded the first tea towel lengthwise and wrapped it around his wrist. Her hands shook.

'Not tight enough.' Unwrapping it, a fleck of blood hitting her face. Breathing, trying to steady herself. *Get it right.* Rewrapping, pulling the cloth as taut as she could, pressing down with her thumbs over the place where the red kept soaking through.

The same with the second tea towel, and then a third. Keeping her hands on the place, pressing, pressing. Skidding in the blood as she changed position.

'Got your mobile?' Patting his pants, glancing at his face. He made no move to help, just looked up at her, tongue working at colourless lips.

Pressing, pressing, fingers sticky, kneeling in blood. Feeling the oblong shape of the phone, drawing it out.

She dialled, thumb awkward on the unfamiliar keypad, spoke to someone, answered their questions. She hung up.

She rang Pete, without hesitation, without thinking. He answered, and she gabbled something. Put the phone down. Clamped the free hand back over the other.

'They'll be here soon,' she said to Doug.

There was a hush, then, the two of them waiting. The cold, clear night, the arms of the lemon tree open to the sky. Far-off car noises, and a dog barking. No siren, yet.

'They'll be here soon,' she said again, flicking her eyes up to Doug's face and then down again, back to her hands on the lumpy band of sodden cloth.

His eyes were closed, his mouth too. She noticed his cheekbones, how high they were.

'Doug?' She checked his face again. 'You okay?'

He didn't answer.

'Doug?'

His eyes stayed closed. When he spoke it was quietly, almost whispering. 'Who'd fucken miss me?'

'Oh, of course people would miss you.' Her voice came out too bright, too sure. 'Your friends, your ...' She faltered, looked back down at her hands. The blood was soaking through the outside tea towel. She could feel the weight of all the liquid in the cloth, the squish of it under her fingers. 'Anyway,' she said, 'there's no need for that kind of talk.' She strained her ears for the ambulance. *Come on.* She thought she could hear it now, faintly, the rise and dip of the siren.

Doug made a hissing sound between his teeth, and his shoulders shook, but she couldn't tell if he was laughing or crying. He tipped back his head into the cold air and hooted. Threw out his hands, Bonnie clinging to the bandaged one like a limpet. 'Who'd fucken miss *me?*'

She sat on the top step and watched as they bent over him with their blue gloves. Filling the front yard with their uniforms, their practised, steady movements, their calm voices.

'Well done. You did well,' said one of them, reaching up, touching her on the arm.

The smooth lowering of the stretcher on its wheels, the points of Doug's knees through his pants as they lifted him.

'One. Two. And three.' The stretcher up and rolling towards the gate.

Pete there, standing aside as they passed. Moving to her in a few quick steps.

'You okay?' Bending, hands on her shoulders.

'Yeah.'

His eyes, staring right into hers. 'You sure?' Him touching her cheek. 'There's blood on your face.'

'I'm fine.' Her voice distant and warped. 'It was Doug. He — I don't know, he's really drunk, he just turned up here, and then he had a beer, a bottle, and he fell ...'

Pete standing again. The slamming of doors behind him, out in the street. The lights flashing red. 'I'm going to go with him, okay? Will you be okay?'

Bonnie looking up at him, his face full of shadows. 'Yeah.'

'Is anyone here? Where's your mum?'

'I'll be okay.'

'Okay.' Him turning, going back down the path. 'You sure?

It's just — I'd better catch them, before they go.'

'Okay.' Trying to focus on him. 'Pete?'

'Yeah?'

'Is he all right? I mean, is he awake?'

Pete just a figure at the gate. 'I think so. He's breathing anyway.' Starting towards the ambulance, but then pausing. 'I'll come back.'

'WHAT DO YOU WANT?' SAYS PETE. 'I MEAN — DO YOU KNOW WHAT you actually want?'

'Yes,' she says. 'I want us to be together. I want everything to be how it was. Before.'

There's a waiting feeling in the early quiet of the house, the children still asleep.

Pete leans his elbows on the table. He's still in his clothes. He speaks softly — 'Me too' — and hope balloons in Bonnie, quick and clumsy. But then he looks at her, and in the morning light lines show on his face. 'But you know it can't ...' Sad creases at the corners of his eyes. 'It can't ever be the same.'

And the hope sinks as fast as it rose.

'Bon?'

'Yeah.' Her voice scratches out. 'Yeah. Of course.'

They sit there, not speaking, and down the hall Jess makes her first cry, and the day begins.

And of course it's not the same.

But the way in which it's different changes, as the days take them, lift and sweep them on like waves. Kinder, library, swimming. Supermarket, park, dinner. And it loosens, very slowly, the strangeness between them, the web of it.

They kiss again, one night, and Pete pushes her back on the couch. His mouth, his tongue, the taste of him so familiar it's hard to believe any of it happened. She reaches down and undoes his belt. He lifts her top, tugs her bra straps off her shoulders, puts his mouth to her breast. She kisses his hair, smells his sweet sawdust smell, hooks her fingers around the button of his jeans. Their bodies fit together. It isn't difficult, or awkward, or strange. It's like it has been for years — two people who know what to do to make each other come. Bonnie stops thinking, goes into that blind, beautiful place, and it could be any time, any one of the countless times they've done this. They could be right back in Pete's share-house bedroom.

Afterwards, though, when she cries, when she leans over him and kisses his face and whispers, 'I'm so sorry. I love you so much,' he moves from underneath her, sits up and reaches for his clothes.

For a moment he stays like that, with his jeans and shirt in his hands, and then he puts his arm around her and lands a fumbling kiss on her ear.

'I don't want to talk about that,' he says, looking at the floor.

She sees Doug, one afternoon, two or three weeks afterwards. She's driving with the kids and she sees him come out of the sports bar of a pub. He has someone with him, another man, short and slight. The word *crony* flicks through Bonnie's mind. In the moment of her passing she sees the dirty white edge of the bandage at the cuff of Doug's shirt, the swagger of his shoulders, the wag of his head as he shoots off some sideways comment.

And then she's past, and he shrinks in her mirror like any other person, any other dot on the street.

She turns from making porridge one morning and there's Jess, up on all fours, rocking, chubby knees edging forwards, eyes alight with uncertain triumph. 'Quick!' calls Bonnie, and then hesitates. *Pete!* she wants to yell, but her throat clogs. It feels too bold, an imposition. 'Everyone!' she calls instead. 'Quick!'

'What?' Edie and Louie run in.

'Look.' Bonnie points. 'Jess's almost crawling.'

'She is crawling!' Louie and Edie fling themselves down beside the baby. 'Jess! Jess!' they cry, patting the floor in front of her.

Jess, dribble running in a clear string from her chin, mouth agape in an astonished smile, shuffles one hand an inch over the lino.

'She's crawling!' yells Edie. 'Dad, Dad — Jess is crawling!'

Pete comes in, and Bonnie watches his face. She sees the gentleness there, the smile that comes so easily for the baby, and then the caution when he glances at her, and she feels the jaws of a lunging helpless need swing open. She closes her hands into fists. She turns bluntly back to the stove.

But then Pete comes over and touches her, his hand warm on her arm, and there's something, some shy offer there, and her heart takes off in soaring, fraught hope.

A delivery arrives, a giant cardboard box. Corrugated plastic tubing in a loop on top, tied with wire. They all stand round it.

'What is it?' says Edie.

'It's a dishwasher,' says Pete. He bends and pulls away the plastic packet that's taped to the side, tears it open and takes out the invoice. Glances at Bonnie. 'It's from your mum.'

'Wow,' she says. 'I think it might be a good one.'

There's a pause, and then Pete grins. 'So,' he says, 'Suzanne comes through with the goods.'

They stand each side of the hulking box, smiling nervously at each other.

Mickey sends new demos, wants to book in more studio time. Bonnie sits up late with headphones on and plays and plays. Her calluses harden again. She drifts away from the children during the daytimes, goes to the living room, picks up the acoustic.

'I like that song.'

It's Edie, hanging over the end of the couch. She comes round to sit, back straight, hands in her lap, trying so hard to be good that Bonnie's chest is squeezed with love.

Bonnie smiles, and before Jess can start to cry or Louie run in, or Edie get bored and fidget and bump the guitar, she shifts round to face her daughter, and she plunges back into the song, and the chords roll full and open around the two of them.

An afternoon wears on. The twins bicker. Jess cries and grabs at Bonnie's legs. Pete comes in late from the workshop, and she clangs a saucepan lid down and yells, 'Fuck this!'

And Pete says, quietly, 'You wanted this. This is what you wanted.'

And he picks up the baby and turns and leaves the room, and she is left standing there, gasping, breathless.

But later he puts his arms around her and says 'Sorry', and Bonnie feels the strength in his arms, the heat of his body, his face, his scratchy chin as he kisses her. She feels it, close and alive.

Sometimes she looks at Pete, and he looks back at her, straight, the way he always did, and it comes so easily, the hugeness of their old love. And for a moment they slip out from under it, the shadow that flaps and skims, waiting, ready to bring them undone. And the love flares bright between them like nothing ever happened, and it doesn't matter that it's only for a moment.

He'll come back, one day, Bonnie knows. Doug.

She tries to prepare herself, to rehearse the scenario.

She puts herself outside, returning to the house with a load of washing from the line. It's night. She'll climb the steps

274

holding the laundry basket, stop at the kitchen door and look in through the glass.

Pete will be at the bench with Jess in his arms. The twins kneeling on chairs. Doug standing directly under the hanging light, in its beam, arms spread, eyebrows jerking, lips curved away from the wreckage of his grin. He'll bend his knees, bob his head, bounce back up with the triumph of a story's end.

And Bonnie, out in the dark, will watch her children, their keen interest, their open faces. And she'll watch Pete. She'll see his ease, his generous smile. And it will come leaping up, that love, like a living thing. And she will pull it close around her, hold on to it. And she'll open the door, and go in.

Acknowledgements

Thank you to The Readings Foundation, The Wheeler Centre, and Writing at Rosebank via the Victorian Writers' Centre for providing valuable time and space during the development of this book. I'd also like to acknowledge the Victorian Government's investment in new writing through the Victorian Premier's Prize for an Unpublished Manuscript by an Emerging Victorian Writer.

For help in various forms thank you to Claudia Murray-White, Naomi Rottem, Trisha Valliappan, Edward Frew, Tim Frew, Ian See, Robin Lucas, Miriam Rosenbloom and Caroline Kennedy-McCracken.

For her assistance, encouragement and good humour, I'm grateful to my agent, Clare Forster.

Special thanks to Louisa Syme for all her reading and insights, and to Mick Turner for many late-night discussions.

Extra-special thanks to Aviva Tuffield, publisher and editor at Scribe, for her thoughtfulness, her honesty, and her incredible hard work. It's been a pleasure to share this project with her.

And to my family, as always, my gratitude and my love.